PENGUIN BOOKS

THE PENGUIN HENRY LAWSON

HENRY LAWSON (1867–1922) was born at Grenfell, New South Wales, where his father, a Norwegian sailor (originally Larsen), was unsuccessfully prospecting for gold. Partially deaf from the age of nine, he had little formal education, and was an apprentice in Sydney when he began to write verse and short stories. His first published work was in 1887 in the *Bulletin*, an influential weekly with which he was associated for the rest of his life. His reputation as a short story writer was established with the publication of *While the Billy Boils* in 1896. During two years (1900–02) that he spent in England, he enjoyed the friendship and critical support of Edward Garnett, and wrote some of his best stories, which were collected in *Joe Wilson and His Mates* in 1901. After his return to Australia his work showed a marked decline, and the rest of his life was darkened by alcoholism and the bitterness generated by the breakdown of his marriage. A national figure, identified strongly with Australian values, he died in poverty in Sydney, where he was given a State funeral.

JOHN BARNES is reader in English at La Trobe University and editor of *Meridian: The La Trobe University English Review*. He has published widely on Australian literature, his works including critical studies of Lawson, Furphy and early Australian novelists, and *The Writer in Australia: A Collection of Literary Documents*. He is currently working on a biography of Joseph Furphy.

THE PENGUIN HENRY LAWSON

SHORT STORIES

edited with an introduction by John Barnes

PENGUIN BOOKS

Penguin Books Australia Ltd,
487 Maroondah Highway, P.O. Box 257
Ringwood, Victoria 3134, Australia
Penguin Books Ltd,
Harmondsworth, Middlesex, England
Penguin Books,
40 West 23rd Street, New York, N.Y. 10010, U.S.A.
Penguin Books Canada Limited,
2801 John Street, Markham, Ontario, Canada L3R 1B4
Penguin Books (N.Z.) Ltd,
182-190 Wairau Road, Auckland 10, New Zealand

First published by Penguin Books Australia, 1986
Reprinted 1986, 1987
Introduction copyright © John Barnes, 1986

Typeset in Times by Abb-typesetting Pty Ltd, Melbourne
Made and printed in Australia by
The Book Printer, Maryborough, Victoria

CIP

Lawson, Henry, 1867-1922.
The Penguin Henry Lawson short stories.

ISBN 0 14 009215 3.

I. Barnes, John, 1931- . II. Title. III. Title:
Henry Lawson short stories.

A823'.2

CONTENTS

The Penguin Henry Lawson

INTRODUCTION

INTRODUCTION

STORY-TELLING is an ancient art, but the idea of the short story as a distinct literary form is comparatively recent. Today the term 'short story' covers a range of possibilities, and we are less likely than the readers of a century ago to regard the short story as the poor relation of the novel. There perhaps still lingers a suspicion that the fiction writer without a novel to his credit has, so to speak, failed to measure up to the real test of creativity, no matter how fine that writer's short fiction may impress us as being. And in our assessment of the achievements of a short-story writer, we incline perhaps to regard most highly those stories which best bear comparison with novels. It is certainly true that critical discussion of Henry Lawson's prose writing has been coloured by the assumption – sometimes unconscious – that in being 'only a short-story writer' he was less than if he had been a novelist. That is an assumption challenged in this selection, which aims to show Lawson as an original and distinctive artist whose prose fiction is only now receiving the right kind of recognition.

In Lawson's lifetime a combination of factors tended to cloud perception of what was distinctive about his writing. There was the general expectation that as he matured he would write a novel (or a sequence of connected stories), a 'big' work, no matter how commonplace, being regarded as of a higher order of creation than a piece of short fiction. The prevailing taste was for short stories with a strong narrative interest – 'story' in the simplest sense – and Lawson was most highly praised by local critics for those works in which he came nearest to the conventional. But probably the most influential factor was

Lawson's standing as a national figure. 'Henry Lawson is the voice of the bush, and the bush is the heart of Australia', proclaimed A. G. Stephens of the *Bulletin*, when reviewing his first book, *Short Stories in Prose and Verse*, in 1895, and that view of his uniquely representative status is still potent, at least for older readers. For some of us, our responses to Lawson's writing still tend to get mixed up with feelings about 'the real, the true Australia'. Manning Clark's recent *In Search of Henry Lawson* (which he describes as 'a hymn of praise to a man who was great of heart') states the basic proposition on which the 'Lawson legend' rests: 'Australia is Lawson writ large'. Clark's book shows just how strong the romantic conception of the 'national voice' remains, at least where Lawson is concerned.

The historical function of Lawson's writing is undeniable. At a time of burgeoning nationalism, he was stimulated by a notion of 'Australianness', and was himself a source of stimulus to others. In his stories where he writes as one of the bush people he describes, Lawson impressed his contemporaries as a reporter and observer, opening their eyes to the reality around them. Reviewing *While the Billy Boils* in 1896, Price Warung clearly had reservations about the literary quality of the stories, but no doubt about their documentary value. 'We do not yet, we Australians, know our country', he wrote, going on to praise Lawson's knowledge and concluding, 'Whatever else may be said of it, certain it is that this book must make Australians know their Australia better'. Another reviewer – like Price Warung, inclined to devalue Lawson's stories as being no more than 'photographs' – thought that they would help 'to correct false and create fresh impressions of Australian life among all who are amiably or earnestly interested in learning what our National Characteristics are and towards what they may be tending'. Yet another found 'the genuine Australia' in *While the Billy Boils* and (in the rhetoric to which Lawson's admirers were prone) wrote: 'Of this Australia Henry Lawson is the poet, the prophet, the singer, and the portal-keeper of its temple'. By the end of his life, the belief that Lawson was 'the poet prophet of Australia' (in the words of his aristocratic benefactor, Earl Beauchamp) had taken firm root, and more and more in the years that followed it affected how he was read.

The 'Lawson legend' was not groundless – legends seldom are – but it was a partial and distorting view of a writer of individual gifts, and it fostered an uncritical attitude which discouraged intelligent scrutiny of what he had written. Lawson's writing did strike his contemporaries with the effect of a revelation. What he offered, though, was not an inclusive transcript of bush life but an intense and narrow personal vision. His famed knowledge of the bush was comparatively limited, his direct experience of the Outback being confined to that one soul-searing trip to Bourke and Hungerford which lasted in all less than a year. The precision of detail and the feeling of intimacy with which life in the countryside was portrayed in his writing led some of the early readers to think of him as primarily concerned with describing various phases of Australian life. Very soon, though, there were objections that his work did not portray the whole truth about the bush or about Australia in general. The argument was really beside the point. As Frank Sargeson – himself a fine short-story writer who learnt from Lawson – once pointed out, Lawson was not a realist, in the usual sense of the word: 'He looked at the desolation of the Australian inland, and he saw his own interior desolation'. Lawson, he went on to say, 'uses naturalistic phenomena to express his inward-looking vision'.

This 'inward-looking vision' was very different from the 'gospel of mateship' with which Lawson has been identified, on the basis of a selective reading of his work. True, mateship was a phenomenon of the bush life, and Lawson writes about it often. True also, the impulse to idealise the facts of mateship, and to sentimentalise relationships between men, is there from the beginning (his very first story – of a father and son – is entitled 'His Father's Mate'). But the insistence on the value of mateship as the most important human relationship is an aspect of Lawson's decline. *Children of the Bush*, which appeared in 1902, marks the turning point in Lawson's artistic life. It contains a number of stories in which mateship is celebrated, stories like 'Send Round the Hat', which are heart-warming and quite lacking in the hard-edged authenticity of the best stories in *While the Billy Boils*. The bush life which Lawson now lovingly evokes is a touched-up 'photograph', in which sentiment predominates over emotion. Lawson himself, one might say, could not face reality as he had once done, and retreated into sentimental re-writing of his own achievement. Indeed, one could say that his early collapse contributed to falsification of what he had done in the short creative period of his life.

To those who saluted Lawson as 'the voice of Australia', literary considerations were of secondary importance, and the struggling artist was hardly discernible in the almost mystically conceived National Writer. A most common formulation in the obituary articles was that Lawson was the 'Poet of Australia', a kind of antipodean Burns, whose writings were a treasure house of Australianness. When half a century later Colin Roderick collected Lawson's verse in three substantial volumes, it was apparent how little of it could be considered poetry. The essential criticism had been made as long ago as 1902 by Edward Garnett, the most perceptive critic Lawson encountered, when he wrote: 'Like a voice speaking to you through a bad telephone, the poems convey the speaker's meaning, but all the shades of original tone are muffled, lost or hidden'. There would be general agreement now that Lawson's verse is marginal to his achievement, thus reversing the preference of his own day.

However, although we may now claim that we are no longer blinkered in our view of Lawson – at least, not to the extent that previous generations were – we can hardly claim to have seen him steadily, and certainly not whole. Anyone looking over the quite extensive body of critical comment on Lawson must be struck by the almost patronising way in which his work – especially his prose work – was discussed, even by his admirers, before A. A. Phillips's essay in 1948 argued the case for Lawson as a craftsman. Although Phillips's own acceptance of the essential outline of the Lawson legend did close off lines of speculation that he might profitably have followed, his perception that Lawson was a conscious innovator – aiming at a minimum of 'plot' – directed attention to the previously neglected formal aspects of the stories. Brian Matthews effected a further reorientation of Lawson studies when in the first full-length critical study of the stories, *The Receding Wave* (1972), he argued that Lawson's decline was not mainly the result of personal circumstances but had its origin in the very nature of his talent. Odd though it may seem, considering how much has been written about Lawson, it is only since Matthews's book that the stories have begun to receive sustained critical attention. Scholarly study has now revealed aspects of the man and his writing that hitherto were hidden or ignored. There is as yet no adequate biography, but biographical accounts have now got beyond anecdote and admiration, and an illuminating Freudian study by French academic Xavier Pons has identified psychological issues with which Lawson's eventual biographer will have to deal.

'I don't know about the merit or value of my work', wrote Lawson in ' "Pursuing Literature" in Australia', a bitter *apologia* in the *Bulletin* in 1899, 'all I know is that I started a shy, ignorant lad from the bush, under every disadvantage arising from poverty and lack of education, and with the extra disadvantage of partial deafness thrown in.' He did not exaggerate the disadvantages, but they can be seen in another light as not being disadvantages at all, as far as the writer was concerned. Many have sought to imitate Lawson's simplicity of style, but no other Australian writer has managed so well to create that effect of natural, unaffected Australian speech, which is Lawson's hallmark. A few years of elementary education in 'the old bark school', taught by a teacher whose weak points were 'spelling, English grammar and singing', may not seem much of a preparation for a writing career; and Lawson was always rather defensive on the point, easily hurt by the criticisms of his 'cultured critics'. But though his spelling was always shaky and he suffered from feelings of inferiority, Lawson's very lack of education meant that his style was largely formed on the speech of the people amongst whom he lived. He had learnt to read from *Robinson Crusoe*, and Defoe's plain style undoubtedly had some influence on the formation of his own. Lawson read little throughout his life and took little from what he did read. The absence of pretension, and of self-conscious literariness, enabled Lawson to write in a genuinely simple style. He had confidence in the vernacular as literary language (most other Australian writers have thought it suitable only for humorous effects) because he knew no other. His prose at its best shows him acutely aware of tone and inflection as registers of feeling in the voice. His deafness may have shut out a great deal in his adult life, while preserving uncorrupted the memory of voices heard in childhood.

Asked by an aspiring writer what was the best early training for a writer, Hemingway replied, 'an unhappy childhood'. Lawson might well have given the same answer. More important than the vivid memories of places and people was the intense loneliness he felt. He was the eldest child of a foreign father and an Australian-born mother. His father was Nils Larsen, a Norwegian sailor who had left his ship to join the gold rushes in 1855. His mother, Louisa, who changed the family name when registering her son's birth in 1867, was the dominant parent in the marriage: a remarkable woman of great determination, she had literary talent and encouraged her son to write. Lawson's parents were the models for the couple in 'A Child in the Dark, and a Foreign Father', though it would be a mistake to take the story as straight autobiography. In his 'Fragment of Autobiography', a meandering and patchy account of his early years, Lawson touched on the misery of his childhood, but shied away from looking closely at the family situation:

Home life, I might as well say here, was miserably unhappy, but it was fate – there was no one to blame. It was the result of one of those utterly impossible matches so common in Australia. I remember a child who, after a violent and painful scene, used to slip out in the dark and crouch down behind the pig-stye and sob as if his heart would break.

A weak, dreamy boy, whose aunts always said that he should have been a girl, and whom town boys called 'Barmy Harry', Lawson knew periods when he seemed to live on his own: 'when Mother and brothers, but not so often Father, seemed to go completely out of my life'. Later in the autobiography he remarks: 'As I grew the feeling of loneliness and the desire to be alone increased'. The partial deafness which afflicted him from the age of nine added to his isolation. 'I wasn't a healthy-minded, average boy', says Joe Wilson (in 'Joe Wilson's Courtship'), and there is no doubt that he speaks for Lawson.

The Lawson family was broken up in 1883 when the parents separated. Henry and the other children went with their mother to Sydney, where she became a prominent advocate of women's rights, founding *Dawn*, the first Australian feminist journal in 1888, and publishing her son's first book, *Short Stories in Prose and Verse*, in 1894. Lawson's early years had been spent in the countryside around Mudgee in New South Wales, where his father had variously been a prospector, selector, and carpenter, but from 1883 onward Sydney became his home base. Lawson's life was never settled for very long, but it was always to Sydney that he returned after his various trips – to back o' Bourke, to Western Australia (twice), to New Zealand (twice), and to England. These journeys brought him fresh 'copy' (Lawson favoured the journalist's term though he did not have the journalist's approach to writing) in the shape of new impressions, but they did not fundamentally alter his vision of things. The impulse to write grew out of the keenness of his youthful feeling. Looking back late in his life, Lawson knew that he had lost the power he had possessed when he began to write as 'the lonely boy who felt things deeply and wrote with his heart's blood'.

The *Bulletin*, begun in Sydney in 1880, invited contributions of verse and prose from its readers, and it was here that Lawson was first published, in 1887. The editor and part-founder, J. F. Archibald, was an important figure in Lawson's life – the first, and perhaps the most decisive of the father-figures on whom Lawson depended. A gifted journalist, his attitude towards writing was summed up in the phrase he regularly used: 'Boil it down'. For his part, Lawson had no guiding notions of 'style', and although the influence of Dickens, Bret Harte, and later Mark Twain, is there in some of his stories, he was not apprenticed to any literary master. Archibald encouraged his own natural instinct as a writer, with advice which Lawson remembered as follows:

Every man has at least *one* story; some more. Never write until you have something to write about; *then* write. Write and re-write. Cut out every word from your copy that you can possibly do without. Never strain after effect; and, above all, always avoid anti-climax.

Lawson's comment was 'I think I did all that naturally from the first', and there is no reason to doubt him. In the same passage, Lawson offers a rare insight into his thinking on form:

Archibald in those days, preferred the short story to the short sketch. I thought the short story was a lazy man's game, second to 'free' verse, compared with the sketch. The sketch, to be really good, must be good in every line. But the sketch-story is best of all. ('Three or Four Archibalds and the Writer')

In modern usage the term 'short story' embraces what Lawson and his contemporaries called 'the sketch'. During the twentieth century writers have greatly extended the range of the short story to the point where the 'story' has become inessential. Lawson's preference for the 'sketch-story' aligns him with those modern writers since Chekhov who have aimed at suggestiveness rather than explicitness. Introducing a collection of short stories, *Capajon*, in 1933, Edward Garnett praised Hemingway's 'amazing power of suggesting more in three pregnant words than other authors do in ten', but shrewdly observed in passing that 'Lawson gets even more feeling observation and atmosphere into a page than does Hemingway'.

Apart from Garnett, however, the critics of Lawson's time failed almost completely to appreciate the artistic worth of his sketches. Worse than that, Stephens in his *Bulletin* review of *While the Billy Boils* was dismissive of the 'fragmentary impressions' which he thought could have been written as 'a single plotted, climaxed story which would make a permanent mark'. It was a line of criticism which disturbed Lawson and continued to worry him over the years. Stephens was right in judging the collection to be very uneven – the same point could be made about all the collections of Lawson's stories – but his review, in effect, advised Lawson to write against the grain of his talent. Though Lawson responded by telling his publisher, George Robertson, 'My line is writing short stories and sketches in prose and verse. I'm not a novelist', and asking, 'If you were a builder, would you set the painters to do the carpentering?', the criticism shook his self-confidence and discouraged him from experimenting further with sketches or sketch-stories. Over the next six years Lawson several times persuaded himself that he was capable of writing a novel, and his failures added to the depression and despair that finally broke him.

The stories in this selection are roughly in chronological order – the exact date of composition is not always known – and grouped to highlight themes and preoccupations. In Lawson's writing life two journeys mark important stages: the first was to Bourke and Hungerford in 1892, returning to Sydney in the following year, and the second was to England in 1900, returning in 1902.

Of the stories written before Lawson went out to Bourke, only two are included here, but they are among his most admired works. 'The Drover's Wife', written when he was only twenty-five, was the first in which he found an individual voice. It is more of a sketch than a story (in Lawson's terms), the anecdote of the snake being used to provide a framework within which he evokes the woman's life. What could have been exploited for its external interest, and presented as sensational or farcical (as it would have been by other *Bulletin* writers of the day), becomes typical of the daily threat to existence. Much discussion of the story has concentrated on the ending, which many readers have thought sentimental. Phillips implicitly defends Lawson against the charge in the course of demonstrating his art, asking what naive writer would have resisted the temptation to put an epithet before 'bush' in the final sentence. The point is well made. The writing is firm, restrained, economical; and the two adjectives which are used in that final sentence – the woman's breast is 'worn-out' and the daylight is 'sickly' – show a considerable literary tact. Far from laying it on thick, Lawson attempts to establish the emotional significance of the moment with minimal effects. This concluding tableau of mother and son is not designed to wring further pathos out of the situation, but to give it a symbolic dimension. The boy's attempt to comfort his mother – 'Mother, I won't never go drovin'; blast me if I do!' – brings into focus feelings that inhere in the predicament of the drover's wife. The boy is dependent for his survival on the mother he tries to comfort; he cannot replace the absent father and husband; his 'manly' promise to his mother, with its implication that his father was weak in submitting to necessity and leaving the family, reveals his child's vulnerability and helplessness. If 'The Drover's Wife' is susceptible to a sentimental interpretation, it is partly because the central image of mother and son – I should emphasise that I see the final scene as aiming at something more complex and more subtle than is achieved in the supposed climax of the killing of the snake – is perilously close to cliché in its conception, and throughout the sketch Lawson's notion of the woman is too close to the stereotype of the bush heroine.

Yet 'The Drover's Wife' is an impressive work to come from a young inexperienced writer. Along with 'The Bush Undertaker', it can be accommodated by the conventional view of Lawson as the sympathetic chronicler of bush life, but such an approach does not do justice to either story. In both Lawson is attempting – not wholly successfully – to create images which will define and express feelings he would have been incapable of analysing or explaining. The old hatter muttering 'I am the rassaraction' over the grave is cut off from all consolation, all hope that existence has some meaning. Uncharacteristically, in the final paragraph, Lawson distances himself from the grotesque figure he has portrayed, in sharp contrast to his identification with the 'hollow men' of 'The Union Buries Its Dead', which was written a year or so later, when he was working in the Bourke district.

The trip to Bourke and Hungerford – arranged by Archibald who was concerned by Lawson's heavy drinking – brought a new energy and toughness to his writing, as 'The Union Buries Its Dead' bears witness. He went up-country with no illusions about what he would find. A month or so earlier he had been told by 'Banjo' Paterson in the pages of the *Bulletin*:

> You had better stick to Sydney and make merry with the 'push',
> For the bush will never suit you, and you'll never suit the bush.

The two writers had engaged in a verse controversy, in which Lawson attacked the account Southern poets gave of the inland, and Paterson had written 'In Defence of the Bush'. Arriving in Bourke in a dry season, Lawson wrote to his aunt: 'The bush between here and Bathurst is horrible. I was right and Banjo wrong'. In the same letter he told her 'I got a lot of good points for copy on the way up', and 'Took notes all the way up'. Out of the journey came 'In a Dry Season', which, like 'The Union Buries Its Dead' and probably 'Hungerford', was written close to the event. These three sketches included in this volume are 'good in every line', and repay the close attention which they may not seem to invite. Written as newspaper sketches (the form of which, I suppose, had descended from the periodical essays of the previous century), they assume a local audience, alert to local references (to Tyson in 'The Union Buries Its Dead', and to Clancy in 'Hungerford', for instance). These sketches display a remarkable sureness and economy of treatment, and give the impression of a man writing out of an intensity of feeling untroubled by doubts about form.

It is relevant to note here that a numbr of commentators have been inclined to suggest that Lawson spoiled a good story when he included the passage beginning 'I have left out the wattle . . .' in 'The Union Buries Its Dead'. Such criticism assumes that Lawson's purpose was to tell a story, and that he intruded himself to draw attention to his avoidance of the stock conventions. But this 'Sketch from Life', as it was subtitled when first published, was not thought of by Lawson as a work of fiction: it was a personal impression, and the passage simply emphasised the writer's fidelity to fact in writing up his 'copy'. (That the stock emotive devices he disdains here appealed to him is plain enough from weaker stories in which he falls back upon such consoling falsities.) Placed as it is, following the painfully detailed description of the actual burial, in which the narrator, insisting that 'It doesn't matter much – nothing does', has shown how much he feels it does matter, the comment restores the unemotional reporting tone, which the narrator adopts as the representative of the union. The verbal ironies which accumulate through the sketch (more accurately sketch-story) make it a powerful revelation of what Lawson perceived as 'the Out Back Hell' (as he calls it elsewhere).

'Hungerford' is another expression of Lawson's bleak vision. On the surface a mere 'newspaper sketch', it illustrates superbly his ability to charge detail with emotional significance while leaving the meaning of the whole to emerge through implication. In this instance, the experience of going to Hungerford becomes an experience of human absurdity and futility. As a town, a centre of 'civilisation', Hungerford is a ludicrous and horrifying negation of all meaning in human endeavour. The road stops short of the town; there is a rabbit-proof fence with rabbits on both sides of it; the river on the banks of which the town is sited flows only when it floods; and, most absurd of all, the colonial border divides the town in two. And the surrounding landscape is an image of desolation which appalls the onlooker. The humour of the sketch is in the tradition of bush leg-pulling, but the effect is intentionally the reverse of comic.

Much of what Lawson wrote in the next few years was under the stimulus of the Bourke experience, though nothing else approached the direct personal intensity of these early sketches. The work, collected in *While the Billy Boils*, while uneven, contains some fine examples of sketch-stories with Mitchell as the narrator within the story framework. The economy and poise of such sketch-stories as 'On the Edge of a Plain', 'Some Day', and 'Our Pipes' is very impressive. One thinks of Chekhov's remark in a letter to Gorki: 'When a man spends the least possible number of movements over some definite action, that is grace'. These stories, seemingly insubstantial, suggest much more than they state – and so much more than *can* be stated. They are all implication. To do anything like justice to the delicate precision of their art one would have to explore them in more detail than is possible here. The appropriate comparison is with a poem rather than with a conventional story. Lawson works on a small scale, and the very brevity of the work is essential to its effect. To add and elaborate would be to destroy the effect. The stories I have selected here show, as Edward Garnett said, that Lawson 'has the faculty of bringing life to a focus, of making it typical.'

An important element in Lawson's success with these slight stories is his use of Mitchell, the shrewd, kindly, and philosophical swagman. A version of Lawson, a persona rather than a fully developed character, he replaces the author as narrator or teller of yarns in a number of stories, allowing the author to create perspective. Mitchell is on the track, a man on his own except when he finds a mate to travel with; one could suggest that as a literary creation he is related to the Romantic outcast figure of the Wanderer. Mitchell's stories give glimpses of his past, but the manner of telling and the related small actions that are described work together to have the teller reveal more than he realises. Mitchell is not so much a character to be explored in connected stories as an instrument by which Lawson can create states of feeling and so define his sense of being human. 'On the Edge of a Plain' is, in this respect, a perfect story. To a modern reader of Chekhov, the art of this little story is quickly recognised, but the originality of what Lawson was doing on his own went unremarked when *While the Billy Boils* was published in 1896.

Most critics would now agree that Lawson is at his strongest in *While the Billy Boils* and *Joe Wilson and His Mates*, and that view is reflected in this selection which aims to represent Lawson's characteristic strengths. *Joe Wilson and His Mates* was the product of his first year in England. Lawson's decision to leave Australia grew out of his conviction that if he were to succeed as a writer he had to get away. Although *While the Billy Boils* and *In the Days When the World was Wide* had won acclaim in Australia, his life had become increasingly desperate: he had married in 1896 but by 1900 there were strains in the marriage; his alcoholism had become so bad that he had voluntarily entered an inebriates' home; his writing did not earn him a sufficient income; he was depressed and distracted by the constant need to earn money, and he was tormented by the sense that he could not do himself justice working under the conditions that prevailed in Australia. The encouragement of English editors and publishers led him to decide to try to survive as a full-time writer in London. The ordeal that he underwent during the two-year stay in England (his wife became mentally unstable and had to be hospitalised for long periods, and he was responsible for the care as well as the support of two infants) has only recently been told. By the time he returned to Australia in mid-1902 his marriage was virtually over, he was exhausted, and there had been a marked decline in his writing. Before the end of that year he had attempted suicide. He never recovered from the crisis of that time, and although he continued to write over the next twenty years – he was writing the night he died in September 1922 – after 1902 there are only occasional flickers of the imaginative power he had previously shown. As a writer his life was tragically short: the work on which his current reputation rests was all done between 1892 and 1902.

In this selection I have printed the Joe Wilson stories in the order in which they were written, not as they were arranged in *Joe Wilson and His Mates*. I have done this to encourage readers to consider each story individually. To read the group of four stories as if they constitute 'a single plotted, climaxed story' (the model Stephens had recommended) is to put the emphasis in the wrong place and, incidentally, to pass over quite significant inconsistencies between the stories as a result of changes in conception from one to the other. 'Brighten's Sister-in-law', the first story Lawson wrote after his arrival in England, was the longest he had ever written up to that time. Lawson was aiming at writing a short story rather than his preferred story-sketch, and seeking to respond to the voices that urged on him the superiority of the extended narrative. It is a leisurely story, in which he exploits the freedom allowed by the autobiographical mode of narration, but the core of its meaning is located in the narrator's perception of the woman as a suffering soul. The source of her tragedy is not stated directly, nor does Joe Wilson reflect on what he sees, the woman's behaviour towards the father and son being in itself a form of revelation to the reader. In the final form of the story the link between the lonely woman without husband or child and the Wilsons is delicately suggested: her fate could be theirs.

'Brighten's Sister-in-law' had been an important advance for Lawson, in that he had preserved the essence of the 'sketch-story', with its focus on the moment of awareness, within an extended narrative, such as he had never managed before. His next Joe Wilson story attempted less and was a more even performance. By now Lawson was thinking of a Joe Wilson series, but in the next story he had obvious difficulty in controlling the direction of the narrative, and what was intended as the story of how the Wilsons settled on the land became the story of Mrs Spicer (the drover's wife writ large, as Brian Matthews says). This story has some very fine passages, including the initial episode in which Joe Wilson hears Mrs Spicer summon Annie to 'water them geraniums'. The description of the pathetic flower patch outside the Spicer hut is an outstanding example of how deftly and subtly Lawson could suggest the symbolic dimension of an experience.

There were more attempts at Joe Wilson stories, but the only other one Lawson chose to include in *Joe Wilson and His Mates* was 'Joe Wilson's Courtship', which is set earlier in time than the envisaged sequence and narrated in a gently reminiscent manner. Like the earlier monologue, 'An Old Mate of Your Father's', this story has all the charm of tender recollection without losing a sense of the real. The ending – with Joe Wilson asking Black for permission to marry Mary – is another of those short episodes in which Lawson was so effective: it is virtually a 'story-sketch' in itself.

'Telling Mrs Baker' and 'The Loaded Dog' were both written in England in the same period as the Joe Wilson stories. In the first Lawson displays a confident control of narrative, and it is only after one has started to reflect upon the view of character that it offers that one realises the unexamined emotionalism on which the whole situation is based. The idealising of the bushmen ('They are grand men – they are noble') contrasts with the realistic observation of earlier stories, and signals Lawson's turning away from the painfully real into a consoling dreamworld of the bush, in which the gospel of mateship is lived out.

I have grouped 'The Loaded Dog' with two earlier stories to illustrate Lawson's success as a humorous writer. The term 'humorous writer' is, in itself, a limiting one, and I would agree with the view that, though he wrote many enjoyable comic sketches and stories, Lawson's individual distinction is not to be found there. 'The Geological Spieler', the best of several stories in which Steelman and Smith appear, shows Lawson's characteristic use of ironic reversal, but the story does remain within the conventions of frontier humour which Mark Twain popularised. 'The Iron-bark Chip', which similarly relies upon a sudden twist, has more of the feel of local experience about it.

The hilarious farce of 'The Loaded Dog' centres on the action of the dog, but Lawson raises the story above the level of stock farce by making what happens the result of Dave Regan's bright idea; with a few strokes at the end, Lawson puts the episode into perspective as a Dave Regan yarn, part of the communal memory of the bush. Of the humorous stories in this selection, though, the Mitchell yarn, 'Bill, the Ventriloquial Rooster', is the most successful in giving the flavour of bush humour.

There is no hint of humour in the final story of this selection. I have included 'A Child in the Dark, and a Foreign Father' because it is of very great biographical interest, and also because it so clearly marks the end of Lawson's creative period. In his autobiography Lawson quotes a friend's advice to him on a projected book about bush people: 'Treated ruthlessly, Rousseaulike, without regard to your own or others' feelings, what a notable book yours would be!' 'A Child in the Dark, and a Foreign Father' may well have been begun under the influence of such advice. According to Lawson, he had intended to write a novel, and had begun work in England. The story was finished after his return to Australia in 1902 and before his suicide attempt that same year. In this version of what were obviously distressing childhood memories, there is an impersonality of tone that is quite uncharacteristic, and an absence of those evocative impressionistic descriptions which carry so much emotional force in his best work. Like 'The Drover's Wife' this story deals with the relationship of parent and child, but it is the work of a man who has lost the power to see into the heart of things.

There are a few more stories which might have been included, had space permitted. Lawson's achievement as a short-story writer, however, is not to be measured by the bulk of his collected works. His writing will be read by Australians for all sorts of reasons that have nothing to do with his literary qualities, but his claim to recognition as a writer in the larger English-speaking world rests, I believe, on the stories which have been gathered in this volume. It is in these stories that he stands apart from his *Bulletin* contemporaries – and successors – who understood the short story as a form of yarn-spinning, and no more than that. Reading these stories one starts to develop Lawson's own haunting sense of 'what-might-have-been'. The delicacy of his art met with little appreciation in a culture which valued the 'slap-dash' as being 'dinkum', and he never realised his full potential. Henry

Lawson's fate seems especially bitter in that he was misread and frustrated as an artist in the country which praised him highly while he lived and honoured him with a state funeral when he died.

In the course of this Introduction I have drawn on my *Henry Lawson's Short Stories*, in the Essays in Australian Literature series, published in Melbourne by Shillington House in 1985.

John Barnes

I

THE DROVER'S WIFE

THE two-roomed house is built of round timber, slabs, and stringy bark, and floored with split slabs. A big bark kitchen standing at one end is larger than the house itself, verandah included.

Bush all round – bush with no horizon, for the country is flat. No ranges in the distance. The bush consists of stunted, rotten native apple trees. No undergrowth. Nothing to relieve the eye save the darker green of a few sheoaks which are sighing above the narrow, almost waterless creek. Nineteen miles to the nearest sign of civilisation – a shanty on the main road.

The drover, an ex-squatter, is away with sheep. His wife and children are left here alone.

Four ragged, dried-up-looking children are playing about the house. Suddenly one of them yells: 'Snake! Mother, here's a snake!'

The gaunt, sun-browned bushwoman dashes from the kitchen, snatches her baby from the ground, holds it on her left hip, and reaches for a stick.

'Where is it?'

'Here! gone into the wood-heap!' yells the eldest boy – a sharp-faced, excited urchin of eleven. 'Stop there, mother! I'll have him. Stand back! I'll have the beggar!'

'Tommy, come here, or you'll be bit. Come here at once when I tell you, you little wretch!'

The youngster comes reluctantly, carrying a stick bigger than himself. Then he yells, triumphantly:

'There it goes – under the house!' and darts away with club uplifted.

At the same time the big, black, yellow-eyed dog-of-all-breeds, who has shown the wildest interest in the proceedings, breaks his chain and rushes after that snake. He is a moment late, however, and his nose reaches the crack in the slabs just as the end of its tail disappears. Almost at the same moment the boy's club comes down and skins the aforesaid nose. Alligator takes small notice of this, and proceeds to undermine the building; but he is subdued after a struggle and chained up. They cannot afford to lose him.

The drover's wife makes the children stand together near the dog-house while she watches for the snake. She gets two small dishes of milk and sets them down near the wall to tempt it to come out; but an hour goes by and it does not show itself.

It is near sunset, and a thunderstorm is coming. The children must be brought inside. She will not take them into the house, for she knows the snake is there, and may at any moment come up through the cracks in the rough slab floor; so she carries several armfuls of firewood into the kitchen, and then takes the children there. The kitchen has no floor – or, rather, an earthen one – called a 'ground floor' in this part of the bush. There is a large, roughly made table in the centre of the place. She brings the children in, and makes them get on this table. They are two boys and two girls – mere babies. She gives them some supper, and then, before it gets dark, she goes into the house, and snatches up some pillows and bedclothes – expecting to see or lay her hand on the snake any minute. She makes a bed on the kitchen table for the children, and sits down beside it to watch all night.

She has an eye on the corner, and a green sapling club laid in readiness on the dresser by her side, together with her sewing basket and a copy of the *Young Ladies' Journal*. She has brought the dog into the room.

Tommy turns in, under protest, but says he'll lie awake all night and smash that blinded snake.

His mother asks him how many times she has told him not to swear.

He has his club with him under the bedclothes, and Jacky protests:

'Mummy! Tommy's skinnin' me alive wif his club. Make him take it out.'

Tommy: 'Shet up, you little —! D'yer want to be bit with the snake?'

Jacky shuts up.

'If yer bit,' says Tommy, after a pause, 'you'll swell up, an' smell, an' turn red an' green an' blue all over till yer bust. Won't he, mother?'

'Now then, don't frighten the child. Go to sleep,' she says.

The two younger children go to sleep, and now and then Jacky complains of being 'skeezed.' More room is made for him. Presently Tommy says: 'Mother! listen to them (adjective) little 'possums. I'd like to screw their blanky necks.'

And Jacky protests drowsily:

'But they don't hurt us, the little blanks!'

Mother: 'There, I told you you'd teach Jacky to swear.' But the remark makes her smile. Jacky goes to sleep.

Presently Tommy asks:

'Mother! Do you think they'll ever extricate the (adjective) kangaroo?'

'Lord! How am I to know, child? Go to sleep.'

'Will you wake me if the snake comes out?'

'Yes. Go to sleep.'

Near midnight. The children are all asleep and she sits there still, sewing and reading by turns. From time to time she glances round the floor and wall-plate, and whenever she hears a noise she reaches for the stick. The thunderstorm comes on, and the wind, rushing through the cracks in the slab wall, threatens to blow out her candle. She places it on a sheltered part of the dresser and fixes up a newspaper to protect it. At every flash of lightning, the cracks between the slabs gleam like polished silver. The thunder rolls, and the rain comes down in torrents.

Alligator lies at full length on the floor, with his eyes turned towards the partition. She knows by this that the snake is there. There are large cracks in that wall opening under the floor of the dwelling-house.

She is not a coward, but recent events have shaken her nerves. A little son of her brother-in-law was lately bitten by a snake, and died. Besides, she has not heard from her husband for six months, and is anxious about him.

He was a drover, and started squatting here when they were married.

The drought of 18— ruined him. He had to sacrifice the remnant of his flock and go droving again. He intends to move his family into the nearest town when he comes back, and, in the meantime, his brother, who keeps a shanty on the main road, comes over about once a month with provisions. The wife has still a couple of cows, one horse, and a few sheep. The brother-in-law kills one of the sheep occasionally, gives her what she needs of it, and takes the rest in return for other provisions.

She is used to being left alone. She once lived like this for eighteen months. As a girl she built the usual castles in the air; but all her girlish hopes and aspirations have long been dead. She finds all the excitement and recreation she needs in the *Young Ladies' Journal*, and, Heaven help her! takes a pleasure in the fashion-plates.

Her husband is an Australian, and so is she. He is careless, but a good enough husband. If he had the means he would take her to the city and keep her there like a princess. They are used to being apart, or at least she is. 'No use fretting,' she says. He may forget sometimes that he is married; but if he has a good cheque when he comes back he will give most of it to her. When he had money he took her to the city several times – hired a railway sleeping compartment, and put up at the best hotels. He also bought her a buggy, but they had to sacrifice that along with the rest.

The last two children were born in the bush – one while her husband was bringing a drunken doctor, by force, to attend to her. She was alone on this occasion, and very weak. She had been ill with a fever. She prayed to God to send her assistance. God sent Black Mary – the 'whitest' gin in all the land. Or, at least, God sent 'King Jimmy' first, and he sent Black Mary. He put his black face round the door-post, took in the situation at a glance, and said cheerfully: 'All right, Missis – I bring my old woman, she down alonga creek.'

One of her children died while she was here alone. She rode nineteen miles for assistance, carrying the dead child.

* * *

It must be near one or two o'clock. The fire is burning low. Alligator lies with his head resting on his paws, and watches the wall. He is not a very beautiful dog to look at, and the light shows numerous old wounds where the hair will not grow. He is afraid of nothing on the face of the earth or under it. He will tackle a bullock as readily as he will tackle a flea. He hates all other dogs – except kangaroo-dogs – and has a marked dislike to friends or relations of the family. They seldom call, however. He sometimes makes friends with strangers. He hates snakes and has killed many, but he will be bitten some day and die; most snake-dogs end that way.

Now and then the bushwoman lays down her work and watches, and listens, and thinks. She thinks of things in her own life, for there is little else to think about.

The rain will make the grass grow, and this reminds her how she fought a bush fire once while her husband was away. The grass was long, and very dry, and the fire threatened to burn her out. She put on an old pair of her husband's trousers and beat out the flames with a green bough, till great drops of sooty perspiration stood out on her forehead and ran in streaks down her blackened arms. The sight of his mother in trousers greatly amused Tommy, who worked like a little hero by her side, but the terrified baby howled lustily for his 'mummy'. The fire would have mastered her but for four excited bushmen who arrived in the nick of time. It was a mixed-up affair all round; when she went to take up the baby he screamed and struggled convulsively, thinking it was a 'black man'; and Alligator, trusting more to the child's sense than his own instinct, charged furiously, and (being old and slightly deaf) did not in his excitement at first recognise his mistress's voice, but continued to hang on to the moleskins until choked off by Tommy with a saddle-strap. The dog's sorrow for his blunder, and his anxiety to let it be known that it was all a mistake, was as evident as his ragged tail and a twelve-inch grin could make it. It was a glorious time for the boys; a day to look back to, and talk about, and laugh over for many years.

She thinks how she fought a flood during her husband's absence. She stood for hours in the drenching downpour, and dug an overflow gutter to save the dam across the creek. But she could not save it. There are things that a bushwoman cannot do. Next morning the dam was broken, and her heart was nearly broken too, for she thought how her husband would feel when he came home and saw the result of years of labour swept away. She cried then.

She also fought the *pleuro-pneumonia* – dosed and bled the few remaining cattle, and wept again when her two best cows died.

Again, she fought a mad bullock that besieged the house for a day.

She made bullets and fired at him through cracks in the slabs with an old shotgun. He was dead in the morning. She skinned him and got seventeen-and-six for the hide.

She also fights the crows and eagles that have designs on her chickens. Her plan of campaign is very original. The children cry 'Crows, mother!' and she rushes out and aims a broomstick at the birds as though it were a gun, and says, 'Bung!' The crows leave in a hurry; they are cunning, but a woman's cunning is greater.

Occasionally a bushman in the horrors, or a villainous-looking sundowner, comes and nearly scares the life out of her. She generally tells the suspicious-looking stranger that her husband and two sons are at work below the dam, or over at the yard, for he always cunningly enquires for the boss.

Only last week a gallows-faced swagman – having satisfied himself that there were no men on the place – threw his swag down on the verandah, and demanded tucker. She gave him something to eat; then he expressed his intention of staying for the night. It was sundown then. She got a batten from the sofa, loosened the dog, and confronted the stranger, holding the batten in one hand and the dog's collar with the other. 'Now you go!' she said. He looked at her and at the dog, said 'All right, mum,' in a cringing tone, and left. She was a determined-looking woman, and Alligator's yellow eyes glared unpleasantly – besides, the dog's chawing-up apparatus greatly resembled that of the reptile he was named after.

She has few pleasures to think of as she sits here alone by the fire, on guard against a snake. All days are much the same to her, but on Sunday afternoon she dresses herself, tidies the children, smartens up baby, and goes for a lonely walk along the bush-track, pushing an old perambulator in front of her. She does this every Sunday. She takes as much care to make herself and the children look smart as she would if she were going to do the block in the city. There is nothing to see, however, and not a soul to meet. You might walk for twenty miles along this track without being able to fix a point in your mind, unless you are a bushman. This is because of the everlasting, maddening sameness of the stunted trees – that monotony which makes a man long to break away and travel as far as trains can go, and sail as far as ships can sail – and further.

But this bushwoman is used to the loneliness of it. As a girl-wife she hated it, but now she would feel strange away from it.

She is glad when her husband returns, but she does not gush or make a fuss about it. She gets him something good to eat, and tidies up the children.

She seems contented with her lot. She loves her children, but has no time to show it. She seems harsh to them. Her surroundings are not favourable to the development of the 'womanly' or sentimental side of nature.

*   *   *

It must be near morning now; but the clock is in the dwelling-house. Her candle is nearly done; she forgot that she was out of candles. Some more wood must be got to keep the fire up, and so she shuts the dog inside and hurries round to the wood-heap. The rain has cleared off. She seizes a stick, pulls it out, and – crash! the whole pile collapses.

Yesterday she bargained with a stray blackfellow to bring her some wood, and while he was at work she went in search of a missing cow. She was absent an hour or so, and the native black made good use of his time. On her return she was so astonished to see a good heap of wood by the chimney, that she gave him an extra fig of tobacco, and praised him for not being lazy. He thanked her, and left with head erect and chest well out. He was the last of his tribe and a King; but he had built that wood-heap hollow.

She is hurt now, and tears spring to her eyes as she sits down again by the table. She takes up a handkerchief to wipe the tears away, but pokes her eyes with her bare fingers instead. The handkerchief is full of holes, and she finds that she has put her thumb through one, and her forefinger through another.

This makes her laugh, to the surprise of the dog. She has a keen, very keen, sense of the ridiculous; and some time or other she will amuse bushmen with the story.

She has been amused before like that. One day she sat down 'to have a good cry,' as she said – and the old cat rubbed against her dress and 'cried too.' Then she had to laugh.

*   *   *

It must be near daylight. The room is very close and hot because of the fire. Alligator still watches the wall from time to time. Suddenly he becomes greatly interested; he draws himself a few inches nearer the partition, and a thrill runs through his body. The hair on the back of his neck begins to bristle, and the battle-light is in his yellow eyes. She knows what this means, and lays her hand on the stick. The lower end of one of the partition slabs has a large crack on both sides. An evil pair of small, bright, bead-like eyes glisten at one of these holes. The snake – a black one – comes slowly out, about a foot, and moves its head up and down. The dog lies still, and the woman sits as one fascinated. The snake comes out a foot further. She lifts her stick, and the reptile, as though suddenly aware of danger, sticks his head in through the crack on the other side of the slab, and hurries to get his tail round afer him. Alligator springs, and his jaws come together with a snap. He misses, for his nose is large and the snake's body close down in the angle formed by the slabs and the floor. He snaps again as the tail comes round. He has the snake now, and tugs it out eighteen inches. Thud, thud comes the woman's club on the ground. Alligator pulls again. Thud, thud. Alligator gives another pull and he has the snake out – a black brute, five feet long. The head rises to dart about, but the dog has the enemy close to the neck. He is a big, heavy dog, but quick as a terrier. He shakes the snake as though he felt the original curse in common with mankind. The eldest boy wakes up, seizes his stick, and tries to get out of bed, but his mother forces him back with a grip of iron. Thud, thud – the snake's back is broken in several places. Thud, thud – its head is crushed, and Alligator's nose skinned again.

She lifts the mangled reptile on the point of her stick, carries it to the fire, and throws it in; then piles on the wood, and watches the snake burn. The boy and dog watch, too. She lays her hand on the dog's head, and all the fierce, angry light dies out of his yellow eyes. The younger children are quieted, and presently go to sleep. The dirty-legged boy stands for a moment in his shirt, watching the fire. Presently he looks up at her, sees the tears in her eyes, and throwing his arms round her neck, exclaims:

'Mother, I won't never go drovin'; blast me if I do!'

And she hugs him to her worn-out breast and kisses him; and they sit thus together while the sickly daylight breaks over the bush.

THE BUSH UNDERTAKER

'FIVE BOB!'

The old man shaded his eyes and peered through the dazzling glow of that broiling Christmas Day. He stood just within the door of a slab-and-bark hut situated upon the bank of a barren creek; sheep-yards lay to the right, and a low line of bare brown ridges formed a suitable background to the scene.

'Five Bob!' shouted he again; and a dusty sheep-dog rose wearily from the shaded side of the hut and looked inquiringly at his master, who pointed towards some sheep which were straggling from the flock.

'Fetch 'em back,' he said confidently.

The dog went off, and his master returned to the interior of the hut.

'We'll yard 'em early,' he said to himself; 'the super won't know. We'll yard 'em early, and have the arternoon to ourselves.'

'We'll get dinner,' he added, glancing at some pots on the fire, 'I cud do a bit of doughboy, an' that theer boggabri'll eat like tater-marrer along of the salt meat.' He moved one of the black buckets from the blaze. 'I likes to keep it jist on the sizzle,' he said in explanation to himself; 'hard bilin' makes it tough – I'll keep it jist a-simmerin'.'

Here his soliloquy was interrupted by the return of the dog.

'All right, Five Bob,' said the hatter, 'dinner'll be ready dreckly. Jist keep yer eye on the sheep till I calls yer; keep 'em well rounded up, an' we'll yard 'em afterwards and have a holiday.'

This speech was accompanied by a gesture evidently intelligible, for the dog retired as though he understood English, and the cooking proceeded.

'I'll take a pick an' shovel with me an' root up that old blackfellow,' mused the shepherd, evidently following up a recent train of thought; 'I reckon it'll do now. I'll put in the spuds.'

The last sentence referred to the cooking, the first to a blackfellow's grave about which he was curious.

'The sheep's a-campin',' said the soliloquiser, glancing through the door. 'So me an' Five Bob'll be able to get our dinner in peace. I wish I had just enough fat to make the pan siss; I'd treat myself to a leather-jacket; but it took three weeks' skimmin' to get enough for them theer doughboys.'

In due time the dinner was dished up; and the old man seated himself on a block, with the lid of a gin-case across his knees for a table. Five Bob squatted opposite with the liveliest interest and appreciation depicted on his intelligent countenance.

Dinner proceeded very quietly, except when the carver paused to ask the dog how some tasty morsel went with him, and Five Bob's tail declared that it went very well indeed.

'Here y'are, try this,' cried the old man, tossing him a large piece of doughboy. A click of Five Bob's jaws and the dough was gone.

'Clean into his liver!' said the old man with a faint smile.

He washed up the tinware in the water the duff had been boiled in, and then, with the assistance of the dog, yarded the sheep.

This accomplished, he took a pick and shovel and an old sack, and started out over the ridge, followed, of course, by his four-legged mate. After tramping some three miles he reached a spur, running out from the main ridge. At the extreme end of this, under some gum trees, was a little mound of earth, barely defined in the grass, and indented in the centre as all blackfellows' graves were.

He set to work to dig it up, and sure enough, in about half-an-hour he bottomed on payable dirt.

When he had raked up all the bones, he amused himself by putting them together on the grass and by speculating as to whether they had belonged to black or white, male or female. Failing, however, to arrive at any satisfactory conclusion, he dusted them with great care, put them in the bag, and started for home.

He took a short cut this time over the ridge and down a gully which was full of ring-barked trees and long white grass. He had nearly reached its mouth when a great greasy black goanna clambered up a sapling from under his feet and looked fightable.

'Dang the jumpt-up thing!' cried the old man. 'It gin me a start!'

At the foot of the sapling he espied an object which he at first thought was the blackened carcass of a sheep, but on closer examination discovered to be the body of a man; it lay with its forehead resting on its hands, dried to a mummy by the intense heat of the western summer.

'Me luck's in for the day and no mistake!' said the shepherd, scratching the back of his head, while he took stock of the remains. He picked up a stick and tapped the body on the shoulder; the flesh sounded like leather. He turned it over on its side; it fell flat on its back like a board, and the shrivelled eyes seemed to peer up at him from under the blackened wrists.

He stepped back involuntarily, but, recovering himself, leant on his stick and took in all the ghastly details.

There was nothing in the blackened features to tell aught of name or race, but the dress proclaimed the remains to be those of a European. The old man caught sight of a black bottle in the grass, close beside the corpse. This set him thinking. Presently he knelt down and examined the soles of the dead man's blucher boots, and then, rising with an air of conviction, exclaimed: 'Brummy! by gosh! – busted up at last!'

'I tole yer so, Brummy,' he said impressively, addressing the corpse, 'I allers told yer as how it'ud be – an' here y'are, you thundering jumpt-up cuss-o'-God fool. Yer cud earn mor'n any man in the colony, but yer'd lush it all away. I allers sed as how it 'ud end, an' now yer kin see fur y'self.'

'I spect yer was a-comin' t' me t' get fixt up an' set straight agin; then yer was agoin' to swear off, same as yer allers did; an' here y'are, an' now I expect I'll have t' fix yer up for the last time an' make yer decent, for 'twon't do t' leave yer a-lyin' out here like a dead sheep.'

He picked up the corked bottle and examined it. To his great surprise it was nearly full of rum.

'Well, this gits me,' exclaimed the old man; 'me luck's in, this Christmas, an' no mistake. He must a' got the jams early in his spree, or he wouldn't be a-making for me with near a bottleful left. Howsome-never, here goes.'

Looking round, his eyes lit up with satisfaction as he saw some waste bits of bark which had been left by a party of strippers who had been getting bark there for the stations. He picked up two pieces, one about four and the other six feet long, and each about two feet wide, and brought them over to the body. He laid the longest strip by the side of the corpse, which he proceeded to lift on to it.

'Come on, Brummy,' he said, in a softer tone than usual, 'yer ain't as bad as yer might be, considerin' as it must be three good months since yer slipped yer wind. I spect it was the rum as preserved yer. It was the death of yer when yer was alive, an' now yer dead, it preserves yer like – like a mummy.'

Then he placed the other strip on top, with the hollow side downwards – thus sandwiching the defunct between the two pieces – removed the saddle strap, which he wore for a belt, and buckled it round one end, while he tried to think of something with which to tie up the other.

'I can't take any more strips off my shirt,' he said, critically examining the skirts of the old blue overshirt he wore. 'I might get a strip or two more off, but it's short enough already. Let's see; how long have I been awearin' of that shirt? Oh, I remember, I bought it jist two days afore Five Bob was pupped. I can't afford a new shirt jist yet; howsomenever, seein' it's Brummy, I'll jist borrow a couple more strips and sew 'em on agen when I git home.'

He up-ended Brummy, and placing his shoulder against the middle of the lower sheet of bark, lifted the corpse to a horizontal position; then taking the bag of bones in his hand, he started for home.

'I ain't a-spendin' sech a dull Christmas arter all,' he reflected, as he plodded on; but he had not walked above a hundred yards when he saw a black goanna sidling into the grass by the side of the path.

'That's another of them theer dang things!' he exclaimed. 'That's two I've seed this mornin'.'

Presently he remarked: 'Yer don't smell none too sweet, Brummy. It must 'a' been jist about the middle of shearin' when yer pegged out. I wonder who got yer last cheque? Shoo! theer's another black gohanner – theer must be a flock on 'em.'

He rested Brummy on the ground while he had another pull at the bottle, and, before going on, packed the bag of bones on his shoulder under the body, but he soon stopped again.

'The thunderin' jumpt-up bones is all skew-whift,' he said. ' 'Ole on, Brummy, an' I'll fix 'em;' and he leaned the dead man against a tree while he settled the bones on his shoulder, and took another pull at the bottle.

About a mile further on he heard a rustling in the grass to the right, and, looking around, saw another goanna gliding off sideways, with its long snaky neck turned towards him.

This puzzled the shepherd considerably, the strangest part of it being that Five Bob wouldn't touch the reptile, but slunk off with his tail down when ordered to 'sick 'em.'

'Theer's sothin' comic about them theer gohanners,' said the old man at last. 'I've seed swarms of grasshoppers an' big mobs of kangaroos, but dang me if ever I seed a flock of black gohanners afore!'

On reaching the hut the old man dumped the corpse against the wall, wrong end up, and stood scratching his head while he endeavoured to collect his muddled thoughts; but he had not placed Brummy at the correct angle, and, consequently, that individual fell forward and struck him a violent blow on the shoulder with the iron toes of his blucher boots.

The shock sobered him. He sprang a good yard, instinctively hitching up his moleskins in preparation for flight; but a backward glance revealed to him the true cause of this supposed attack from the rear. Then he lifted the body, stood it on its feet against the chimney, and ruminated as to where he should lodge his mate for the night, not noticing that the shorter sheet of bark had slipped down on the boots and left the face exposed.

'I spect I'll have ter put yer into the chimney trough for the night, Brummy,' said he, turning round to confront the corpse. 'Yer can't expect me to take yer into the hut, though I did it when yer was in a worse state than – Lord!'

The shepherd was not prepared for the awful scrutiny that gleamed on him from those empty sockets; his nerves received a shock, and it was some time before he recovered himself sufficiently to speak.

'Now look a-here, Brummy,' said he, shaking his finger severely at the delinquent, 'I don't want to pick a row with yer; I'd do as much for yer an' more than any other man, an' well yer knows it; but if yer starts playin' any of yer jumpt-up pranktical jokes on me, and a scarin' of me after a-humpin' of yer 'ome, by the 'oly frost I'll kick yer to jim-rags, so I will.'

This admonition delivered, he hoisted Brummy into the chimney trough, and with a last glance towards the sheep-yards, he retired to his bunk to have, as he said, a snooze.

He had more than a 'snooze', however, for when he woke it was dark, and the bushman's instinct told him it must be nearly nine o'clock.

He lit a slush lamp and poured the remainder of the rum into a pannikin; but, just as he was about to lift the draught to his lips, he heard a peculiar rustling sound overhead, and put the pot down on the table with a slam that spilled some of the precious liquor.

Five Bob whimpered, and the old shepherd, though used to the weird and dismal, as one living alone in the bush must necessarily be, felt the icy breath of fear at his heart.

He reached hastily for his old shot-gun, and went out to investigate. He walked round the hut several times and examined the roof on all sides, but saw nothing. Brummy appeared to be in the same position.

At last, persuading himself that the noise was caused by 'possums or the wind, the old man went inside, boiled his billy, and after composing his nerves somewhat with a light supper and a meditative smoke, retired for the night. He was aroused several times before midnight by the same mysterious sound overhead, but, though he rose and examined the roof on each occasion by the light of the rising moon, he discovered nothing.

At last he determined to sit up and watch until daybreak, and for this purpose took up a position on a log a short distance from the hut, with his gun laid in readiness across his knee.

After watching for about an hour, he saw a black object coming over the ridge-pole. He grabbed his gun and fired. The thing disappeared. He ran round to the other side of the hut, and there was a great black goanna in violent convulsions on the ground.

Then the old man saw it all. 'The thunderin' jumpt-up thing has been a-havin' o' me,' he exclaimed. 'The same cuss-o'-God wretch has a-follered me 'ome, an' has been a-havin' its Christmas dinner off of Brummy, an' a-hauntin' o' me into the bargain, the jumpt-up tinker!'

As there was no one by whom he could send a message to the station, and the old man dared not leave the sheep and go himself, he determined to bury the body the next afternoon, reflecting that the authorities could disinter it for inquest if they pleased.

So he brought the sheep home early, and made arrangements for the burial by measuring the outer casing of Brummy and digging a hole according to those dimensions.

'That 'minds me,' he said, 'I never rightly knowed Brummy's religion, blest if ever I did. Howsomenever, there's one thing sartin – none o' them theer pianer-fingered parsons is a-goin' ter take the trouble ter travel out inter this God-forgotten part to hold sarvice over him, seein' as how his last cheque's blued. But as I've got the fun'ral arrangements all in me own hands, I'll do jestice to it, and see that Brummy has a good comfortable buryin' – and more's unpossible.'

'It's time yer turned in, Brum,' he said, lifting the body down.

He carried it to the grave and dropped it into one corner like a post. He arranged the bark so as to cover the face, and, by means of a piece of clothes-line, lowered the body to a horizontal position. Then he threw in an armful of gum leaves, and then, very reluctantly, took the shovel and dropped in a few shovelfuls of earth.

'An' this is the last of Brummy,' he said, leaning on his spade and looking away over the tops of the ragged gums on the distant range.

This reflection seemed to engender a flood of memories, in which the old man became absorbed.

'Arter all,' he murmured sadly, 'arter all – it were Brummy.'

'Brummy,' he said at last, 'it's all over now; nothin' matters now – nothin' didn't ever matter, nor – nor don't. You uster say as how it 'ud be all right termorrer' (pause); 'termorrer's come, Brummy – come fur you – it ain't come fur me yet, but – it's a-comin'.'

He threw in some more earth.

'Yer don't remember, Brummy, an' mebbe yer don't want to remember – I don't want to remember – but – well, but, yer see that's where yer got the pull on me.'

He shovelled in some more earth and paused again.

The dog rose, with ears erect, and looked anxiously first at his master, and then into the grave.

'Theer oughter be somethin' sed,' muttered the old man; ' 'tain't right to put 'im under like a dog. There oughter to be some sort o' sarmin.' He sighed heavily in the listening silence that followed this remark, and proceeded with his work. He filled the grave to the brim this time, and fashioned the mound carefully with his spade. Once or twice he muttered the words, 'I am the rassaraction.' As he laid the tools quietly aside, and stood at the head of the grave, he was evidently trying to remember the something that ought to be said. He removed his hat, placed it carefully on the grass, held his hands out from his sides and a little to the front, drew a long deep breath, and said with a solemnity that greatly disturbed Five Bob, 'Hashes ter hashes, dus ter dus, Brummy, – an' – an' in hopes of a great an' gerlorious rassaraction!'

He sat down on a log near by, rested his elbows on his knees and passed his hand wearily over hs forehead – but only as one who was tired and felt the heat; and presently he rose, took up the tools, and walked back to the hut.

And the sun sank again on the grand Australian bush – the nurse and tutor of eccentric minds, the home of the weird, and of much that is different from things in other lands.

II

IN A DRY SEASON

DRAW a wire fence and a few ragged gums, and add some scattered sheep running away from the train. Then you'll have the bush all along the New South Wales Western line from Bathurst on.

The railway town consists of a public house and a general store, with a square tank and a schoolhouse on piles in the nearer distance. The tank stands at the end of the school and is not many times smaller than the building itself. It is safe to call the pub 'The Railway Hotel', and the store 'The Railway Stores', with an 's'. A couple of patient, ungroomed hacks are probably standing outside the pub, while their masters are inside having a drink – several drinks. Also it's safe to draw a sundowner sitting listlessly on a bench on the verandah, reading *The Bulletin*.

The Railway Stores seem to exist only in the shadow of the pub, and it is impossible to conceive either as being independent of the other. There is sometimes a small, oblong weatherboard building – unpainted, and generally leaning in one of the eight possible directions, and perhaps with a twist in another – which, from its half-obliterated sign, seems to have started as a rival to the Railway Stores; but the shutters are up and the place empty.

The only town I saw that differed much from the above consisted of a box-bark humpy with a clay chimney, and a woman standing at the door throwing out the wash-up water.

By way of variety, the artist might make a watercolour-sketch of a fettler's tent on the line, with a billy hanging over the fire in front, and three fettlers standing round filling their pipes.

Slop sac suits, red faces, and old-fashioned flat-brimmed hats, with wire round the brims, begin to drop into the train on the other side of Bathurst; and here and there a hat with three inches of crape round the crown, which perhaps signifies death in the family at some remote date, and perhaps doesn't. Sometimes, I believe, it only means grease under the band. I notice that when a bushman puts crape round his hat he generally leaves it there till the hat wears out, or another friend dies. In the latter case, he buys a new piece of crape. This outward sign of bereavement usually has a jolly red face beneath it. Death is about the only cheerful thing in the bush.

We crossed the Macquarie – a narrow, muddy gutter with a dog swimming across, and three goats interested.

A little further on we saw the first sundowner. He carried a Royal Alfred, and had a billy in one hand and a stick in the other. He was dressed in a tailcoat turned yellow, a print shirt, and a pair of moleskin trousers, with big square calico patches on the knees; and his old straw hat was covered with calico. Suddenly he slipped his swag, dropped his billy, and ran forward, boldly flourishing the stick. I thought that he was mad, and was about to attack the train, but he wasn't; he was only killing a snake. I didn't have time to see whether he cooked the snake or not – perhaps he only thought of Adam.

Somebody told me that the country was very dry on the other side of Nevertire. It is. I wouldn't like to sit down on it anywhere. The least horrible spot in the bush, in a dry season, is where the bush isn't – where it has been cleared away and a green crop is trying to grow. They talk of settling people on the land! Better settle *in* it. I'd rather settle on the water; at least, until some gigantic system of irrigation is perfected in the West.

Along about Byrock we saw the first shearers. They dress like the unemployed, but differ from that body in their looks of independence. They sat on trucks and wool-bales and the fence, watching the train, and hailed Bill, and Jim, and Tom, and asked how those individuals were getting on.

Here we came across soft felt hats with straps round the crowns, and full-bearded faces under them. Also a splendid-looking black tracker in a masher uniform and a pair of Wellington boots.

One or two square-cuts and stand-up collars struggle dismally through to the bitter end. Often a member of the unemployed starts cheerfully out, with a letter from the Government Labour Bureau in his pocket, and nothing else. He has an idea that the station where he has the job will be within easy walking distance of Bourke. Perhaps he thinks there'll be a cart or a buggy waiting for him. He travels for a night and day without a bite to eat, and, on arrival, he finds that the station is eighty or a hundred miles away. Then he has to explain matters to a publican and a coach-driver. God bless the publican and the coach-driver! God forgive our social system!

Native industry was represented at one place along the line by three tiles, a chimney-pot, and a length of piping on a slab.

Somebody said to me, 'Yer wanter go out back, young man, if yer wanter see the country. Yer wanter get away from the line.' I don't wanter; I've been there.

You could go to the brink of eternity as far as Australia is concerned and yet meet an animated mummy of a swagman who will talk of going 'out back'. Out upon the out-back fiend!

About Byrock we met the bush liar in all his glory. He was dressed like – like a bush larrikin. His name was Jim. He had been to a ball where some blank had 'touched' his blanky overcoat. The overcoat had a cheque for ten 'quid' in the pocket. He didn't seem to feel the loss much. 'Wot's ten quid?' He'd been everywhere, including the Gulf country. He still had three or four sheds to go. He had telegrams in his pocket from half-a-dozen squatters and supers offering him pens on any terms. He didn't give a blank whether he took them or no. He thought at first he had the telegrams on him, but found that he had left them in the pocket of the overcoat aforesaid. He had learned butchering in a day. He was a bit of a scrapper himself and talked a lot about the ring. At the last station where he shore he gave the super the father of a hiding. The super was a big chap, about six foot three, and had knocked out Paddy Somebody in one round. He worked with a man who shore 400 sheep in nine hours.

Here a quiet-looking bushman in a corner of the carriage grew restless, and presently he opened his mouth and took the liar down in about three minutes.

At 5.30 we saw a long line of camels moving out across the sunset. There's something snaky about camels. They remind me of turtles and goannas.

Somebody said, 'Here's Bourke.'

THE UNION BURIES ITS DEAD

WHILE out boating one Sunday afternoon on a billabong across the river, we saw a young man on horseback driving some horses along the bank. He said it was a fine day, and asked if the water was deep there. The joker of our party said it was deep enough to drown him, and he laughed and rode farther up. We didn't take much notice of him.

Next day a funeral gathered at a corner pub and asked each other in to have a drink while waiting for the hearse. They passed away some of the time dancing jigs to a piano in the bar parlour. They passed away the rest of the time sky-larking and fighting.

The defunct was a young union labourer, about twenty-five, who had been drowned the previous day while trying to swim some horses across a billabong of the Darling.

He was almost a stranger in town, and the fact of his having been a union man accounted for the funeral. The police found some union papers in his swag, and called at the General Labourers' Union Office for information about him. That's how we knew. The secretary had very little information to give. The departed was a 'Roman', and the majority of the town were otherwise – but unionism is stronger than creed. Drink, however, is stronger than unionism; and, when the hearse presently arrived, more than two-thirds of the funeral were unable to follow. They were too drunk.

The procession numbered fifteen, fourteen souls following the broken shell of a soul. Perhaps not one of the fourteen possessed a soul any more than the corpse did – but that doesn't matter.

Four or five of the funeral, who were boarders at the pub, borrowed a trap which the landlord used to carry passengers to and from the railway station. They were strangers to us who were on foot, and we to them. We were all strangers to the corpse.

A horseman, who looked like a drover just returned from a big trip, dropped into our dusty wake and followed us a few hundred yards, dragging his pack-horse behind him, but a friend made wild and demonstrative signals from a hotel verandah – hooking at the air in front with his right hand and jobbing his left thumb over his shoulder in the direction of the bar – so the drover hauled off and didn't catch up to us any more. He was a stranger to the entire show.

We walked in twos. There were three twos. It was very hot and dusty; the heat rushed in fierce dazzling rays across every iron roof and light-coloured wall that was turned to the sun. One or two pubs closed respectfully until we got past. They closed their bar doors and the patrons went in and out through some side or back entrance for a few minutes. Bushmen seldom grumble at an inconvenience of this sort, when it is caused by a funeral. They have too much respect for the dead.

On the way to the cemetery we passed three shearers sitting on the shady side of a fence. One was drunk – very drunk. The other two covered their right ears with their hats, out of respect for the departed – whoever he might have been – and one of them kicked the drunk and muttered something to him.

He straightened himself up, stared, and reached helplessly for his hat, which he shoved half off and then on again. Then he made a great effort to pull himself together – and succeeded. He stood up, braced his back against the fence, knocked off his hat, and remorsefully placed his foot on it – to keep it off his head till the funeral passed.

A tall, sentimental drover, who walked by my side, cynically quoted Byronic verses suitable to the occasion – to death – and asked with pathetic humour whether we thought the dead man's ticket would be recognised 'over yonder'. It was a G.L.U. ticket, and the general opinion was that it would be recognised.

Presently my friend said:

'You remember when we were in the boat yesterday, we saw a man driving some horses along the bank?'

'Yes.'

He nodded at the hearse and said:

'Well, that's him.'

I thought awhile.

'I didn't take any particular notice of him,' I said. 'He said something, didn't he?'

'Yes; said it was a fine day. You'd have taken more notice if you'd known that he was doomed to die in the hour, and that those were the last words he would say to any man in this world.'

'To be sure,' said a full voice from the rear. 'If ye'd known that, ye'd have prolonged the conversation.'

We plodded on across the railway line and along the hot, dusty road which ran to the cemetery, some of us talking about the accident, and lying about the narrow escapes we had had ourselves. Presently some one said:

'There's the Devil.'

I looked up and saw a priest standing in the shade of the tree by the cemetery gate.

The hearse was drawn up and the tail-boards were opened. The funeral extinguished its right ear with its hat as four men lifted the coffin out and laid it over the grave. The priest – a pale, quiet young fellow – stood under the shade of a sapling which grew at the head of the grave. He took off his hat, dropped it carelessly on the ground, and proceeded to business. I noticed that one or two heathens winced slightly when the holy water was sprinkled on the coffin. The drops quickly evaporated, and the little round black spots they left were soon dusted over; but the spots showed, by contrast, the cheapness and shabbiness of the cloth with which the coffin was covered. It seemed black before; now it looked a dusky grey.

Just here man's ignorance and vanity made a farce of the funeral. A big, bull-necked publican, with heavy, blotchy features, and a supremely ignorant expression, picked up the priest's straw hat and held it about two inches over the head of his reverence during the whole of the service. The father, be it remembered, was standing in the shade. A few shoved their hats on and off uneasily, struggling between their disgust for the living and their respect for the dead. The hat had a conical crown and a brim sloping down all round like a sunshade, and the publican held it with his great red claw spread over the crown. To do the priest justice, perhaps he didn't notice the incident. A stage priest or parson in the same position might have said, 'Put the hat down, my friend; is not the memory of our departed brother worth more than my complexion?' A wattlebark layman might have expressed himself in stronger language, none the less to the point. But my priest seemed unconscious of what was going on. Besides, the publican was a great and important pillar of the Church. He couldn't, as an ignorant and conceited ass, lose such a good opportunity of asserting his faithfulness and importance to his Church.

The grave looked very narrow under the coffin, and I drew a breath of relief when the box slid easily down. I saw a coffin get stuck once, at Rookwood, and it had to be yanked out with difficulty, and laid on the sods at the feet of the heart-broken relations, who howled dismally while the grave-diggers widened the hole. But they don't cut contracts so fine in the West. Our grave-digger was not altogether bowelless, and, out of respect for that human quality described as 'feelin's', he scraped up some light and dusty soil and threw it down to deaden the fall of the clay lumps on the coffin. He also tried to steer the first few shovelsful gently down against the end of the grave with the back of the shovel turned outwards, but the hard, dry Darling River clods rebounded and knocked all the same. It didn't matter much – nothing does. The fall of lumps of clay on a stranger's coffin doesn't sound any different from the fall of the same things on an ordinary wooden box – at least I didn't notice anything awesome or unusual in the sound; but, perhaps, one of us – the most sensitive – might have been impressed by being reminded of a burial of long ago, when the thump of every sod jolted his heart.

I have left out the wattle – because it wasn't there. I have also neglected to mention the heart-broken old mate, with his grizzled head bowed and great pearly drops streaming down his rugged cheeks. He was absent – he was probably 'Out Back'. For similar reasons I have omitted reference to the suspicious moisture in the eyes of a bearded bush ruffian named Bill. Bill failed to turn up, and the only moisture was that which was induced by the heat. I have left out the 'sad Australian sunset' because the sun was not going down at the time. The burial took place exactly at mid-day.

The dead bushman's name was Jim, apparently; but they found no portraits, nor locks of hair, nor any love letters, nor anything of that kind in his swag – not even a reference to his mother; only some papers relating to union matters. Most of us didn't know the name till we saw it on the coffin; we knew him as 'that poor chap that got drowned yesterday'.

'So his name's James Tyson,' said my drover acquaintance, looking at the plate.

'Why! Didn't you know that before?' I asked.

'No; but I knew he was a union man.'

It turned out, afterwards, that J.T. wasn't his real name – only 'the name he went by'.

Anyhow he was buried by it, and most of the 'Great Australian Dailies' have mentioned in their brevity columns that a young man named James John Tyson was drowned in a billabong of the Darling last Sunday.

We did hear, later on, what his real name was; but if we ever chance to read it in the 'Missing Friends Column', we shall not be able to give any information to heart-broken Mother or Sister or Wife, nor to any one who could let him hear something to his advantage – for we have already forgotten the name.

HUNGERFORD

ONE of the hungriest cleared roads in New South Wales runs to within a couple of miles of Hungerford, and stops there; then you strike through the scrub to the town. There is no distant prospect of Hungerford – you don't see the town till you are quite close to it, and then two or three white-washed galvanised-iron roofs start out of the mulga.

They say that a past Ministry commenced to clear the road from Bourke, under the impression that Hungerford was an important place, and went on, with the blindness peculiar to Governments, till they got to within two miles of the town. Then they ran short of rum and rations, and sent a man on to get them, and make inquiries. The member never came back, and two more were sent to find him – or Hungerford. Three days later the two returned in an exhausted condition, and submitted a motion of want-of-confidence, which was lost. Then the whole House went on and was lost also. Strange to relate, that Government was never missed.

However, we found Hungerford and camped there for a day. The town is right on the Queensland border, and an interprovincial rabbit-proof fence – with rabbits on both sides of it – runs across the main street.

This fence is a standing joke with Australian rabbits – about the only joke they have out there, except the memory of Pasteur and poison and inoculation. It is amusing to go a little way out of town, about sunset, and watch them crack Noah's Ark rabbit jokes about that fence, and burrow under and play leap-frog over till they get tired. One old buck rabbit sat up and nearly laughed his ears off at a joke of his own about that fence. He laughed so much that he couldn't get away when I reached for him. I could hardly eat him for laughing. I never saw a rabbit laugh before; but I've seen a 'possum do it.

Hungerford consists of two houses and a humpy in New South Wales, and five houses in Queensland. Characteristically enough, both the pubs are in Queensland. We got a glass of sour yeast at one and paid sixpence for it – we had asked for English ale.

The post-office is in New South Wales, and the police-barracks in Bananaland. The police cannot do anything if there's a row going on across the street in New South Wales, except to send to Brisbane and have an extradition warrant applied for; and they don't do much if there's a row in Queensland. Most of the rows are across the border, where the pubs are.

At least, I believe that's how it is, though the man who told me might have been a liar. Another man said he was a liar, but then *he* might have been a liar himself – a third person said he was one. I heard that there was a fight over it, but the man who told me about the fight might not have been telling the truth.

One part of the town swears at Brisbane when things go wrong, and the other part curses Sydney.

The country looks as though a great ash-heap had been spread out there, and mulga scrub and firewood planted – and neglected. The country looks just as bad for a hundred miles round Hungerford, and beyond that it gets worse – a blasted, barren wilderness that doesn't even howl. If it howled it would be a relief.

I believe that Burke and Wills found Hungerford, and it's a pity they did; but, if I ever stand by the graves of the men who first travelled through this country, when there were neither roads nor stations, nor tanks, nor bores, nor pubs, I'll – I'll take my hat off. There were brave men in the land in those days.

It is said that the explorers gave the district its name chiefly because of the hunger they found there, which has remained there ever since. I don't know where the ford comes in – there's nothing to ford, except in flood-time. Hungerthirst would have been better. The town is supposed to be situated on the banks of a river called the Paroo, but we saw no water there, except what passed for it in a tank. The goats and sheep and dogs and the rest of the population drink there. It is dangerous to take too much of that water in a raw state.

Except in flood-time you couldn't find the bed of the river without the aid of a spirit level and a long straight-edge. There is a Custom-house against the fence on the northern side. A pound of tea often costs six shillings on that side, and you can get a common lead pencil for fourpence at the rival store across the street in the mother province. Also, a small loaf of sour bread sells for a shilling at the humpy afore-mentioned. Only about sixty per cent of the sugar will melt.

We saw one of the storekeepers give a deadbeat swagman five shil-lings' worth of rations to take him on into Queensland. The store-keepers often do this, and put it down on the loss side of their books. I hope the recording angel listens, and puts it down on the right side of his book.

We camped on the Queensland side of the fence, and after tea had a yarn with an old man who was minding a mixed flock of goats and sheep; and we asked him whether he thought Queensland was better than New South Wales, or the other way about.

He scratched the back of his head, and thought awhile, and hesitated like a stranger who is going to do you a favour at some personal in-convenience.

At last, with the bored air of a man who has gone through the same performance too often before, he stepped deliberately up to the fence and spat over it into New South Wales. After which he got leisurely through and spat back on Queensland.

'That's what *I* think of the blanky colonies!' he said.

He gave us time to become sufficiently impressed; then he said:

'And if I was at the Victorian and South Australian border I'd do the same thing.'

He let that soak into our minds, and added: 'And the same with West Australia – and – and Tasmania.' Then he went away.

The last would have been a long spit – and he forgot Maoriland.

We heard afterwards that his name was Clancy, and he had that day been offered a job droving at 'twenty-five shillings a week and find your own horse'. Also find your own horse-feed and tobacco and soap and other luxuries, at station prices. Moreover, if you lost your own horse you would have to find another, and if that died or went astray you would have to find a third – or forfeit your pay and return on foot. The boss drover agreed to provide flour and mutton – when such things were procurable.

Consequently, Clancy's decidedly unfavourable opinion of the colonies.

My mate and I sat down on our swags against the fence to talk things over. One of us was very deaf. Presently a black tracker went past and looked at us, and returned to the pub. Then a trooper in Queensland uniform came along and asked us what the trouble was about, and where we came from and were going, and where we camped. We said we were discussing private business, and he explained that he thought it was a row, and came over to see. Then he left us, and later on we saw him sitting with the rest of the population on a bench under the hotel veranda. Next morning we rolled up our swags and left Hungerford to the North-West.

III

'RATS'

'WHY, there's two of them, and they're having a fight! Come on.'

It seemed a strange place for a fight – that hot, lonely, cotton-bush plain. And yet not more than half-a-mile ahead there were apparently two men struggling together on the track.

The three travellers postponed their smoke-oh! and hurried on. They were shearers – a little man and a big man, known respectively as 'Sunlight' and 'Macquarie', and a tall, thin, young jackeroo whom they called 'Milky'.

'I wonder where the other man sprang from? I didn't see him before,' said Sunlight.

'He muster bin layin' down in the bushes,' said Macquarie. 'They're goin' at it proper, too. Come on! Hurry up and see the fun!'

They hurried on.

'It's a funny-lookin' feller, the other feller,' panted Milky. 'He don't seem to have no head. Look! he's down – they're both down! They must ha' clinched on the ground. No! they're up an' at it again . . . Why, good Lord! I think the other's a woman!'

'My oath! so it is!' yelled Sunlight. 'Look! the brute's got her down again! He's kickin' her! Come on, chaps; come on, or he'll do for her!'

They dropped swags, water-bags and all, and raced forward; but presently Sunlight, who had the best eyes, slackened his pace and dropped behind. His mates glanced back at his face, saw a peculiar expression there, looked ahead again, and then dropped into a walk.

They reached the scene of the trouble, and there stood a little withered old man by the track, with his arms folded close up under his chin; he was dressed mostly in calico patches; and half-a-dozen corks, suspended on bits of string from the brim of his hat, dangled before his bleared optics to scare away the flies. He was scowling malignantly at a stout, dumpy swag which lay in the middle of the track.

'Well, old Rats, what's the trouble,' asked Sunlight.

'Oh, nothing, nothing,' answered the old man, without looking round. 'I fell out with my swag, that's all. He knocked me down, but I've settled him.'

'But look here,' said Sunlight, winking at his mates, 'we saw you jump on him when he was down. That ain't fair, you know.'

'But you didn't see it all,' cried Rats, getting excited. 'He hit *me* down first! And, look here, I'll fight him again for nothing, and you can see fair play.'

They talked awhile; then Sunlight proposed to second the swag, while his mate supported the old man, and after some persuasion, Milky agreed, for the sake of the lark, to act as time-keeper and referee.

Rats entered into the spirit of the thing; he stripped to the waist, and while he was getting ready the travellers pretended to bet on the result.

Macquarie took his place behind the old man, and Sunlight up-ended the swag. Rats shaped and danced round; then he rushed, feinted, ducked, retreated, darted in once more, and suddenly went down like a shot on the broad of his back. No actor could have done it better; he went down from that imaginary blow as if a cannon-ball had struck him in the forehead.

Milky called time, and the old man came up, looking shaky. However, he got in a tremendous blow which knocked the swag into the bushes.

Several rounds followed with varying success.

The men pretended to get more and more excited, and betted freely; and Rats did his best. At last they got tired of the fun, Sunlight let the swag lie after Milky called time, and the jackeroo awarded the fight to Rats. They pretended to hand over the stakes, and then went back for their swags, while the old man put on his shirt.

Then he calmed down, carried his swag to the side of the track, sat down on it and talked rationally about bush matters for awhile; but

presently he grew silent and began to feel his muscles and smile idiotic-
ally.

'Can you len' us a bit o' meat?' said he suddenly.

They spared him half-a-pound; but he said he didn't want it all, and
cut off about an ounce, which he laid on the end of his swag. Then he
took the lid off his billy and produced a fishing-line. He baited the
hook, threw the line across the track, and waited for a bite. Soon he got
deeply interested in the line, jerked it once or twice, and drew it in
rapidly. The bait had been rubbed off in the grass. The old man
regarded the hook disgustedly.

'Look at that!' he cried, 'I had him, only I was in such a hurry. I
should ha' played him a little more.'

Next time he was more careful, he drew the line in warily, grabbed an
imaginary fish and laid it down on the grass. Sunlight and Co. were
greatly interested by this time.

'Wot yer think o' that?' asked Rats. 'It weighs thirty pound if it
weighs an ounce! Wot yer think o' that for a cod?' The hook's half-way
down his blessed gullet?'

He caught several cod and a bream while they were there, and
invited them to camp and have tea with him. But they wished to reach
a certain shed next day, so – after the ancient had borrowed about a
pound of meat for bait – they went on, and left him fishing contentedly.

But first Sunlight went down into his pocket and came up with half-
a-crown, which he gave to the old man, along with some tucker. 'You'd
best push on to the water before dark, old chap,' he said, kindly.

When they turned their heads again, Rats was still fishing: but when
they looked back for the last time before entering the timber, he was
having another row with his swag; and Sunlight reckoned that the
trouble arose out of some lies which the swag had been telling about the
bigger fish it caught.

An Old Mate of Your Father's

YOU remember when we hurried home from the old bush school how we were sometimes startled by a bearded apparition, who smiled kindly down on us, and whom our mother introduced, as we raked off our hats, as, 'An old mate of your father's on the diggings, Johnny.' And he would pat our heads and say we were fine boys, or girls – as the case may have been – and that we had our father's nose but our mother's eyes, or the other way about; and say that the baby was the dead spit of its mother, and then add, for father's benefit: 'But yet he's like you, Tom.' It did seem strange to the children to hear him address the old man by his Christian name – considering that the mother always referred to him as 'Father'. She called the old mate Mr So-and-so, and father called him Bill, or something to that effect.

Occasionally the old mate would come dressed in the latest city fashion, and at other times in a new suit of reach-me-downs, and yet again he would turn up in clean white moleskins, washed tweed coat, Crimean shirt, blucher boots, soft felt hat, with a fresh-looking speckled handkerchief round his neck. But his face was mostly round and brown and jolly, his hands were always horny, and his beard grey. Sometimes he might have seemed strange and uncouth to us at first, but the old man never appeared the least surprised at anything he said or did – they understood each other so well – and we would soon take to this relic of our father's past, who would have fruit or lollies for us – strange that he always remembered them – and would surreptitiously slip 'shilluns' into our dirty little hands, and tell us stories about the old days, 'when me an' yer father was on the diggin's, an' you wasn't thought of, my boy.'

Sometimes the old mate would stay over Sunday, and in the fore-noon or after dinner he and father would take a walk amongst the deserted shafts of Sapling Gully or along Quartz Ridge, and criticise old ground, and talk of past diggers' mistakes, and second bottoms, and feelers, and dips, and leads – also outcrops – and absently pick up pieces of quartz and slate, rub them on their sleeves, look at them in an abstracted manner, and drop them again; and they would talk of some old lead they had worked on: 'Hogan's party was here on one side of us, Macintosh was here on the other, Mac was getting good gold and so was Hogan, and now, why the blanky blank weren't we on gold?' And the mate would always agree that there was 'gold in them ridges and gullies yet, if a man only had the money behind him to git at it.' And then perhaps the guv'nor would show him a spot where he intended to put down a shaft some day – the old man was always thinking of putting down a shaft. And these two old 'Fifty-Niners would mooch round and sit on their heels on the sunny mullock heaps and break clay lumps between their hands, and lay plans for the putting down of shafts, and smoke, till an urchin was sent to 'look for his father and Mr So-and-so, and tell 'em to come to their dinner.'

And again – mostly in the fresh of the morning – they would hang about the fences on the selection and review the live stock: five dusty skeletons of cows, a hollow-sided calf or two, and one shocking piece of equine scenery – which, by the way, the old mate always praised. But the selector's heart was not in farming nor on selections – it was far away with the last new rush in West Australia or Queensland, or per-haps buried in the worked-out ground of Tambaroora, Married Man's Creek, or Araluen; and by-and-by the memory of some half-forgotten reef or lead or 'Last Chance', 'Nil Desperandum', or 'Brown Snake' claim would take their thoughts far back and away from the dusty patch of sods and struggling sprouts called the crop, or the few dis-couraged, half-dead slips which comprised the orchard. Then their conversation would be pointed with many Golden Points, Baikery Hills, Deep Creeks, Maitland Bars, Specimen Flats, and Chinamen's Gullies. And so they'd yarn till the youngster came to tell them that 'Mother sez the breakfus is gettin' cold,' and then the old mate would rouse himself and stretch and say, 'Well, we mustn't keep the missus waitin', Tom!'

And, after tea, they would sit on a log of the wood-heap, or the edge of the veranda – that is, in warm weather – and yarn about Ballarat and Bendigo – of the days when we spoke of being 'on' a place oftener than 'at' it; *on* Ballarat, *on* Gulgong, *on* Lambing Flat, *on* Creswick – and they would use the definite article before the names, as: 'on The Turon; The Lachlan; The Home Rule; The Canadian Lead.' Then again they'd yarn of old mates, such as Tom Brook, Jack Henright, and poor Martin Ratcliffe – who was killed in his golden hole – and of other men whom they didn't seem to have known much about, and who went by the names of 'Adelaide Adolphus', 'Corney George', and other names which might have been more or less applicable.

And sometimes they'd get talking, low and mysterious like, about 'Th' Eureka Stockade'; and if we didn't understand and asked questions, 'What was the Eureka Stockade?' or 'What did they do it for?' father'd say: 'Now, run away, sonny, and don't bother; me and Mr So-and-so want to talk.' Father had the mark of a hole on his leg, which he said he got through a gun accident when a boy, and a scar on his side, that we saw when he was in swimming with us; he said he got that in an accident in a quartz-crushing machine. Mr. So-and-so had a big scar on the side of his forehead that was caused by a pick accidentally slipping out of a loop in the rope, and falling down a shaft where he was working. But how was it they talked low, and their eyes brightened up, and they didn't look at each other, but away over sunset, and had to get up and walk about, and take a stroll in the cool of the evening when they talked about Eureka?

And, again they'd talk lower and more mysterious like, and perhaps mother would be passing the wood-heap and catch a word, and ask:

'Who was she, Tom?'

And Tom – father – would say:

'Oh, you didn't know her, Mary; she belonged to a family Bill knew at home.'

And Bill would look solemn till mother had gone, and then they would smile a quiet smile, and stretch and say, 'Ah, well!' and start something else.

They had yarns for the fireside, too, some of those old mates of our father's, and one of them would often tell how a girl – a queen of the diggings – was married, and had her wedding-ring made out of the gold of that field; and how the diggers weighed their gold with the new wedding-ring – for luck – by hanging the ring on the hook of the scales and attaching their chamois-leather gold bags to it (whereupon she boasted that four hundred ounces of the precious metal passed through her wedding-ring); and how they lowered the young bride, blindfolded, down a golden hole in a big bucket, and got her to point out the drive from which the gold came that her ring was made out of. The point of this story seems to have been lost – or else we forgot it – but it was characteristic. Had the girl been lowered down a duffer, and asked to point out the way to the gold, and had she done so successfully, there would have been some sense in it.

And they would talk of King, and Maggie Oliver, and G. V. Brooke, and others, and remember how the diggers went five miles out to meet the coach that brought the girl actress, and took the horses out and brought her in in triumph, and worshipped her, and sent her off in glory, and threw nuggets into her lap. And how she stood upon the box-seat and tore her sailor hat to pieces, and threw the fragments amongst the crowd; and how the diggers fought for the bits and thrust them inside their shirt bosoms; and how she broke down and cried, and could in her turn have worshipped those men – loved them, every one. They were boys all, and gentlemen all. There were college men, artists, poets, musicians, journalists – Bohemians all. Men from all the lands and one. They understood art – and poverty was dead.

And perhaps the old mate would say slyly, but with a sad, quiet smile:

'Have you got that bit of straw yet, Tom?'

Those old mates had each three pasts behind them. The two they told each other when they became mates, and the one they had shared.

And when the visitor had gone by the coach we noticed that the old man would smoke a lot, and think as much, and take great interest in the fire, and be a trifle irritable perhaps.

Those old mates of our father's are getting few and far between, and only happen along once in a way to keep the old man's memory fresh, as it were. We met one to-day, and had a yarn with him, and afterwards we got thinking, and somehow began to wonder whether those ancient friends of ours were, or were not, better and kinder to their mates than we of the rising generation are to our fathers; and the doubt is painfully on the wrong side.

MITCHELL: A CHARACTER SKETCH

IT was a very mean station, and Mitchell thought he had better go himself and beard the overseer for tucker. His mates were for waiting till the overseer went out on the run, and then trying their luck with the cook; but the self-assertive and diplomatic Mitchell decided to go.

'Good day,' said Mitchell.

'Good day,' said the manager.

'It's hot,' said Mitchell.

'Yes it's hot.'

'I don't suppose,' said Mitchell; 'I don't suppose it's any use asking you for a job?'

'Naw.'

'Well, I won't ask you,' said Mitchell, 'but I don't suppose you want any fencing done?'

'Naw.'

'Nor boundary-riding?'

'Naw.'

'You ain't likely to want a man to knock round?'

'Naw.'

I thought not. Things are pretty bad just now.'

'Na – yes – they are.'

'Ah, well; there's a lot to be said on the squatter's side as well as the men's. I suppose I can get a bit of rations?'

'Ye – yes. (*Shortly*) – Wot d'yer want?'

'Well, let's see; we want a bit of meat and flour – I think that's all. Got enough tea and sugar to carry us on.'

'All right. Cook! have you got any meat?'

'No!'

To Mitchell: 'Can you kill a sheep?'

'Rather!'

To the cook: 'Give this man a cloth and knife and steel, and let him go up to the yard and kill a sheep.' (To Mitchell): 'You can take a fore-quarter and get a bit of flour.'

Half-an-hour later Mitchell came back with the carcase wrapped in the cloth.

'Here yer are; here's your sheep,' he said to the cook.

'That's all right; hand it in there. Did you take a fore-quarter?'

'No.'

'Well, why didn't you? The boss told you to.'

'I didn't want a fore-quarter. I don't like it. I took a hind-quarter.'

So he had.

The cook scratched his head; he seemed to have nothing to say. He thought about trying to think, perhaps, but gave it best. It was too hot and he was out of practice.

'Here, fill these up, will you,' said Mitchell, 'that's the tea-bag, and that's the sugar-bag, and that's the flour-bag.'

He had taken them from the front of his shirt.

'Don't be frightened to stretch 'em a little, old man, I've got two mates to feed.'

The cook took the bags mechanically and filled them well before he knew what he was doing. Mitchell talked all the time.

'Thank you,' said he – 'got a bit of baking-powder?'

'Ye – yes, here you are.'

'Thank you. Find it dull here, don't you?'

'Well, yes, pretty dull. There's a bit of cooked beef and some bread and cake there, if you want it!'

'Thanks,' said Mitchell, sweeping the broken victuals into an old pillow-slip which he carried on his person for such an emergency. 'I 'spose you find it dull round here.'

'Yes, pretty dull.'

'No one to talk to much?'

'No, not many.'

'Tongue gets rusty?'

'Ye-es, sometimes.'

'Well, so long, and thank yer.'

'So long,' said the cook (he nearly added 'thank yer').

'Well, good day; I'll see you again.'

'Good day.'

Mitchell shouldered his spoil and left.

The cook scratched his head; he had a chat with the overseer afterwards, and they agreed that the traveller was a bit gone.

But Mitchell's head wasn't gone – not much: he was a Sydney jackeroo who had been round a bit – that was all.

On the Edge of a Plain

'I'D been away from home for eight years,' said Mitchell to his mate, as they dropped their swags in the mulga shade and sat down. 'I hadn't written a letter – kept putting it off, and a blundering fool of a fellow that got down the day before me told the old folks that he'd heard I was dead.'

Here he took a pull at his water-bag.

'When I got home they were all in mourning for me. It was night, and the girl that opened the door screamed and fainted away like a shot.'

He lit his pipe.

'Mother was upstairs howling and moaning in a chair, with all the girls boo-hooing round her for company. The old man was sitting in the back kitchen crying to himself.'

He put his hat down on the ground, dinted in the crown, and poured some water into the hollow for his cattle-pup.

'The girls came rushing down. Mother was so pumped out that she couldn't get up. They thought at first I was a ghost, and then they all tried to get holt of me at once – nearly smothered me. Look at that pup! You want to carry a tank of water on a dry stretch when you've got a pup that drinks as much as two men.'

He poured a drop more water into the top of his hat.

'Well, mother screamed and nearly fainted when she saw me. Such a picnic you never saw. They kept it up all night. I thought the old cove was gone off his chump. The old woman wouldn't let go my hand for three mortal hours. Have you got the knife?'

He cut up some more tobacco.

'All next day the house was full of neighbours, and the first to come was an old sweetheart of mine; I never thought she cared for me till then. Mother and the girls made me swear never to go away any more; and they kept watching me, and hardly let me go outside for fear I'd – '

'Get drunk?'

'No, – you're smart – for fear I'd clear. At last I swore on the Bible that I'd never leave home while the old folks were alive; and then mother seemed easier in her mind.'

He rolled the pup over and examined its feet. 'I expect I'll have to carry him a bit – his feet are very sore. Well, he's done pretty well this morning, and anyway he won't drink so much when he's carried.'

'You broke your promise about leaving home,' said his mate.

Mitchell stood up, stretched himself, and looked dolefully from his heavy swag to the wide, hot, shadeless cotton-bush plain ahead.

'Oh, yes,' he yawned, 'I stopped at home for a week, and then they began to growl because I couldn't get any work to do.'

The mate guffawed and Mitchell grinned. They shouldered the swags, with the pup on top of Mitchell's, took up their billies and water-bags, turned their unshaven faces to the wide, hazy distance, and left the timber behind them.

'SOME DAY'

THE two travellers had yarned late in their camp, and the moon was getting low down through the mulga. Mitchell's mate had just finished a rather 'racy' yarn, but it seemed to fall flat on Mitchell; he was in a sentimental mood. He smoked a while, and thought, and then said:

'Ah! there was one little girl that I was properly struck on. She came to our place on a visit to my sister. I think she was the best little girl that ever lived, and about the prettiest. She was just eighteen, and didn't come up to my shoulder; the biggest blue eyes you ever saw, and she had hair that reached down to her knees, and so thick you couldn't span it with your two hands – brown and glossy – and her skin was like lilies and roses. Of course, I never thought she'd look at a rough, ugly, ignorant brute like me, and I used to keep out of her way and act a little stiff towards her; I didn't want the others to think I was gone on her, because I knew they'd laugh at me, and maybe she'd laugh at me more than all. She would come and talk to me, and sit near me at table; but I thought that that was on account of her good nature, and she pitied me because I was such a rough, awkward chap. I was gone on that girl, and no joking; and I felt quite proud to think she was a countrywoman of mine. But I wouldn't let her know that, for I felt sure she'd only laugh.

'Well, things went on till I got the offer of two or three years' work on a station up near the border, and I had to go, for I was hard up; besides, I wanted to get away. Stopping round where she was only made me miserable.

'The night I left they were all down at the station to see me off –

including the girl I was gone on. When the train was ready to start she was standing away by herself on the dark end of the platform, and my sister kept nudging me and winking, and fooling about, but I didn't know what she was driving at. At last she said:

' "Go and speak to her, you noodle; go and say good-bye to Edie."

'So I went up to where she was, and, when the others turned their backs –

' "Well, good-bye, Miss Brown," I said, holding out my hand; "I don't suppose I'll ever see you again, for Lord knows when I'll be back. Thank you for coming to see me off."

'Just then she turned her face to the light, and I saw she was crying. She was trembling all over. Suddenly she said, "Jack! Jack!" just like that, and held up her arms like this.'

Mitchell was speaking in a tone of voice that didn't belong to him, and his mate looked up. Mitchell's face was solemn, and his eyes were fixed on the fire.

'I suppose you gave her a good hug then, and a kiss?' asked the mate.

'I s'pose so,' snapped Mitchell. 'There is some things a man doesn't want to joke about . . . Well, I think we'll shove on one of the billies, and have a drink of tea before we turn in.'

'I suppose,' said Mitchell's mate, as they drank their tea, 'I suppose you'll go back and marry her some day?'

'Some day! That's it; it looks like it, doesn't it? We all say "Some day." I used to say it ten years ago, and look at me now. I've been knocking round for five years, and the last two years constant on the track, and no show of getting off it unless I go for good, and what have I got for it? I look like going home and getting married, without a penny in my pocket or a rag to my back scarcely, and no show of getting them. I swore I'd never go back home without a cheque, and, what's more, I never will; but the cheque days are past. Look at that boot! If we were down among the settled districts we'd be called tramps and beggars; and what's the difference? I've been a fool, I know, but I've paid for it; and now there's nothing for it but to tramp, tramp, tramp for your tucker, and keep tramping till you get old and careless and dirty, and older, and more careless and dirtier, and you get used to the dust and sand, and heat, and flies, and mosquitoes, just as a bullock does, and lose ambition and hope, and get contented with this animal life, like a dog, and till your swag seems part of yourself, and you'd be lost and uneasy and light-shouldered without it, and you don't care a damn if you'll ever get work again, or live like a Christian; and you go on like this till the spirit of a bullock takes the place of the heart of a man. Who cares? If we hadn't found the track yesterday we might have lain and rotted in that lignum, and no one been any the wiser – or sorrier – who knows? Somebody might have found us in the end, but it mightn't have been worth his while to go out of his way and report us. Damn the world, say I!'

He smoked for a while in savage silence; then he knocked the ashes out of his pipe, felt for his tobacco with a sigh, and said:

'Well, I am a bit out of sorts to-night. I've been thinking . . . I think we'd best turn in, old man; we've got a long, dry stretch before us to-morrow.'

They rolled out their swags on the sand, lay down, and wrapped themselves in their blankets. Mitchell covered his face with a piece of calico, because the moonlight and wind kept him awake.

SHOOTING THE MOON

WE lay in camp in the fringe of the mulga, and watched the big, red, smoky, rising moon out on the edge of the misty plain, and smoked and thought together sociably. Our nose-bags were nice and heavy, and we still had about a pound of nail-rod between us.

The moon reminded my mate, Jack Mitchell, of something – anything reminded him of something, in fact.

'Did you ever notice,' said Jack, in a lazy tone, just as if he didn't want to tell a yarn – 'Did you ever notice that people always shoot the moon when there's no moon? Have you got the matches?'

He lit up; he was always lighting up when he was reminded of something.

'This reminds me – Have you got the knife? My pipe's stuffed up.'

He dug it out, loaded afresh, and lit up again.

'I remember once, at a pub I was staying at, I had to leave without saying good-bye to the landlord. I didn't know him very well at that time.

'My room was upstairs at the back, with the window opening onto the backyard. I always carried a bit of clothes-line in my swag or portmanteau those times. I travelled along with a portmanteau those times. I carried the rope in case of accident, or in case of fire, to lower my things out of the window – or hang myself, maybe, if things got too bad. No, now I come to think of it, I carried a revolver for that, and it was the only thing I never pawned.'

'To hang yourself with?'

'Yes – you're very smart,' snapped Mitchell; 'never mind – . This reminds me that I got a chap at a pub to pawn my last suit, while I stopped inside and waited for an old mate to send me a pound; but I kept the shooter, and if he hadn't sent it I'd have been the late John Mitchell long ago.'

'And sometimes you lower'd out when there wasn't a fire.'

'Yes, that will pass; you're improving in the funny business. But about the yarn. There was two beds in my room at the pub, where I had to go away without shouting for the boss, and, as it happened, there was a strange chap sleeping in the other bed that night, and, just as I raised the window and was going to lower my bag out, he woke up.

' "Now, look here," I said, shaking my fist at him, like that, "if you say a word, I'll stoush yer!"

' "Well," he said, "well, you needn't be in such a sweat to jump down a man's throat. I've got my swag under the bed, and I was just going to ask you for the loan of the rope when you're done with it."

'Well, we chummed. His name was Tom – Tom – something, I forget the other name, but it doesn't matter. Have you got the matches?'

He wasted three matches, and continued –

'There was a lot of old galvanised iron lying about under the window, and I was frightened the swag would make a noise; anyway, I'd have to drop the rope, and that was sure to make a noise. So we agreed for one of us to go down and land the swag. If we were seen going down without the swags it didn't matter, for we could say we wanted to go out in the yard for something.'

'If you had the swag you might pretend you were walking in your sleep,' I suggested, for the want of something funnier to say.

'Bosh,' said Jack, 'and get woke up with a black eye. Bushies don't generally carry their swags out of pubs in their sleep, or walk neither; it's only city swells who do that. Where's the blessed matches?

'Well, Tom agreed to go, and presently I saw a shadow under the window, and lowered away.

' "All right?" I asked in a whisper.

' "All right!" whispered the shadow.

'I lowered the other swag.

' "All right?"

' "All right!" said the shadow, and just then the moon came out.

' "All right!" says the shadow.

'But it wasn't all right. It was the landlord himself!

'It seems he got up and went out to the back in the night, and just happened to be coming in when my mate Tom was sneaking out of the back door. He saw Tom, and Tom saw him, and smoked through a hole in the palings into the scrub. The boss looked up at the window, and dropped to it. I went down, funky enough, I can tell you, and faced him. He said:

' "Look here, mate, why didn't you come straight to me, and tell me how you was fixed, instead of sneaking round the trouble in that fashion? There's no occasion for it."

'I felt mean at once, but I said: "Well, you see, we didn't know you, boss."

' "So it seems. Well, I didn't think of that. Anyway, call up your mate and come and have a drink; we'll talk it over afterwards." So I called Tom. "Come on," I shouted. "It's all right."

'And the boss kept us a couple of days, and then gave us as much tucker as we could carry, and a drop of stuff and a few bob to go on the track again with.'

'Well, he was white, any road.'

'Yes. I knew him well after that, and only heard one man say a word against him.'

'And did you stoush him?'

'No; I was going to, but Tom wouldn't let me. He said he was frightened I might make a mess of it, and he did it himself.'

'Did what? Make a mess of it?'

'He made a mess of the other man that slandered that publican. I'd be funny if I was you. Where's the matches?'

'And could Tom fight?'

'Yes. Tom could fight.'

'Did you travel long with him after that!'

'Ten years.'

'And where is he now?'

'Dead. – Give us the matches.'

OUR PIPES

THE moon rose away out on the edge of a smoky plain, seen through a sort of tunnel or arch in the fringe of mulga behind which we were camped – Jack Mitchell and I. The 'timber' proper was just behind us, very thick and very dark. The moon looked like a big new copper boiler set on edge on the horizon of the plain, with the top turned towards us and a lot of old rags and straw burning inside.

We had tramped twenty-five miles on a dry stretch on a hot day – swagmen know what that means. We reached the water about two hours 'after dark' – swagmen know what that means. We didn't sit down at once and rest – we hadn't rested for the last ten miles. We knew that if we sat down we wouldn't want to get up again in a hurry – that, if we did, our leg-sinews, especially those of our calves, would 'draw' like redhot wires. You see, we hadn't been long on the track this time – it was only our third day out. Swagmen will understand.

We got the billy boiled first, and some leaves laid down for our beds and the swags rolled out. We thanked the Lord that we had some cooked meat and a few johnny-cakes left, for we didn't feel equal to cooking. We put the billy of tea and our tucker-bags between the heads of our beds, and the pipes and tobacco in the crown of an old hat, where we could reach them without having to get up. Then we lay down on our stomachs and had a feed. We didn't eat much – we were too tired for that – but we drank a lot of tea. We gave our calves time to tone down a bit; then we lit up and began to answer each other. It got to be pretty comfortable, so long as we kept those unfortunate legs of ours straight, and didn't move round much.

We cursed society because we weren't rich men, and then we felt better and conversation drifted lazily round various subjects and ended in that of smoking.

'How I came to start smoking?' said Mitchell. 'Let's see.' He reflected. 'I started smoking first when I was about fourteen or fifteen. I smoked some sort of weed – I forget the name of it – but it wasn't tobacco; and then I smoked cigarettes – not the ones we get now, for those cost a penny each. Then I reckoned that, if I could smoke those, I could smoke a pipe.'

He reflected.

'We lived in Sydney then – Surry Hills. Those were different times; the place was nearly all sand. The old folks were alive then, and we were all at home, except Tom.'

He reflected.

'Ah, well! . . . Well, one evening I was playing marbles out in front of our house when a chap we knew gave me his pipe to mind while he went into a church-meeting. The little church was opposite – a 'chapel' they called it.'

He reflected.

'The pipe was alight. It was a clay pipe and nigger-head tobacco. Mother was at work out in the kitchen at the back, washing up the tea-things, and, when I went in, she said; 'You've been smoking!'

'Well, I couldn't deny it – I was too sick to do so, or care much, anyway.'

' "Give me that pipe!" she said.

'I said I hadn't got it.

' "*Give – me – that – pipe!*" she said.

'I said I hadn't got it.

' "Where is it?" she said.

' "Jim Brown's got it," I said, "it's his."

' "Then I'll give it to Jim Brown," she said; and she did; though it wasn't Jim's fault, for he only gave it to me to mind. I didn't smoke the pipe so much because I wanted to smoke a pipe just then, as because I had such a great admiration for Jim.'

Mitchell reflected, and took a look at the moon. It had risen clear and had got small and cold and pure-looking, and had floated away back out amongst the stars.

'I felt better towards morning, but it didn't cure me – being sick and nearly dead all night, I mean. I got a clay pipe and tobacco, and the old lady found it and put it in the stove. Then I got another pipe and tobacco, and she laid for it, and found it out at last; but she didn't put the tobacco in the stove this time – she'd got experience. I don't know what she did with it. I tried to find it, but couldn't. I fancy the old man got hold of it, for I saw him with a plug that looked very much like mine.'

He reflected.

'But I wouldn't be done. I got a cherry pipe. I thought it wouldn't be so easy to break if she found it. I used to plant the bowl in one place and the stem in another because I reckoned that if she found one she mightn't find the other. It doesn't look much of an idea now, but it seemed like an inspiration then. Kids get rum ideas.'

He reflected.

'Well, one day I was having a smoke out at the back, when I heard her coming, and I pulled out the stem in a hurry and put the bowl behind the water-butt and the stem under the house. Mother was coming round for a dipper of water. I got out of her way quick, for I hadn't time to look innocent; but the bowl of the pipe was hot and she got a whiff of it. She went sniffing round, first on one side of the cask and then on the other, until she got on the scent and followed it up and found the bowl. Then I had only the stem left. She looked for that, but she couldn't scent it. But I couldn't get much comfort out of that. Have you got the matches?

'Then I gave it best for a time and smoked cigars. They were the safest and most satisfactory under the circumstances, but they cost me two shillings a week, and I couldn't stand it, so I started a pipe again and then mother gave in at last. God bless her, and God forgive me, and us all – we deserve it. She's been at rest these seventeen long years.'

Mitchell reflected.

'And what did your old man do when he found out that you were smoking?' I asked.

'The old man?'

He reflected.

'Well, he seemed to brighten up at first. You see, he was sort of pensioned off by mother and she kept him pretty well inside his income . . . Well, he seemed to sort of brighten up – liven up – when he found out that I was smoking.'

'Did he? So did my old man, and he livened me up, too. But what did your old man do – what did he say?'

'Well,' said Mitchell, very slowly, 'about the first thing he did was to ask me for a fill.'

He reflected.

'Ah! many a solemn, thoughtful old smoke we had together on the quiet – the old man and me.'

He reflected.

'Is your old man dead, Mitchell?' I asked softly.

'Long ago – these twelve years,' said Mitchell.

BILL, THE VENTRILOQUIAL ROOSTER

'WHEN we were up-country on the selection, we had a rooster at our place, named Bill,' said Mitchell; 'a big mongrel of no particular breed, though the old lady said he was a "brammer" – and many an argument she had with the old man about it too; she was just as stubborn and obstinate in her opinion as the governor was in his. But, anyway, we called him Bill, and didn't take any particular notice of him till a cousin of some of us came from Sydney on a visit to the country, and stayed at our place because it was cheaper than stopping at a pub. Well, somehow this chap got interested in Bill, and studied him for two or three days, and at last he says:

' "Why, that rooster's a ventriloquist!"

' "A what?"

' "A ventriloquist!"

' "Go along with yer!"

' "But he is. I've heard of cases like this before; but this is the first I've come across. Bill's a ventriloquist right enough."

'Then we remembered that there wasn't another rooster within five miles – our only neighbour, an Irishman named Page, didn't have one at the time – and we'd often heard another cock crow, but didn't think to take any notice of it. We watched Bill, and sure enough he *was* a ventriloquist. The "ka-cocka" would come all right, but the "co-ka-koo-oi-oo" seemed to come from a distance. And sometimes the whole crow would go wrong, and come back like an echo that had been lost for a year. Bill would stand on tiptoe, and hold his elbows out, and curve his neck, and go two or three times as if he was swallowing nest-eggs, and nearly break his neck and burst his gizzard; and then there'd be no sound at all where he was – only a cock crowing in the distance.

'And pretty soon we could see that Bill was in great trouble about it himself. You see, he didn't know it was himself – thought it was another rooster challenging him, and he wanted badly to find that other bird. He would get up on the wood-heap, and crow and listen – crow and listen again – crow and listen, and then he'd go up to the top of the paddock, and get up on the stack, and crow and listen there. Then down to the other end of the paddock, and get up on a mullock-heap, and crow and listen there. Then across to the other side and up on a log among the saplings, and crow 'n' listen some more. He searched all over the place for that other rooster, but of course, couldn't find him. Sometimes he'd be out all day crowing and listening all over the country, and then come home dead tired, and rest and cool off in a hole that the hens had scratched for him in a damp place under the water-cask sledge.

'Well, one day Page brought home a big white rooster, and when he let it go it climbed up on Page's stack and crowed, to see if there was any more roosters round there. Bill had come home tired; it was a hot day, and he'd rooted out the hens, and was having a spell-oh under the cask when the white rooster crowed. Bill didn't lose any time getting out and on to the wood-heap, and then he waited till he heard the crow again; then he crowed, and the other rooster crowed again, and they crowed at each other for three days, and called each other all the wretches they could lay their tongues to, and after that they implored each other to come out and be made into chicken soup and feather pillows. But neither'd come. You see, there were *three* crows – there was Bill's crow, and the ventriloquist crow, and the white rooster's crow – and each rooster thought that there was *two* roosters in the opposition camp, and that he mightn't get fair play, and, consequently, both were afraid to put up their hands.

'But at last Bill couldn't stand it any longer. He made up his mind to go and have it out, even if there was a whole agricultural show of prize and honourable-mention fighting-cocks in Page's yard. He got down from the wood-heap and started off across the ploughed field, his head down, his elbows out, and his thick awkward legs prodding away at the furrows behind for all they were worth.

'I wanted to go down badly and see the fight, and barrack for Bill. But

I daren't, because I'd been coming up the road late the night before with my brother Joe, and there was about three panels of turkeys roosting along on the top rail of Page's front fence; and we brushed 'em with a bough, and they got up such a blessed gobbling fuss about it that Page came out in his shirt and saw us running away; and I knew he was laying for us with a bullock-whip. Besides, there was friction between the two families on account of a thorough-bred bull that Page borrowed and wouldn't lend to us, and that got into our paddock on account of me mending a panel in the party fence, and carelessly leaving the top rail down after sundown while our cows was moving round there in the saplings.

'So there was too much friction for me to go down, but I climbed a tree as near the fence as I could and watched. Bill reckoned he'd found that rooster at last. The white rooster wouldn't come down from the stack, so Bill went up to him, and they fought there till they tumbled down the other side, and I couldn't see any more. Wasn't I wild? I'd have given my dog to have seen the rest of the fight. I went down to the far side of Page's fence and climbed a tree there, but, of course I couldn't see anything, so I came home the back way. Just as I got home Page came round to the front and sung out, "Insoid there!" And me and Jim went under the house like snakes and looked out round a pile. But Page was all right – he had a broad grin on his face, and Bill safe under his arm. He put Bill down on the ground very carefully, and says he to the old folks:

' "Yer rooster knocked the stuffin' out of my rooster, but I bear no malice. 'Twas a grand foight."

'And then the old man and Page had a yarn, and got pretty friendly after that. And Bill didn't seem to bother about any more ventriloquism; but the white rooster spent a lot of time looking for that other rooster. Perhaps he thought he'd have better luck with him. But Page was on the look-out all the time to get a rooster that would lick ours. He did nothing else for a month but ride round and inquire about roosters; and at last he borrowed a game-bird in town, left five pounds deposit on him, and brought him home. And Page and the old man agreed to have a match – about the only thing they'd agreed about for five years. And they fixed it up for a Sunday when the old lady and the girls and kids were going on a visit to some relations, about fifteen miles away – to stop all night. The guv'nor made me go with them on horseback; but

I knew what was up, and so my pony went lame about a mile along the road, and I had to come back and turn him out in the top paddock, and hide the saddle and bridle in a hollow log, and sneak home and climb up on the roof of the shed. It was an awful hot day, and I had to keep climbing backward and forward over the ridge-pole all the morning to keep out of sight of the old man, for he was moving about a good deal.

'Well, after dinner, the fellows from round about began to ride in and hang up their horses round the place till it looked as if there was going to be a funeral. Some of the chaps saw me, of course, but I tipped them the wink, and they gave me the office whenever the old man happened around.

'Well, Page came along with his game-rooster. Its name was Jim. It wasn't much to look at, and it seemed a good deal smaller and weaker than Bill. Some of the chaps were disgusted, and said it wasn't a game-rooster at all; Bill'd settle it in one lick, and they wouldn't have any fun.

'Well, they brought the game one out and put him down near the wood-heap, and routed Bill out from under his cask. He got interested at once. He looked at Jim, and got up on the wood-heap and crowed and looked at Jim again. He reckoned *this* at last was the fowl that had been humbugging him all along. Presently his trouble caught him, and then he'd crow and take a squint at the game 'un, and crow again, and have another squint at gamey, and try to crow and keep his eye on the game-rooster at the same time. But Jim never committed himself, until at last he happened to gape just after Bill's whole crow went wrong, and Bill spotted him. He reckoned he'd caught him this time, and he got down off that wood-heap and went for the foe. But Jim ran away – and Bill ran after him.

'Round and round the wood-heap they went, and round the shed, and round the house and under it, and back again, and round the wood-heap and over it and round the other way, and kept it up for close on an hour. Bill's bill was just within an inch or so of the game-rooster's tail feathers most of the time, but he couldn't get any nearer, do how he liked. And all the time the fellers kep chyackin' Page and singing out, "What price yer game un, Page! Go it, Bill! Go it, old cock!" and all that sort of thing. Well, the game-rooster went as if it was a go-as-you-please, and he didn't care if it lasted a year. He didn't seem to take any interest in the business, but Bill got excited, and by and by he got mad. He held his head lower and lower and his wings further and further out from his sides, and prodded away harder and harder at the ground behind, but it wasn't any use. Jim seemed to keep ahead without trying. They stuck to the wood-heap towards the last. They went round first one way for a while, and then the other for a change, and now and then they'd go over the top to break the monotony; and the chaps got more interested in the race than they would have been in the fight – and bet on it, too. But Bill was handicapped with his weight. He was done up at last; he slowed down till he couldn't waddle, and then, when he was thoroughly knocked up, that game-rooster turned on him, and gave him the father of a hiding.

'And my father caught me when I'd got down in the excitement, and wasn't thinking, and *he* gave *me* the step-father of a hiding. But he had a lively time with the old lady afterwards, over the cock-fight.

'Bill was so disgusted with himself that he went under the cask and died.'

IV

The Geological Spieler

THERE'S nothing so interesting as Geology, even to common and ignorant people, especially when you have a bank or the side of a cutting, studded with fossil fish and things and oysters that were stale when Adam was fresh to illustrate by. (*Remark made by Steelman, professional wanderer, to his pal and pupil, Smith.*)

THE first man that Steelman and Smith came up to on the last embankment, where they struck the new railway line, was a heavy, gloomy, labouring man with bow-yangs on and straps round his wrists. Steelman bade him the time of day and had a few words with him over the weather. The man of mullick gave it as his opinion that the fine weather wouldn't last, and seemed to take a gloomy kind of pleasure in that reflection; he said there was more rain down yonder, pointing to the south-east, than the moon could swallow up – the moon was in its first quarter, during which time it is popularly believed in some parts of Maoriland that the south-easter is most likely to be out on the wallaby and the weather bad. Steelman regarded that quarter of the sky with an expression of gentle remonstrance mingled as it were with a sort of fatherly indulgence, agreed mildly with the labouring man, and seemed lost for a moment in a reverie from which he roused himself to inquire cautiously after the boss. There was no boss, it was a co-operative party. That chap standing over there by the dray in the end of the cutting was their spokesman – their representative: they called him Boss, but that was only his nickname in camp. Steelman expressed his thanks and moved on towards the cutting, followed respectfully by Smith.

Steelman wore a snuff-coloured sac suit, a wide-awake hat, a pair of professional-looking spectacles, and a scientific expression; there was a clerical atmosphere about him, strengthened however by an air as of unconscious dignity and superiority, born of intellect and knowledge. He carried a black bag, which was an indispensable article in his profession in more senses than one. Smith was decently dressed in sober tweed and looked like a man of no account, who was mechanically devoted to his employer's interests, pleasures, or whims, whatever they may have been.

The Boss was a decent-looking young fellow with a good face – rather solemn – and a quiet manner.

'Good day, sir,' said Steelman.

'Good day, sir,' said the Boss.

'Nice weather this.'

'Yes, it is, but I'm afraid it won't last.'

'I am afraid it will not by the look of the sky down there,' ventured Steelman.

'No, I go mostly by the look of our weather prophet,' said the Boss with a quiet smile, indicating the gloomy man.

'I suppose bad weather would put you back in your work?'

'Yes, it will; we didn't want any bad weather just now.'

Steelman got the weather question satisfactorily settled; then he said:

'You seem to be getting on with the railway.'

'Oh, yes, we are about over the worst of it.'

'The worst of it?' echoed Steelman, with mild surprise: 'I should have thought you were just coming into it' and he pointed to the ridge ahead.

'Oh, our section doesn't go any further than that pole you see sticking up yonder. We had the worst of it back there across the swamps – working up to our waists in water most of the time, in mid-winter too – and at eighteenpence a yard.'

'That was bad.'

'Yes, rather rough. Did you come from the terminus?'

'Yes, I sent my baggage on in the brake.'

'Commercial traveller, I suppose,' asked the Boss, glancing at Smith, who stood a little to the rear of Steelman, seeming interested in the work.

'Oh no,' said Steelman, smiling – 'I am – well – I'm a geologist; this is my man here,' indicating Smith. '(You may put down the bag, James, and have a smoke.) My name is Stoneleigh – you might have heard of it.'

The Boss said 'oh,' and then presently he added 'indeed,' in an undecided tone.

There was a pause – embarrassed on the part of the Boss – he was silent not knowing what to say. Meanwhile Steelman studied his man and concluded that he would do.

'Having a look at the country, I suppose?' asked the Boss presently.

'Yes,' said Steelman; then after a moment's reflection: 'I am travelling for my own amusement and improvement, and also in the interest of science, which amounts to the same thing. I am a member of the Royal Geological Society – vice-president in fact of a leading Australian branch'; and then, as if conscious that he had appeared guilty of egotism, he shifted the subject a bit. 'Yes. Very interesting country this – very interesting indeed. I should like to make a stay here for a day or so. Your work opens right into my hands. I cannot remember seeing a geological formation which interested me so much. Look at the face of that cutting, for instance. Why! you can almost read the history of the geological world from yesterday – this morning as it were – beginning with the super-surface on top and going right down through the different layers and stratas – through the vanished ages – right down and back to the prehistorical – to the very primeval or fundamental geological formations!' And Steelman studied the face of the cutting as if he could read it like a book, with every layer or stratum a chapter, and every streak a note of explanation. The Boss seemed to be getting interested, and Steelman gained confidence and proceeded to identify and classify the different 'stratas and layers,' and fix their ages, and describe the conditions and politics of Man in their different times, for the Boss's benefit.

'Now,' continued Steelman, turning slowly from the cutting, removing his glasses, and letting his thoughtful eyes wander casually over the general scenery – 'now the first impression that this country would leave on an ordinary intelligent mind – though maybe unconsciously, would be as of a new country – new in a geological sense; with patches of an older geological and vegetable formation cropping out here and there; as for instance that clump of dead trees on that clear alluvial slope there, that outcrop of lime-stone, or that timber yonder,' and he indicated a dead forest which seemed alive and green because of the parasites. 'But the country is old – old; perhaps the oldest geological formation in the world is to be seen here, as is the oldest vegetable formation in Australia. I am not using the words old and new in an ordinary sense, you understand, but in a geological sense.'

The Boss said, 'I understand,' and that geology must be a very interesting study.

Steelman ran his eye meditatively over the cutting again, and turning to Smith said,

'Go up there, James, and fetch me a specimen of that slaty out-crop you see there – just above the coeval strata.'

It was a stiff climb and slippery, but Smith had to do it, and he did it.

'This,' said Steelman, breaking the rotten piece between his fingers, 'belongs probably to an older geological period than its position would indicate – a primitive sandstone level perhaps. Its position on that layer is no doubt due to volcanic upheavals – such disturbances, or rather the results of such disturbances, have been and are the cause of the greatest trouble to geologists – endless errors and controversy. You see we must study the country, not as it appears now, but as it would appear had the natural geological growth been left to mature undisturbed; we must restore and reconstruct such disorganised portions of the mineral kingdom, if you understand me.'

The Boss said he understood.

Steelman found an opportunity to wink sharply and severely at Smith, who had been careless enough to allow his features to relapse into a vacant grin.

'It is generally known even amongst the ignorant that rock grows – grows from the outside – but the rock here, a specimen of which I hold in my hand, is now in the process of decomposition; to be plain it is rotting – in an advanced stage of decomposition – so much so that you are not able to identify it with any geological period or formation, even as you may not be able to identify any other extremely decomposed body.'

The Boss blinked and knitted his brow, but had the presence of mind to say: 'Just so.'

'Had the rock on that cutting been healthy – been alive, as it were – you would have had your work cut out; but it is dead and has been dead for ages perhaps. You find less trouble in working it than you would ordinary clay or sand, or even gravel, which formations together are really rock in embryo – before birth as it were.'

The Boss's brow cleared.

'The country round here is simply rotting down – simply rotting down.'

He removed his spectacles, wiped them, and wiped his face; then his attention seemed to be attracted by some stones at his feet. He picked one up and examined it.

'I shouldn't wonder,' he mused, absently, 'I shouldn't wonder if there is alluvial gold in some of these creeks and gullies, perhaps tin or even silver, quite probably antimony.'

The Boss seemed interested.

'Can you tell me if there is any place in this neighbourhood where I could get accommodation for myself and my servant for a day or two?' asked Steelman presently. 'I should very much like to break my journey here.'

'Well, no,' said the Boss. 'I can't say I do – I don't know of any place nearer than Pahiatua, and that's seven miles from here.'

'I know that,' said Steelman reflectively, 'but I fully expected to have found a house of accommodation of some sort on the way, else I would have gone on in the van.'

'Well,' said the Boss. 'If you like to camp with us for to-night, at least, and don't mind roughing it, you'll be welcome, I'm sure.'

'If I was sure that I would not be putting you to any trouble, or interfering in any way with your domestic economy – '

'No trouble at all,' interrupted the Boss. 'The boys will be only too glad, and there's an empty whare where you can sleep. Better stay. It's going to be a rough night.'

After tea Steelman entertained the Boss and a few of the more thoughtful members of the party with short chatty lectures on geology and other subjects.

In the meantime Smith, in another part of the camp, gave selections on a tin whistle, sang a song or two, contributed, in his turn, to the sailor yarns, and ensured his popularity for several nights at least. After several draughts of something that was poured out of a demijohn into a pint pot, his tongue became loosened, and he expressed an opinion that geology was all bosh, and said if he had half his employer's money he'd be dashed if he would go rooting round in the mud like a blessed old ant-eater; he also irreverently referred to his learned boss as 'Old Rocks' over there. He had a pretty easy billet of it though, he said, taking it all round, when the weather was fine; he got a couple of notes a week and all expenses paid, and the money was sure; he was only required to look after the luggage and arrange for accommodation, grub out a chunk of rock now and then, and (what perhaps was the most irksome of his duties) he had to appear interested in old rocks and clay.

Towards midnight Steelman and Smith retired to the unoccupied whare which had been shown them, Smith carrying a bundle of bags, blankets, and rugs, which had been placed at their disposal by their good-natured hosts. Smith lit a candle and proceeded to make the beds. Steelman sat down, removed his specs and scientific expression, placed the glasses carefully on a ledge close at hand, took a book from his bag, and commenced to read. The volume was a cheap copy of Jules Verne's 'Journey to the Centre of the Earth'. A little later there was a knock at the door. Steelman hastily resumed the spectacles, together with the scientific expression, took a note-book from his pocket, opened it on the table, and said 'Come in.' One of the chaps appeared with a billy of hot coffee, two pint pots, and some cake. He said he thought you chaps might like a drop of coffee before you turned in, and the boys had forgot to ask you to wait for it down in the camp. He also wanted to know whether Mr Stoneleigh and his man would be all right and quite comfortable for the night, and whether they had blankets enough. There was some wood at the back of the whare and they could light a fire if they liked.

Mr Stoneleigh expressed his thanks and his appreciation of the kindness shown him and his servant. He was extremely sorry to give them any trouble.

The navvy, a serious man, who respected genius or intellect in any shape or form, said that it was no trouble at all, the camp was very dull and the boys were always glad to have some one come round. Then, after a brief comparison of opinions concerning the probable duration of the weather which had arrived, they bade each other good night, and the darkness swallowed the serious man.

Steelman turned into the top bunk on one side and Smith took the lower on the other. Steelman had the candle by his bunk, as usual; he lit his pipe for a final puff before going to sleep, and held the light up for a moment so as to give Smith the full benefit of a solemn, uncompromising wink. The wink was silently applauded and dutifully returned by Smith. Then Steelman blew out the light, lay back, and puffed at his pipe for a while. Presently he chuckled, and the chuckle was echoed by Smith; by-and-bye Steelman chuckled once more, and then Smith chuckled again. There was silence in the darkness, and after a bit Smith chuckled twice. Then Steelman said:

'For God's sake give her a rest, Smith, and give a man a show to get some sleep.'

Then the silence in the darkness remained unbroken.

The invitation was extended next day, and Steelman sent Smith on to see that his baggage was safe. Smith stayed out of sight for two or three hours, and then returned and reported all well.

They stayed on for several days. After breakfast and when the men were going to work Steelman and Smith would go out along the line with the black bag and poke round amongst the 'layers and stratas' in sight of the works for a while, as an evidence of good faith; then they'd drift off casually into the bush, camp in a retired and sheltered spot, and light a fire when the weather was cold, and Steelman would lie on the grass and read and smoke and lay plans for the future and improve Smith's mind until they reckoned it was about dinner time. And in the evening they would come home with the black bag full of stones and bits of rock, and Steelman would lecture on those minerals after tea.

On about the fourth morning Steelman had a yarn with one of the men going to work. He was a lanky young fellow with a sandy complexion, and seemingly harmless grin. In Australia he might have been regarded as a 'cove' rather than a 'chap', but there was nothing of the 'bloke' about him. Presently the cove said:

'What do you think of the Boss, Mr Stoneleigh? He seems to have taken a great fancy for you, and he's fair gone on geology.'

'I think he is a very decent fellow indeed, a very intelligent young man. He seems very well read and well informed.'

'You wouldn't think he was a University man,' said the cove.

'No, indeed! Is he?'

'Yes. I thought you knew!'

Steelman knitted his brows. He seemed slightly disturbed for the moment. He walked on a few paces in silence and thought hard.

'What might have been his special line?' he asked the cove.

'Why, something the same as yours. I thought you knew. He was reckoned the best – what do you call it? – the best minrologist in the country. He had a first-class billet in the Mines Department, but he lost it – you know – the booze.'

'I think we will be making a move, Smith,' said Steelman, later on, when they were private. 'There's a little too much intellect in this camp to suit me. But we haven't done so bad anyway. We've got three days' good board and lodging with entertainments and refreshments thrown in.' Then he said to himself: 'We'll stay for another day any-way. If those beggars are having a lark with us, we're getting the worth of it any-way, and I'm not thin-skinned. They're the mugs and not us, any-how it goes, and I can take them down before I leave.'

But on the way home he had a talk with another man whom we might set down as a 'chap'.

'I wouldn't have thought the Boss was a college man,' said Steelman to the chap.

'A what?'

'A University man – University education.'

'Why! Who's been telling you that?'

'One of your mates.'

'Oh, he's been getting at you, why: it's all the Boss can do to write his own name. Now that lanky sandy cove with the birth-mark grin – it's him that's had the college education.'

'I think we'll make a start to-morrow,' said Steelman to Smith in the privacy of their whare. 'There's too much humour and levity in this camp to suit a serious scientific gentleman like myself.'

THE IRON-BARK CHIP

  DAVE Regan and party – bush-fencers, tank-sinkers, and rough carpenters – were finishing the third and last culvert of their contract on the last section of the new railway line, and had already sent in their vouchers for the completed contract, so that there might be no excuse for extra delay in connection with the cheque.

Now it had been expressly stipulated in the plans and specifications that the timber for certain beams and girders was to be iron-bark and no other, and government inspectors were authorised to order the removal from the ground of any timber or material they might deem inferior, or not in accordance with the stipulations. The railway contractor's foreman and inspector of sub-contractors was a practical man and a bushman, but he had been a timber-getter himself; his sympathies were bushy, and he was on winking terms with Dave Regan. Besides, extended time was expiring, and the contractors were in a hurry to complete the line. But the government inspector was a reserved man who poked round on his independent own and appeared in lonely spots at unexpected times – with apparently no definite object in life – like a grey kangaroo bothered by a new wire fence, but un-suspicious of the presence of humans. He wore a grey suit, rode, or mostly led, an ashen-grey horse; the grass was long and grey, so he was seldom spotted until he was well within the horizon and bearing leisurely down on a party of sub-contractors, leading his horse.

Now iron-bark was scarce and distant on those ridges, and another timber, similar in appearance, but much inferior in grain and 'standing' quality, was plentiful and close at hand. Dave and party were 'about full of' the job and place, and wanted to get their cheque and be gone to another 'spec' they had in view. So they came to reckon they'd get the last girder from a handy tree, and have it squared, in place, and carefully and conscientiously tarred before the inspector happened along, if he did. But they didn't. They got it squared, and ready to be lifted into its place; the kindly darkness of tar was ready to cover a fraud that took four strong men with crowbars and levers to shift; and now (such is the regular cussedness of things) as the fraudulent piece of timber lay its last hour on the ground, looking and smelling, to their guilty imaginations, like anything but iron-bark, they were aware of the government inspector drifting down upon them obliquely, with something of the atmosphere of a casual Bill or Jim who had dropped out of his easygoing track to see how they were getting on, and borrow a match. They had more than half hoped that, as he had visited them pretty frequently during the progress of the work, and knew how near it was to completion, he wouldn't bother coming any more. But it's the way with the Government. You might move heaven and earth in vain endeavour to get the 'guvermunt' to flutter an eyelash over something of the most momentous importance to yourself and mates and the district – even to the country; but just when you are leaving authority severely alone, and have strong reasons for not wanting to worry or interrupt it, and not desiring it to worry about you, it will take a fancy into its head to come along and bother.

'It's always the way!' muttered Dave to his mates. 'I knew the beggar would turn up! . . . And the only cronk log we've had, too!' he added, in an injured tone. 'If this had 'a' been the only blessed iron-bark in the whole contract, it would have been all right . . . Good day, sir!' (to the inspector). 'It's hot?'

The inspector nodded. He was not of an impulsive nature. He got down from his horse and looked at the girder in an abstracted way; and presently there came into his eyes a dreamy, far-away, sad sort of expression, as if there had been a very sad and painful occurrence in his family, way back in the past, and that piece of timber in some way reminded him of it and brought the old sorrow home to him. He blinked three times, and asked, in a subdued tone:

'Is that iron-bark?'

Jack Bentley, the fluent liar of the party, caught his breath with a jerk and coughed, to cover the gasp and gain time. 'I – iron-bark? Of course it is! I thought you would know iron-bark, mister.' (Mister was silent.) 'What else d'yer think it is?'

The dreamy, abstracted expression was back. The inspector, by the way, didn't know much about timber, but he had a great deal of instinct, and went by it when in doubt.

'L – look here, mister!' put in Dave Regan, in a tone of innocent puzzlement and with a blank bucolic face. 'B – but don't the plans and specifications say iron-bark? Ours does, anyway. I – I'll git the papers from the tent and show yer, if yer like.'

It was not necessary. The inspector admitted the fact slowly. He stooped, and with an absent air picked up a chip. He looked at it abstractedly for a moment, blinked his threefold blink; then, seeming to recollect an appointment, he woke up suddenly and asked briskly:

'Did this chip come off that girder?'

Blank silence. The inspector blinked six times, divided in threes, rapidly, mounted his horse, said 'Day,' and rode off.

Regan and party stared at each other.

'Wha – what did he do that for?' asked Andy Page, the third in the party.

'Do what for, you fool?' inquired Dave.

'Ta – take that chip for?'

'He's taking it to the office!' snarled Jack Bentley.

'What – what for? What does he want to do that for?'

'To get it blanky well analysed! You ass! Now are yer satisfied?' And Jack sat down hard on the timber, jerked out his pipe, and said to Dave, in a sharp, toothache tone:

'Gimmiamatch!'

'We – well! what are we to do now?' inquired Andy, who was the hardest grafter, but altogether helpless, hopeless, and useless in a crisis like this.

'Grain and varnish the bloomin' culvert!' snapped Bentley.

But Dave's eyes, that had been ruefully following the inspector, suddenly dilated. The inspector had ridden a short distance along the line, dismounted, thrown the bridle over a post, laid the chip (which was too big to go in his pocket) on top of it, got through the fence, and was now walking back at an angle across the line in the direction of the fencing party, who had worked up on the other side, a little more than opposite the culvert.

Dave took in the lay of the country at a glance and thought rapidly.

'Gimme an iron-bark chip!' he said suddenly.

Bentley, who was quick-witted when the track was shown him, as is a kangaroo-dog (Jack ran by sight, not scent), glanced in the line of Dave's eyes, jumped up, and got a chip about the same size as that which the inspector had taken.

Now the 'lay of the country' sloped generally to the line from both sides, and the angle between the inspector's horse, the fencing party, and the culvert was well within a clear concave space; but a couple of hundred yards back from the line and parallel to it (on the side on which Dave's party worked their timber) a fringe of scrub ran to within a few yards of a point which would be about in line with a single tree on the cleared slope, the horse, and the fencing party.

Dave took the iron-bark chip, ran along the bed of the watercourse into the scrub, raced up the siding behind the bushes, got safely through without breathing, across the exposed space, and brought the tree into line between him and the inspector who was talking to the fencers. Then he began to work quickly down the slope towards the tree (which was a thin one), keeping it in line, his arms close to his sides, and working, as it were, down the trunk of the tree, as if the fencing party were kangaroos and Dave was trying to get a shot at them. The inspector, by the by, had a habit of glancing now and then in the direction of his horse, as though under the impression that it was flighty and restless and inclined to bolt on opportunity. It was an anxious moment for all parties concerned – except the inspector. They didn't want *him* to be perturbed. And, just as Dave reached the foot of the tree, the inspector finished what he had to say to the fencers, turned, and started to walk briskly back to his horse. There was a thunderstorm coming. Now was the critical moment – there were certain prearranged signals between Dave's party and the fencers which might have interested the inspector, but none to meet a case like this.

Jack Bentley gasped, and started forward with an idea of intercepting the inspector and holding him for a few minutes in bogus conversation. Inspirations come to one at a critical moment, and it flashed on Jack's mind to send Andy instead. Andy looked as innocent and guileless as he was, but was uncomfortable in the vicinity of 'funny business', and must have an honest excuse. 'Not that that mattered,' commented Jack afterwards; 'it would have taken the inspector ten minutes to get at what Andy was driving at, whatever it was.'

'Run, Andy! Tell him there's a heavy thunderstorm coming and he'd better stay in our humpy till it's over. Run! Don't stand staring like a blanky fool. He'll be gone!'

Andy started. But just then, as luck would have it, one of the fencers started after the inspector, hailing him as 'Hi, mister!' He wanted to be set right about the survey or something – or to pretend to want to be set right – from motives of policy which I haven't time to explain here.

That fencer explained afterwards to Dave's party that he 'seen what you coves was up to,' and that's why he called the inspector back. But he told them that after they had told their yarn – which was a mistake.

'Come back, Andy!' cried Jack Bentley.

Dave Regan slipped round the tree, down on his hands and knees, and made quick time through the grass which, luckily, grew pretty tall on the thirty or forty yards of slope between the tree and the horse. Close to the horse, a thought struck Dave that pulled him up, and sent a shiver along his spine and a hungry feeling under it. The horse would break away and bolt! But the case was desperate. Dave ventured an interrogatory 'Cope, cope, cope?' The horse turned its head wearily and regarded him with a mild eye, as if he'd expected him to come, and come on all fours, and wondered what had kept him so long; then he went on thinking. Dave reached the foot of the post; the horse obligingly leaning over on the other leg. Dave reared head and shoulders cautiously behind the post, like a snake; his hand went up twice, swiftly – the first time he grabbed the inspector's chip, and the second time he put the iron-bark one in its place. He drew down and back, and scuttled off for the tree like a gigantic tailless goanna.

A few minutes later he walked up to the culvert from along the creek, smoking hard to settle his nerves.

The sky seemed to darken suddenly; the first great drops of the thunderstorm came pelting down. The inspector hurried to his horse, and cantered off along the line in the direction of the fettlers' camp.

He had forgotten all about the chip, and left it on top of the post!

Dave Regan sat down on the beam in the rain and swore comprehensively.

THE LOADED DOG

DAVE Regan, Jim Bently, and Andy Page were sinking a shaft at Stony Creek in search of a rich gold quartz reef which was supposed to exist in the vicinity. There is always a rich reef supposed to exist in the vicinity; the only questions are whether it is ten feet or hundreds beneath the surface, and in which direction. They had struck some pretty solid rock, also water which kept them bailing. They used the old-fashioned blasting-powder and time-fuse. They'd make a sausage or cartridge of blasting-powder in a skin of strong calico or canvas, the mouth sewn and bound round the end of the fuse; they'd dip the cartridge in melted tallow to make it watertight, get the drill-hole as dry as possible, drop in the cartridge with some dry dust, and wad and ram with stiff clay and broken brick. Then they'd light the fuse and get out of the hole and wait. The result was usually an ugly pot-hole in the bottom of the shaft and half a barrow-load of broken rock.

There was plenty of fish in the creek, fresh-water bream, cod, cat-fish, and tailers. The party were fond of fish, and Andy and Dave of fishing. Andy would fish for three hours at a stretch if encouraged by a 'nibble' or a 'bite' now and then – say once in twenty minutes. The butcher was always willing to give meat in exchange for fish when they caught more than they could eat; but now it was winter, and these fish wouldn't bite. However, the creek was low, just a chain of muddy waterholes, from the hole with a few bucketfuls in it to the sizable pool with an average depth of six or seven feet, and they could get fish by bailing out the smaller holes or muddying up the water in the larger ones till the fish rose to the surface. There was the cat-fish, with spikes growing out of the sides of its head, and if you got pricked you'd know it, as Dave said. Andy took off his boots, tucked up his trousers, and went into a hole one day to stir up the mud with his feet, and he knew it. Dave scooped one out with his hand and got pricked, and he knew it too; his arm swelled, and the pain throbbed up into his shoulder, and down into his stomach, too, he said, like a toothache he had once, and kept him awake for two nights – only the toothache pain had a 'burred edge,' Dave said.

Dave got an idea.

'Why not blow the fish up in the big waterhole with a cartridge?' he said. 'I'll try it.'

He thought the thing out and Andy Page worked it out. Andy usually put Dave's theories into practice if they were practicable, or bore the blame for the failure and the chaffing of his mates if they weren't.

He made a cartridge about three times the size of those they used in the rock. Jim Bently said it was big enough to blow the bottom out of the river. The inner skin was of stout calico; Andy stuck the end of a six-foot piece of fuse well down in the powder and bound the mouth of the bag firmly to it with whipcord. The idea was to sink the cartridge in the water with the open end of the fuse attached to a float on the surface, ready for lighting. Andy dipped the cartridge in melted bees-wax to make it watertight. 'We'll have to leave it some time before we light it,' said Dave, 'to give the fish time to get over their scare when we put it in, and come nosing round again; so we'll want it well water-tight.'

Round the cartridge Andy, at Dave's suggestion, bound a strip of sail canvas – that they used for making water-bags – to increase the force of the explosion, and round that he pasted layers of stiff brown paper – on the plan of the sort of fireworks we called 'gun-crackers.' He let the paper dry in the sun, then he sewed a covering of two thicknesses of canvas over it, and bound the thing from end to end with stout fishing-line. Dave's schemes were elaborate, and he often worked his inventions out to nothing. The cartridge was rigid and solid enough now – a formidable bomb; but Andy and Dave wanted to be sure. Andy sewed on another layer of canvas, dipped the cartridge in melted tallow, twisted a length of fencing-wire round it as an afterthought, dipped it in tallow again, and stood it carefully against a tent-peg, where he'd know where to find it, and wound the fuse loosely round it. Then he went to the camp-fire to try some potatoes which were boiling in their jackets in a billy, and to see about frying some chops for dinner. Dave and Jim were at work in the claim that morning.

They had a big black young retriever dog – or rather an overgrown pup, a big, foolish, four-footed mate, who was always slobbering round them and lashing their legs with his heavy tail that swung round like a stock-whip. Most of his head was usually a red, idiotic slobbering grin of appreciation of his own silliness. He seemed to take life, the world, his two-legged mates, and his own instinct as a huge joke. He'd retrieve anything; he carted back most of the camp rubbish that Andy threw away. They had a cat that died in hot weather, and Andy threw it a good distance away in the scrub; and early one morning the dog found the cat, after it had been dead a week or so, and carried it back to camp, and laid it just inside the tent-flaps, where it could best make its presence known when the mates should rise and begin to sniff suspiciously in the sickly smothering atmosphere of the summer sunrise. He used to retrieve them when they went in swimming; he'd jump in after them, and take their hands in his mouth, and try to swim out with them, and scratch their naked bodies with his paws. They loved him for his good-heartedness and his foolishness, but when they wished to enjoy a swim they had to tie him up in camp.

He watched Andy with great interest all the morning making the cartridge, and hindered him considerably, trying to help; but about noon he went off to the claim to see how Dave and Jim were getting on, and to come home to dinner with them. Andy saw them coming, and put a panful of mutton-chops on the fire. Andy was cook to-day; Dave and Jim stood with their backs to the fire, as Bushmen do in all weathers, waiting till dinner should be ready. The retriever went nosing round after something he seemed to have missed.

Andy's brain still worked on the cartridge; his eye was caught by the glare of an empty kerosene-tin lying in the bushes, and it struck him that it wouldn't be a bad idea to sink the cartridge packed with clay, sand, or stones in the tin, to increase the force of the explosion. He may have been all out, from a scientific point of view, but the notion looked all right to him. Jim Bently, by the way, wasn't interested in their 'damned silliness.' Andy noticed an empty treacle-tin – the sort with the little tin neck or spout soldered on to the top for the convenience of pouring out the treacle – and it struck him that this would have made the best kind of cartridge-case: he would only have had to pour in the powder, stick the fuse in through the neck, and cork and seal it with bees-wax. He was turning to suggest this to Dave, when Dave glanced over his shoulder to see how the chops were doing – and bolted. He explained afterwards that he thought he heard the pan spluttering extra, and looked to see if the chops were burning. Jim Bently looked behind and bolted after Dave. Andy stood stock-still, staring after them.

'Run, Andy! Run!' they shouted back at him. 'Run! Look behind you, you fool!' Andy turned slowly and looked, and there, close behind him, was the retriever with the cartridge in his mouth – wedged into his broadest and silliest grin. And that wasn't all. The dog had come round the fire to Andy, and the loose end of the fuse had trailed and waggled over the burning sticks into the blaze; Andy had slit and nicked the firing end of the fuse well, and now it was hissing and spitting properly.

Andy's legs started with a jolt; his legs started before his brain did, and he made after Dave and Jim. And the dog followed Andy.

Dave and Jim were good runners — Jim the best — for a short distance; Andy was slow and heavy, but he had the strength and the wind and could last. The dog capered round him, delighted as a dog could be to find his mates, as he thought, on for a frolic. Dave and Jim kept shouting back, 'Don't foller us! Don't foller us, you coloured fool!' But Andy kept on, no matter how they dodged. They could never explain, any more than the dog, why they followed each other, but so they ran, Dave keeping in Jim's track in all its turnings, Andy after Dave, and the dog circling round Andy – the live fuse swishing in all directions and hissing and spluttering and stinking. Jim yelling to Dave not to follow him, Dave shouting to Andy to go in another direction – to 'spread out,' and Andy roaring at the dog to go home. Then Andy's brain began to work, stimulated by the crisis: he tried to get a running kick at the dog, but the dog dodged; he snatched up sticks and stones and threw them at the dog and ran on again. The retriever saw that he'd made a mistake about Andy, and left him and bounded after Dave. Dave, who had the presence of mind to think that the fuse's time wasn't up yet, made a dive and a grab for the dog, caught him by the tail, and as he swung round snatched the cartridge out of his mouth and flung it as far as he could; the dog immediately bounded after it and retrieved it. Dave roared and cursed at the dog, who, seeing that Dave was

offended, left him and went after Jim, who was well ahead. Jim swung
to a sapling and went up it like a native bear; it was a young sapling, and
Jim couldn't safely get more than ten or twelve feet from the ground.
The dog laid the cartridge, as carefully as if it was a kitten, at the foot of
the sapling, and capered and leaped and whooped joyously round
under Jim. The big pup reckoned that this was part of the lark – he was
all right now – it was Jim who was out for a spree. The fuse sounded as if
it were going a mile a minute. Jim tried to climb higher and the sapling
bent and cracked. Jim fell on his feet and ran. The dog swooped on the
cartridge and followed. It all took but a very few moments. Jim ran to a
digger's hole, about ten feet deep, and dropped down into it – landing
on soft mud – and was safe. The dog grinned sardonically down on
him, over the edge, for a moment, as if he thought it would be a good
lark to drop the cartridge down on Jim.

'Go away, Tommy,' said Jim feebly, 'go away.'

The dog bounded off after Dave, who was the only one in sight now;
Andy had dropped behind a log, where he lay flat on his face, having
suddenly remembered a picture of the Russo-Turkish war with a circle
of Turks lying flat on their faces (as if they were ashamed) round a
newly-arrived shell.

There was a small hotel or shanty on the creek, on the main road, not
far from the claim. Dave was desperate, the time flew much faster in
his stimulated imagination than it did in reality, so he made for the
shanty. There were several casual Bushmen on the veranda and in the
bar; Dave rushed into the bar, banging the door to behind him. 'My
dog!' he gasped, in reply to the astonished stare of the publican, 'the
blanky retriever – he's got a live cartridge in his mouth – '

The retriever, finding the front door shut against him, had bounded
round and in by the back way, and now stood smiling in the doorway
leading from the passage, the cartridge still in his mouth and the fuse
spluttering. They burst out of that bar. Tommy bounded first after one
and then after another, for, being a young dog, he tried to make friends
with everybody.

The Bushmen ran round corners, and some shut themselves in the
stable. There was a new weather-board and corrugated-iron kitchen
and wash-house on piles in the backyard, with some women washing
clothes inside. Dave and the publican bundled in there and shut the
door – the publican cursing Dave and calling him a crimson fool,

in hurried tones, and wanting to know what the hell he came here for.

The retriever went in under the kitchen, amongst the piles, but, luckily for those inside, there was a vicious yellow mongrel cattle-dog sulking and nursing his nastiness under there – a sneaking, fighting, thieving canine, whom neighbours had tried for years to shoot or poison. Tommy saw his danger – he'd had experience from this dog – and started out and across the yard, still sticking to the cartridge. Halfway across the yard the yellow dog caught him and nipped him. Tommy dropped the cartridge, gave one terrified yell, and took to the Bush. The yellow dog followed him to the fence and then ran back to see what he had dropped. Nearly a dozen other dogs came from round all the corners and under the buildings – spidery, thievish, cold-blooded kangaroo dogs, mongrel sheep- and cattle-dogs, vicious black and yellow dogs – that slip after you in the dark, nip your heels, and vanish without explaining – and yapping, yelping small fry. They kept at a respectable distance round the nasty yellow dog, for it was danger-ous to go near him when he thought he had found something which might be good for a dog to eat. He sniffed at the cartridge twice, and was just taking a third cautious sniff when –

It was very good blasting-powder – a new brand that Dave had recently got up from Sydney; and the cartridge had been excellently well made. Andy was very patient and painstaking in all he did, and nearly as handy as the average sailor with needles, twine, canvas and rope.

Bushmen say that that kitchen jumped off its piles and on again. When the smoke and dust cleared away, the remains of the nasty yellow dog were lying against the paling fence of the yard looking as if he had been kicked into a fire by a horse and afterwards rolled in the dust under a barrow, and finally thrown against the fence from a dis-tance. Several saddle-horses, which had been 'hanging-up' round the veranda, were galloping wildly down the road in clouds of dust, with broken bridle-reins flying; and from a circle round the outskirts, from every point of the compass in the scrub, came the yelping of dogs. Two of them went home, to the place where they were born, thirty miles away, and reached it the same night and stayed there; it was not till towards evening that the rest came back cautiously to make inquiries. One was trying to walk on two legs, and most of 'em looked more or less singed; and a little, singed, stumpy-tailed dog, who had been in the habit of hopping the back half of him along on one leg, had reason to be glad that he'd saved up the other leg all those years, for he needed it now. There was one old one-eyed cattle-dog round that shanty for years afterwards, who couldn't stand the smell of a gun being cleaned. He it was who had taken an interest, only second to that of the yellow dog, in the cartridge. Bushmen said that it was amusing to slip up on his blind side and stick a dirty ramrod under his nose: he wouldn't wait to bring his solitary eye to bear – he'd take to the Bush and stay out all night.

For half an hour or so after the explosion there were several Bushmen round behind the stable who crouched, doubled up, against the wall, or rolled gently on the dust, trying to laugh without shrieking. There were two white women in hysterics at the house, and a half-caste rushing aimlessly round with a dipper of cold water. The publican was holding his wife tight and begging her between her squawks, to 'hold up for my sake, Mary, or I'll lam the life out of ye.'

Dave decided to apologise later on, 'when things had settled a bit,' and went back to camp. And the dog that had done it all, Tommy, the great, idiotic mongrel retriever, came slobbering round Dave and lashing his legs with his tail, and trotted home after him, smiling his broadest, longest, and reddest smile of amiability, and apparently satisfied for one afternoon with the fun he'd had.

Andy chained the dog up securely, and cooked some more chops, while Dave went to help Jim out of the hole.

And most of this is why, for years afterwards, lanky, easygoing Bushmen, riding lazily past Dave's camp, would cry, in a lazy drawl and with just a hint of the nasal twang:

''El-lo, Da-a-ve! How's the fishin' getting on, Da-a-ve?'

V

BRIGHTEN'S SISTER-IN-LAW

JIM was born on Gulgong, New South Wales. We used to say 'on' Gulgong – and old diggers still talked of being 'on th' Gulgong' – though the goldfield there had been worked out for years, and the place was only a dusty little pastoral town in the scrubs. Gulgong was about the last of the great alluvial 'rushes' of the 'roaring days' – and dreary and dismal enough it looked when I was there. The expression 'on' came from being on the 'diggins' or goldfield – the workings or the goldfield was all underneath, of course, so we lived (or starved) *on* them – not in nor at 'em.

Mary and I had been married about two years when Jim came – His name wasn't 'Jim', by the way, it was 'John Henry', after an uncle godfather; but we called him Jim from the first – (and before it) – because Jim was a popular bush name, and most of my old mates were Jims. The Bush is full of good-hearted scamps called Jim.

We lived in an old weather-board shanty that had been a sly-grog shop, and the Lord knows what else! in the palmy days of Gulgong; and I did a bit of digging ('fossicking', rather), a bit of shearing, a bit of fencing, a bit of Bush-carpentering, tank-sinking – anything, just to keep the billy boiling.

We had a lot of trouble with Jim with his teeth. He was bad with every one of them, and we had most of them lanced – couldn't pull him through without. I remember we got one lanced and the gum healed over before the tooth came through, and we had to get it cut again. He was a plucky little chap, and after the first time he never whimpered when the doctor was lancing his gum: he used to say 'tar' afterwards, and want to bring the lance home with him.

The first turn we got with Jim was the worst. I had had the wife and Jim camping with me in a tent at a dam I was making at Cattle Creek; I had two men working for me, and a boy to drive one of the tip-drays, and I took Mary out to cook for us. And it was lucky for us that the contract was finished and we got back to Gulgong, and within reach of a doctor, the day we did. We were just camping in the house, with our goods and chattels anyhow, for the night; and we were hardly back home an hour when Jim took convulsions for the first time.

Did you ever see a child in convulsions? You wouldn't want to see it again: it plays the devil with a man's nerves. I'd got the beds fixed up on the floor and the billies on the fire – I was going to make some tea, and put a piece of corned beef on to boil overnight – when Jim (he'd been queer all day, and his mother was trying to hush him to sleep) – Jim, he screamed out twice. He'd been crying a good deal, and I was dog-tired and worried (over some money a man owed me) or I'd have noticed at once that there was something unusual in the way the child cried out: as it was I didn't turn round till Mary screamed 'Joe! Joe!' You know how a woman cries out when her child is in danger or dying – short, and sharp, and terrible. 'Joe! Look! Look! Oh, my God, our child! Get the bath, quick! quick! it's convulsions!'

Jim was bent back like a bow, stiff as a bullock-yoke, in his mother's arms, and his eyeballs were turned up and fixed – a thing I saw twice afterwards and don't want ever to see again.

I was falling over things getting the tub and the hot water, when the woman who lived next door rushed in. She called to her husband to run for the doctor, and before the doctor came she and Mary had got Jim into a hot bath and pulled him through.

The neighbour woman made me up a shake-down in another room and stayed with Mary that night; but it was a long while before I got Jim and Mary's screams out of my head and fell asleep.

You may depend I kept the fire in, and a bucket of water hot over it for a good many nights after that; but (it always happens like this) there came a night, when the fright had worn off, when I was too tired to bother about the fire, and that night Jim took us by surprise. Our wood-heap was done, and I broke up a new chair to get a fire, and had to run a quarter of a mile for water; but this turn wasn't so bad as the first, and we pulled thim through.

You never saw a child in convulsions? Well, you don't want to. It must be only a matter of seconds, but it seems long minutes; and half an hour afterwards the child might be laughing and playing with you, or stretched out dead. It shook me up a lot. I was always pretty high-strung and sensitive. After Jim took the first fit, every time he cried, or turned over, or stretched out in the night, I'd jump: I was always feeling his forehead in the dark to see if he was feverish, or feeling his limbs to see if he was 'limp' yet. Mary and I often laughed about it – afterwards. I tried sleeping in another room, but for nights after Jim's first attack I'd just be dozing off into a sound sleep, when I'd hear him scream, as plain as could be, and I'd hear Mary cry, 'Joe! – Joe!' – short, sharp, and terrible – and I'd be up and into their room like a shot, only to find them sleeping peacefully. Then I'd feel Jim's head and his breathing for signs of convulsions, see to the fire and water, and go back to bed and try to sleep. For the first few nights I was like that all night, and I'd feel relieved when daylight came. I'd be in first thing to see if they were all right; then I'd sleep till dinner-time if it was Sunday or I had no work. But then I was run down about that time: I was worried about some money for a woolshed I put up and never got paid for; and besides, I'd been pretty wild before I met Mary.

I was fighting hard then – struggling for something better. Both Mary and I were born to better things, and that's what made the life so hard for us.

Jim got on all right for a while: we used to watch him well, and have his teeth lanced in time.

It used to hurt and worry me to see how – just as he was getting fat and rosy and like a natural happy child, and I'd feel proud to take him out – a tooth would come along, and he'd get thin and white and pale and bigger-eyed; and old-fashioned. We'd say, 'He'll be safe when he gets his eye-teeth;' but he didn't get them till he was two; then, 'He'll be safe when he gets his two-year-old teeth;' they didn't come till he was going on for three.

He was a wonderful little chap – Yes, I know all about parents thinking that their child is the best in the world. If your boy is small for his age, friends will say that small children make big men; that he's a very bright, intelligent child, and that it's better to have a bright, intelligent child than a big, sleepy lump of fat. And if your boy is dull and sleepy, they say that the dullest boys make the cleverest men – and all the rest of it. I never took any notice of that sort of chatter – took it for what it was worth; but, all the same, I don't think I ever saw such a child as Jim was when he turned two. He was everybody's favourite. They spoilt him rather. I had my own ideas about bringing up a child. I reckoned Mary was too soft with Jim. She'd say, 'Put that' (whatever it was) 'out of Jim's reach, will you, Joe?' and I'd say, 'No! leave it there, and make him understand he's not to have it. Make him have his meals without any nonsense and go to bed at a regular hour,' I'd say. Mary and I had many a breeze over Jim. She'd say that I forgot he was only a baby: but I held that a baby could be trained from the first week; and I believe I was right.

But, after all, what are you to do? You'll see a boy that was brought up strict turn out a scamp; and another that was dragged up anyhow (by the hair of the head, as the saying is) turn out well. Then, again, when a child is delicate – and you might lose him any day – you don't like to spank him, though he might be turning out a little fiend, as delicate children often do. Suppose you gave a child a hammering, and the same night he took convulsions, or something, and died – how'd you feel about it? You never know what a child is going to take, any more than you can tell what some women are going to say or do.

I was very fond of Jim, and we were great chums. Sometimes I'd sit and wonder what the deuce he was thinking about, and often, the way he talked, he'd make me uneasy. When he was two he wanted a pipe above all things, and I'd get him a clean new clay and he'd sit by my side, on the edge of the veranda, or on a log of the wood-heap, in the cool of the evening, and suck away at his pipe, and try to spit when he saw me do it. He seemed to understand that a cold empty pipe wasn't quite the thing, yet to have the sense to know that he couldn't smoke tobacco yet: he made the best he could of things. And if he broke a clay pipe he wouldn't have a new one, and there'd be a row; the old one had to be mended up, somehow, with string or wire. If I got my hair cut, he'd want his cut too; and it always troubled him to see me shave – as if he thought there must be something wrong somewhere, else he ought to have to be shaved too. I lathered him one day, and pretended to shave him: he sat through it as solemn as an owl, but didn't seem to appreciate it – perhaps he had sense enough to know that it couldn't possibly be the real thing. He felt his face, looked very hard at the lather I scraped off, and whimpered, 'No blood, daddy!'

I used to cut myself a good deal: I was always impatient over shaving.

Then he went in to interview his mother about it. She understood his lingo better than I did.

But I wasn't always at ease with him. Sometimes he'd sit looking into the fire, with his head on one side, and I'd watch him and wonder what he was thinking about (I might as well have wondered what a Chinaman was thinking about) till he seemed at least twenty years older than me: sometimes, when I moved or spoke, he'd glance round just as if to see what that old fool of a dadda of his was doing now.

I used to have a fancy that there was something Eastern, or Asiatic – something older than our civilisation or religion – about old-fashioned children. Once I started to explain my idea to a woman I thought would understand – and as it happened she had an old-fashioned child, with very slant eyes – a little tartar he was too. I suppose it was the sight of him that unconsciously reminded me of my infernal theory, and set me off on it, without warning me. Anyhow it got me mixed up in an awful row with the woman and her husband – and all their tribe. It wasn't an easy thing to explain myself out of it, and the row hasn't been fixed up yet. There were some Chinamen in the district.

I took a good-sized fencing contract, the frontage of a ten-mile paddock, near Gulgong, and did well out of it. The railway had got as far as the Cudgegong River – some twenty miles from Gulgong and two hundred from the coast – and 'carrying' was good then. I had a couple of draught-horses, that I worked in the tip-drays when I was tank-sinking, and one or two others running in the bush. I bought a broken-down wagon cheap, tinkered it up myself – christened it 'The Same Old Thing' – and started carrying from the railway terminus through Gulgong and along the bush roads and tracks that branch out fanlike through the scrubs to the one-pub towns and sheep and cattle stations out there in the howling wilderness. It wasn't much of a team. There were the two heavy horses for 'shafters'; a stunted colt, that I'd bought out of the pound for thirty shillings; a light, spring-cart horse; an old grey mare, with points like a big red-and-white Australian store bullock, and with the grit of an old washerwoman to work; and a horse that had spanked along in Cobb & Co's mail-coach in his time. I had a couple there that didn't belong to me: I worked them for the feeding of them in the dry weather. And I had all sorts of harness, that I mended and fixed up myself. It was a mixed team, but I took light stuff, got through pretty quick, and freight rates were high. So I got along.

Before this, whenever I made a few pounds I'd sink a shaft some-where, prospecting for gold; but Mary never let me rest till she had talked me out of that.

I made up my mind to take on a small selection farm – that an old mate of mine had fenced in and cleared, and afterwards chucked up – about thirty miles out west of Gulgong, at a place called Lahey's Creek. (The places were all called Lahey's Creek, or Spicer's Flat, or Murphy's Flat, or Ryan's Crossing, or some such name – round there.) I reckoned I'd have a run for the horses and be able to grow a bit of feed. I always had a dread of taking Mary and the children too far away from a doctor – or a good woman neighbour; but there were some people came to live on Lahey's Creek, and besides, there was a young brother of Mary's – a young scamp (his name was Jim, too, and we called him 'Jimmy' at first to make room for our Jim – he hated the name 'Jimmy' – or James). He came to live with us – without asking – and I thought he'd find enough work at Lahey's Creek to keep him out of mischief. He wasn't to be depended on much – he thought nothing of riding off, five hundred miles or so, 'to have a look at the country' – but he was fond of Mary, and he'd stay by her till I got someone else to keep her company while I was on the road. He would be a protection against 'sundowners' or any shearers who happened to wander that way in the 'D.T.'s' after a spree. Mary had a married sister come to live at Gulgong just before we left, and nothing would suit her and her husband but we must leave little Jim with them for a month or so – till we got settled down at Lahey's Creek. They were newly married.

Mary was to have driven into Gulgong, in the spring-cart, at the end of the month, and taken Jim home; but when the time came she wasn't too well – and, besides, the tyres of the cart were loose, and I hadn't time to get them cut, so we let Jim's time run on a week or so longer, till I happened to come out through Gulgong from the river with a small load of flour for Lahey's Creek way. The roads were good, the weather grand – no chance of it raining, and I had a spare tarpaulin if it did – I would only camp out one night; so I decided to take Jim home with me.

Jim was turning three then, and he was a cure. He was so old-fashioned that he used to frighten me sometimes – I'd almost think that there was something supernatural about him; though, of course, I never took any notice of that rot about some children being too old-fashioned to live. There's always the ghoulish old hag (and some not so old nor haggish either) who'll come round and shake up young parents with such croaks as, 'You'll never rear that child – he's too bright for his age.' To the devil with them! I say.

But I really thought that Jim was too intelligent for his age, and I often told Mary that he ought to be kept back, and not let talk too much to old diggers and long lanky jokers of bushmen who rode in and hung their horses outside my place on Sunday afternoons.

I don't believe in parents talking about their own children everlastingly – you get sick of hearing them; and their kids are generally little devils, and turn out larrikins as likely as not.

But, for all that, I really think that Jim, when he was three years old, was the most wonderful little chap, in every way, that I ever saw.

For the first hour or so, along the road, he was telling me all about his adventures at his auntie's.

'But they spoilt me too much, dad,' he said, as solemn as a native bear. 'An' besides, a boy ought to stick to his parrans!'

I was taking out a cattle-pup for a drover I knew, and the pup took up a good deal of Jim's time.

Sometimes he'd jolt me the way he talked; and other times I'd have to turn away my head and cough, or shout at the horses, to keep from laughing outright. And once, when I was taken that way, he said:

'What are you jerking your shoulders and coughing, and grunting, and going on that way for, dad? Why don't you tell me something?'

'Tell you what, Jim?'

'Tell me some talk.'

So I told him all the talk I could think of. And I had to brighten up, I can tell you, and not draw too much on my imagination – for Jim was a terror at cross-examination when the fit took him; and he didn't think twice about telling you when he thought you were talking nonsense. Once he said:

'I'm glad you took me home with you, dad. You'll get to know Jim.'

'What!' I said.

'You'll get to know Jim.'

'But don't I know you already?'

'No, you don't. You never has time to know Jim at home.'

And, looking back, I saw that it was cruel true. I had known in my heart all along that this was the truth; but it came to me like a blow from Jim. You see, it had been a hard struggle for the last year or so; and when I was home for a day or two I was generally too busy, or too tired and worried, or full of schemes for the future to take much notice of Jim. Mary used to speak to me about it, sometimes. 'You never take notice of the child,' she'd say. 'You could surely find a few minutes of an evening. What's the use of always worrying and brooding? Your brain will go with a snap some day, and, if you get over it, it will teach you a lesson. You'll be an old man, and Jim a young one, before you realise that you had a child once. Then it will be too late.'

This sort of talk from Mary always bored me and made me impatient with her, because I knew it all too well. I never worried for myself – only for Mary and the children. And often, as the days went by, I said to myself, 'I'll take more notice of Jim and give Mary more of my time, just as soon as I can see things clear ahead a bit.' And the hard days went on, and the weeks, and the months, and the years – Ah, well!

Mary used to say, when things would get worse, 'Why don't you talk to me, Joe? Why don't you tell me your thoughts, instead of shutting yourself up in yourself and brooding – eating your heart out? It's hard for me: I get to think you're tired of me, and selfish. I might be cross and speak sharp to you when you are in trouble. How am I to know, if you don't tell me?'

But I didn't think she'd understand.

And so, getting acquainted, and chumming and dozing, with the gums closing over our heads here and there, and the ragged patches of sunlight and shade passing up, over the horses, over us, on the front of the load, over the load, and down on to the white, dusty road again – Jim and I got along the lonely Bush road and over the ridges some fifteen miles before sunset, and camped at Ryan's Crossing on Sandy Creek for the night. I got the horses out and took the harness off. Jim wanted badly to help me, but I made him stay on the load; for one of the horses – a vicious, red-eyed chestnut – was a kicker; he'd broken a man's leg. I got the feed-bags stretched across the shafts, and the chaff and corn into them; and there stood the horses all round with their rumps north, south, and west, and their heads between the shafts, munching and switching their tails. We use double shafts, you know, for horse-teams

– two pairs side by side – and prop them up, and stretch bags between them, letting the bags sag to serve as feed boxes. I threw the spare tarpaulin over the wheels on one side, letting about half of it lie on the ground in case of damp, and so making a floor and a breakwind. I threw down bags and the blankets and 'possum rug against the wheel to make a camp for Jim and the cattle-pup, and got a gin-case we used for a tucker-box, the frying-pan and billy down, and made a good fire at a log close handy, and soon everything was comfortable. Ryan's Crossing was a grand camp. I stood with my pipe in my mouth, my hands behind my back, and my back to the fire, and took the country in.

Sandy Creek came down along a western spur of the range: the banks here were deep and green, and the water ran clear over the granite bars, boulders, and gravel. Behind us was a dreary flat covered with those gnarled, grey-barked, dry-rotted 'native apple-trees' (about as much like apple-trees as the native bear is like any other), and a nasty bit of sand-dusty road that I was always glad to get over in wet weather. To the left on our side of the creek were reedy marshes, with frogs croaking, and across the creek the dark box-scrub-covered ridges ended in steep 'sidings' coming down to the creek-bank, and to the main road that skirted them, running on west up over a 'saddle' in the ridges and on towards Dubbo. The road by Lahey's Creek to a place called Cobborah branched off, through dreary apple-tree and stringy-bark flats to the left, just beyond the crossing: all these fanlike branch tracks from the Cudgegong were inside a big horse-shoe in the Great Western Line, and so they gave small carriers a chance, now that Cobb & Co's coaches and the big teams and vans had shifted out of the main western terminus. There were tall she-oaks all along the creek and a clump of big ones over a deep waterhole just above the crossing. The creek oaks have rough barked trunks, like English elms, but are much taller and higher to the branches – and the leaves are reedy; Kendall, the Australian poet, calls them the 'she-oak harps Aeolian'. Those trees are always sigh-sigh-sighing – more of a sigh than a sough or the 'whoosh' of gum-trees in the wind. You always hear them sighing, even when you can't feel any wind. It's the same with telegraph wires: put your head against a telegraph-post on a dead, still day, and you'll hear and feel the far-away roar of the wires. But then the oaks are not connected with the distance, where there might be wind; and they don't *roar* in a gale, only sigh louder and softer according to the wind, and never seem to go above or below a certain pitch – like a big harp with all the strings the same. I used to have a theory that those creek oaks got the wind's voice telephoned to them, so to speak, through the ground.

I happened to look down, and there was Jim (I thought he was on the tarpaulin playing with the pup): he was standing close beside me with his legs wide apart, his hands behind his back, and his back to the fire.

He held his head a little on one side, and there was such an old, old, wise expression in his big brown eyes – just as if he'd been a child for a hundred years or so, or as though he were listening to those oaks, and understanding them in a fatherly sort of way.

'Dad!' he said presently – 'Dad! do you think I'll ever grow up to be a man?'

'Why – why, Jim?' I gasped.

'Because I don't want to.'

I couldn't think of anything against this. It made me uneasy. But I remember I used to have a childish dread of growing up to be a man.

'Jim,' I said, to break the silence, 'do you hear what the she-oaks say?'

'No, I don't. Is they talking?'

'Yes,' I said, without thinking.

'What is they saying?' he asked.

I took the bucket and went down to the creek for some water for tea. I thought Jim would follow with a little tin billy he had, but he didn't: when I got back to the fire he was again on the 'possum rug, comforting the pup. I fried some bacon and eggs that I'd brought out with me. Jim sang out from the wagon:

'Don't cook too much, dad – I mightn't be hungry.'

I got the tin plates, and pint-pots and things out on a clean new flour-bag, in honour of Jim, and dished up. He was leaning back on the rug looking at the pup in a listless sort of way. I reckoned he was tired out, and pulled the gin-case up close to him for a table and put his plate on it. But he only tried a mouthful or two, and then he said:

'I ain't hungry, dad! You'll have to eat it all.'

It made me uneasy – I never like to see a child of mine turn from his food. They had given him some tinned salmon in Gulgong and I was afraid that that was upsetting him. I was always against tinned muck.

'Sick, Jim?' I asked.

'No, Dad, I ain't sick; I don't know what's the matter with me.'

'Have some tea, sonny?'

'Yes, dad.'

I gave him some tea, with some milk in it that I'd brought in a bottle from his aunt's for him. He took a sip or two and then put the pint-pot on the gin-case.

'Jim's tired, dad,' he said.

I made him lie down while I fixed up a camp for the night. It had turned a bit chilly, so I let the big tarpaulin down all round – it was made to cover a high load, the flour in the wagon didn't come above the rail, so the tarpaulin came down well on to the ground. I fixed Jim up a comfortable bed under the tail-end of the wagon: when I went to lift him in he was lying back, looking up at the stars in a half-dreamy, half-fascinated way that I didn't like. Whenever Jim was extra old-fashioned, or affectionate, there was danger.

'How do you feel now, sonny?'

It seemed a minute before he heard me and turned from the stars.

'Jim's better, dad.' Then he said something like, 'The stars are looking at me.' I thought he was half asleep. I took off his jacket and boots and carried him in under the wagon and made him comfortable for the night.

'Kiss me 'night-night, daddy,' he said.

I'd rather he hadn't asked me – it was a bad sign. As I was going to the fire he called me back.

'What is it, Jim?'

'Get me my things and the cattle-pup, please, daddy.'

I was scared now. His things were some toys and rubbish he'd brought from Gulgong, and I remembered, the last time he had convulsions, he took all his toys and a kitten to bed with him. And 'night-night' and 'daddy' were two-year-old language to Jim. I'd thought he'd forgotten those words – he seemed to be going back.

'Are you quite warm enough, Jim?'

'Yes, dad.'

I started to walk up and down – I always did this when I was extra worried.

I was frightened now about Jim, though I tried to hide the fact from myself. Presently he called again. 'What is it, Jim?'

'Take the blankets off me, fahver – Jim's sick!' (They'd been teaching him to say father.)

I was scared now. I remembered a neighbour of ours had a little girl die (she swallowed a pin), and when she was going she said:

'Take the blankets off me, muvver – I'm dying.'

And I couldn't get that out of my head.

I threw back a fold of the 'possum rug, and felt Jim's head – he seemed cool enough.

'Where do you feel bad, sonny?'

No answer for a while; then he said suddenly, but in a voice as if he were talking in his sleep:

'Put my boots on, please, daddy. I want to go home to muvver!'

I held his hand, and comforted him for a while; then he slept – in a restless, feverish sort of way.

I got the bucket I used for water for the horses and stood it over the fire; I ran to the creek with the big kerosene-tin bucket and got it full of cold water and stood it handy. I got the spade (we always carried one to dig wheels out of bogs in wet weather) and turned a corner of the tarpaulin back, dug a hole, and trod the tarpaulin down into the hole to serve for a bath, in case of the worst. I had a tin of mustard, and meant to fight a good round for Jim, if death came along.

I stooped in under the tail-board of the wagon and felt Jim. His head was burning hot, and his skin parched and dry as a bone.

Then I lost nerve and started blundering backward and forward between the wagon and the fire, and repeating what I'd heard Mary say the last time we fought for Jim: 'God! don't take my child! God! don't take my boy!' I'd never had much faith in doctors, but, my God! I wanted one then. The nearest was fifteen miles away.

I threw back my head and stared up at the branches in desperation; and – well, I don't ask you to take much stock in this, though most old Bushmen will believe anything of the Bush by night; and – now, it might have been that I was unstrung, or it might have been a patch of the sky outlined in the gently moving branches, or the blue smoke rising up. But I saw the figure of a woman, all white, come down, down, nearly to the limbs of the trees, point on up the main road, and then float up and up and vanish, still pointing. I thought Mary was dead! Then it flashed on me –

Four or five miles up the road, over the 'saddle,' was an old shanty that had been a half-way inn before the Great Western Line got round as far as Dubbo, and took the coach traffic off those old Bush roads. A man named Brighten lived there. He was a selector; did a little farming, and as much sly-grog selling as he could. He was married – but it wasn't that: I'd thought of them, but she was a childish, worn-out, spiritless woman, and both were pretty 'ratty' from hardship and loneliness – they weren't likely to be of any use to me. But it was this: I'd heard talk, among some women in Gulgong, of a sister of Brighten's wife who'd gone out to live with them lately: she'd been a hospital matron in the city, they said; and there were yarns about her. Some said she got the sack for exposing the doctors – or carrying on with them – I didn't remember which. The fact of a city woman going out to live in such a place, with such people, was enough to make talk among women in a town twenty miles away, but then there must have been something extra about her, else Bushmen wouldn't have talked and carried her name so far; and I wanted a woman out of the ordinary now. I even reasoned this way, thinking like lightning, as I knelt over Jim between the big back wheels of the wagon.

I had an old racing mare that I used as a riding hack, following the team. In a minute I had her saddled and bridled; I tied the end of a half-full chaff-bag, shook the chaff into each end and dumped it on to the pommel as a cushion or buffer for Jim; I wrapped him in a blanket, and scrambled into the saddle with him.

The next minute we were stumbling down the steep bank, clattering and splashing over the crossing, and struggling up the opposite bank to the level. The mare, as I told you, was an old racer, but broken-winded – she must have run without wind after the first half-mile. She had the old racing instinct in her strong, and whenever I rode in company I'd have to pull her hard else she'd race the other horse or burst. She ran low fore and aft, and was the easiest horse I ever rode. She ran like wheels on rails, with a bit of a tremble now and then – like a railway carriage – when she settled down to it.

The chaff-bag had slipped off, in the creek I suppose, and I let the bridle-rein go and held Jim up to me like a baby the whole way. Let the strongest man, who isn't used to it, hold a baby in one position for five minutes – and Jim was fairly heavy. But I never felt the ache in my arms that night – it must have gone before I was in a fit state of mind to feel it. And at home I'd often growled about being asked to hold the baby for a few minutes. I could never brood comfortably and nurse a baby at the same time. It was a ghostly moonlight night. There's no timber in the world so ghostly as the Australian Bush in moonlight – or just about daybreak. The all-shaped patches of moonlight falling between ragged, twisted boughs; the ghostly blue-white bark of the 'white-box' trees; a dead, naked white ring-barked tree, or dead white stump starting out here and there, and the ragged patches of shade and light on the road that made anything, from the shape of a spotted bullock to a naked corpse laid out stark. Roads and tracks through the Bush made by moonlight – every one seeming straighter and clearer than the real one; you have to trust to your horse then. Sometimes the naked white trunk of a red stringy-bark tree, where a sheet of bark had been taken off, would start out like a ghost from the dark Bush. And dew or frost glistening on these things according to the season. Now and again a great grey kangaroo, that had been feeding on a green patch down by the road, would start with a 'thump-thump', and away up the siding.

The Bush seemed full of ghosts that night – all going my way – and being left behind by the mare. Once I stopped to look at Jim: I just sat back and the mare 'propped' – she'd been a stock-horse, and was used to 'cutting-out'. I felt Jim's hands and forehead; he was in a burning fever. I bent forward, and the old mare settled down to it again. I kept saying out loud – and Mary and me often laughed about it (afterwards): 'He's limp yet! – Jim's limp yet!' (the words seemed jerked out of me by sheer fright) – 'He's limp yet!' till the mare's feet took it up. Then, just when I thought she was doing her best and racing her hardest, she suddenly started forward, like a cable tram gliding along on its own and the grip put on suddenly. It was just what she'd do when I'd be riding alone and a strange horse drew up from behind – the old racing instinct. I *felt* the thing too! I felt as if a strange horse *was* there! And then – the words just jerked out of me by sheer funk – I started saying, 'Death is riding to-night! ... Death is racing to-night! ... Death is riding to-night!' till the hoof-beats took that up. And I believe the old mare felt the black horse at her side and was going to beat him or break her heart.

I was mad with anxiety and fright: I remember I kept saying, 'I'll be kinder to Mary after this! I'll take more notice of Jim!' and the rest of it.

I don't know how the old mare got up the last 'pinch'. She must have slackened pace, but I never noticed it: I just held Jim up to me and gripped the saddle with my knees – I remember the saddle jerked from the desperate jumps of her till I thought the girth would go. We topped the gap and were going down into a gully they called Dead Man's Hollow, and there, at the back of a ghostly clearing that opened from the road where there were some black-soil springs, was a long, low, oblong weather-board-and-shingle building, with blind, broken windows in the gable-ends, and a wide steep veranda roof slanting down almost to the level of the window-sills – there was something sinister about it, I thought – like the hat of a jail-bird slouched over his eyes. The place looked both deserted and haunted. I saw no light, but that was because of the moonlight outside. The mare turned in at the corner of the clearing to take a short cut to the shanty, and, as she struggled across some marshy ground, my heart kept jerking out the words, 'It's deserted! They've gone away! It's deserted!' The mare went round to the back and pulled up between the back door and a big bark-and-slab kitchen. Someone shouted from inside:

'Who's there?'

'It's me. Joe Wilson. I want your sister-in-law – I've got the boy – he's sick and dying!'

Brighten came out, pulling up his moleskins. 'What boy?' he asked.

'Here, take him,' I shouted, 'and let me get down.'

'What's the matter with him?' asked Brighten, and he seemed to hang back. And just as I made to get my leg over the saddle, Jim's head went back over my arm, he stiffened, and I saw his eyeballs turned up and glistening in the moonlight.

I felt cold all over then and sick in the stomach – but *clear-headed* in a way: strange, wasn't it? I don't know why I didn't get down and rush into the kitchen to get a bath ready. I only felt as if the worst had come, and I wished it were over and gone. I even thought of Mary and the funeral.

Then a woman ran out of the house – a big, hard-looking woman. She had on a wrapper of some sort, and her feet were bare. She laid her hand on Jim, looked at his face, and then snatched him from me and ran into the kitchen – and me down and after her. As great good luck would have it they had some dirty clothes on to boil in a kerosene-tin – dish-cloths or something.

Brighten's sister-in-law dragged a tub out from under the table, wrenched the bucket off the hook, and dumped in the water, dish-cloths and all, snatched a can of cold water from a corner, dashed that in, and felt the water with her hand – holding Jim up to her hip all the time – and I won't say how he looked. She stood him in the tub and started dashing water over him, tearing off his clothes between the splashes.

'Here, that tin of mustard – there on the shelf!' she shouted to me.

She knocked the lid off the tin on the edge of the tub, and went on splashing and spanking Jim.

It seemed an eternity. And I? Why, I never thought clearer in my life. I felt cold-blooded – I felt as if I'd like an excuse to go outside till it was all over. I thought of Mary and the funeral – and wished that that was past. All this in a flash, as it were. I felt that it would be a great relief, and only wished the funeral was months past. I felt – well, altogether selfish. I only thought of myself.

Brighten's sister-in-law splashed and spanked him hard – hard enough to break his back I thought, and – after about half an hour it seemed – the end came; Jim's limbs relaxed, he slipped down into the tub, and the pupils of his eyes came down. They seemed dull and expressionless, like the eyes of a new baby, but he was back for the world again.

I dropped on the stool by the table.

'It's all right,' she said. 'It's all over now. I wasn't going to let him die.' I was only thinking, 'Well, it's over now, but it will come on again. I wish it was over for good. I'm tired of it.'

She called to her sister, Mrs Brighten, a washed-out, helpless little fool of a woman, who'd been running in and out and whimpering all the time:

'Here, Jessie! bring the new white blanket off my bed. And you, Brighten, take some of that wood off the fire, and stuff something in that hole there to stop the draught.'

Brighten – he was a nuggety little hairy man with no expression to be seen for whiskers – had been running in with sticks and back logs from the wood-heap. He took the wood out, stuffed up the crack, and went inside and brought out a black bottle – got a cup from the shelf, and put both down near my elbow.

Mrs Brighten started to get some supper or breakfast, or whatever it was, ready. She had a clean cloth, and set the table tidily. I noticed that all the tins were polished bright (old coffee and mustard-tins and the like, that they used instead of sugar-basins and tea-caddies and salt-cellars), and the kitchen was kept as clean as possible. She was all right at little things. I knew a haggard, worked-out Bushwoman who put her whole soul – or all she'd got left – into polishing old tins till they dazzled your eyes.

I didn't feel inclined for corned beef and damper, and post-and-rail tea. So I sat and squinted, when I thought she wasn't looking, at Brighten's sister-in-law. She was a big woman, her hands and feet were big, but well-shaped and all in proportion – they fitted her. She was a handsome woman – about forty I should think. She had a square chin, and a straight thin-lipped mouth – straight save for a hint of a turn down at the corners, which I fancied (and I have strange fancies) had been a sign of weakness in the days before she grew hard. There was no sign of weakness now. She had hard grey eyes and blue-black hair. She hadn't spoken yet. She didn't ask me how the boy took ill or how I got there, or who or what I was – at least not until the next evening at tea-time.

She sat upright with Jim wrapped in the blanket and laid across her knees, with one hand under his neck and the other laid lightly on him, and she just rocked him gently.

She sat looking hard and straight before her, just as I've seen a tired needlewoman sit with her work in her lap, and look away back into the past. And Jim might have been the work in her lap, for all she seemed to think of him. Now and then she knitted her forehead and blinked.

Suddenly she glanced round and said – in a tone as if I was her husband and she didn't think much of me:

'Why don't you eat something?'

'Beg pardon?'

'Eat something!'

I drank some tea, and sneaked another look at her. I was beginning to feel more natural, and wanted Jim again, now that the colour was coming back into his face, and he didn't look like an unnaturally stiff and staring corpse. I felt a lump rising, and wanted to thank her. I sneaked another look at her.

She was staring straight before her – I never saw a woman's face change so suddenly – I never saw a woman's eyes so haggard and hope-less. Then her great chest heaved twice, I heard her draw a long shud-dering breath, like a knocked-out horse, and two great tears dropped from her wide open eyes down her cheeks like rain-drops on a face of stone. And in the firelight they seemed tinged with blood.

I looked away quick, feeling full up myself. And presently (I hadn't seen her look round) she said:

'Go to bed.'

'Beg pardon?' (Her face was the same as before the tears.)

'Go to bed. There's a bed made for you inside on the sofa.'

'But – the team – I must – '

'What?'

'The team. I left it at the camp. I must look at it.'

'Oh! Well, Brighten will ride down and bring it up in the morning – or send the half-caste. Now you go to bed, and get a good rest. The boy will be all right. I'll see to that.'

I went out – it was a relief to get out – and looked to the mare. Brighten had got her some corn and chaff in a candle-box, but she couldn't eat yet. She just stood or hung resting one hind leg and then the other, with her nose over the box – and she sobbed. I put my arms round her neck and my face down on her ragged mane, and cried for the second time since I was a boy.

As I started to go in I heard Brighten's sister-in-law say, suddenly and sharply:

'Take *that* away, Jessie.'

And presently I saw Mrs Brighten go into the house with the black bottle.

The moon had gone behind the range. I stood for a minute between the house and the kitchen and peeped in through the kitchen win-dow.

She had moved away from the fire and sat near the table. She bent over Jim and held him up close to her and rocked herself to and fro.

I went to bed and slept till the next afternoon. I woke just in time to hear the tail-end of a conversation between Jim and Brighten's sister-in-law. He was asking her out to our place, and she promising to come.

'And now,' says Jim, 'I want to go home to "muffer" in "The Same Ol' Fling." '

'What?'

Jim repeated.

'Oh! "The Same Old Thing" – the wagon.'

The rest of the afternoon I poked round the gullies with old Brighten, looking at some 'indications' (of the existence of gold) he had found. It was no use trying to 'pump' him concerning his sister-in-law; Brighten was an 'old hand', and had learned in the old bushranging and cattle-stealing days to know nothing about other people's business. And, by the way, I noticed then that the more you talk and listen to a bad character, the more you lose your dislike for him.

I never saw such a change in a woman as in Brighten's sister-in-law that evening. She was bright and jolly, and seemed at least ten years younger. She bustled round and helped her sister to get tea ready. She rooted out some old china that Mrs Brighten had stowed away some-where, and set the table as I seldom saw it set out there. She propped Jim up with pillows, and laughed and played with him like a great girl. She described Sydney and Sydney life as I'd never heard it described before; and she knew as much about the Bush and old digging days as I did. She kept old Brighten and me listening and laughing till nearly midnight. And she seemed quick to understand everything when I talked. If she wanted to explain anything that we hadn't seen, she wouldn't say that it was 'like a – like a' – and hesitate (you know what I mean); she'd hit the right thing on the head at once. A squatter with a very round, flaming red face and a white cork hat had gone by in the afternoon; she said it was 'like a mushroom on the rising moon.' She gave me a lot of good hints about children.

But she was quiet again next morning. I harnessed up, and she dressed Jim and gave him his breakfast, and made a comfortable place for him on the load with a 'possum rug and a spare pillow. She got up on the wheel to do it herself. Then was the awkward time. I'd half start to speak to her, and then turn away and go fixing up round the horses, and then make another false start to say good-bye. At last she took Jim up in her arms and kissed him, and lifted him on the wheel; but he put his arms tight round her neck, and kissed her – a thing Jim seldom did with anybody, except his mother, for he wasn't what you'd call an affectionate child – he'd never more than offer his cheek to me, in his old-fashioned way. I'd got up the other side of the load to take him from her.

'Here, take him,' she said.

I saw his mouth twitching as I lifted him. Jim seldom cried now-adays – no matter how much he was hurt. I gained some time fixing Jim comfortable.

'You'd better make a start,' she said. 'You want to get home early with that boy.'

I got down and went round to where she stood. I held out my hand and tried to speak, but my voice went like an ungreased wagon-wheel, and I gave it up, and only squeezed her hand.

'That's all right,' she said; then tears came into her eyes, and she suddenly put her hand on my shoulder and kissed me on the cheek. 'You be off – you're only a boy yourself. Take care of that boy; be kind to your wife, and take care of yourself.'

'Will you come to see us?'

'Some day,' she said.

I started the horses, and looked round once more. She was looking up at Jim, who was waving his hand to her from the top of the load. And I saw that haggard, hungry, hopeless look come into her eyes in spite of the tears.

I smoothed over that story and shortened it a lot when I told it to Mary – I didn't want to upset her. But, some time after I brought Jim home from Gulgong, and while I was at home with the team for a few days, nothing would suit Mary but she must go over to Brighten's shanty and see Brighten's sister-in-law. So James drove her over one morning in the spring-cart: it was a long way, and they stayed at Brighten's over-night and didn't get back till late the next afternoon. I'd got the place in a pig-muck, as Mary said, 'doing for' myself, and I was having a snooze on the sofa when they got back. The first thing I remember was some-one stroking my head and kissing me, and I heard Mary saying, 'My poor boy! My poor old boy!'

I sat up with a jerk. I thought that Jim had gone off again. But it seems that Mary was only referring to me. Then she started to pull grey hairs out of my head and put 'em in an empty match-box – to see how many she'd get. She used to do this when she felt a bit soft. I don't know what she said to Brighten's sister-in-law or what Brighten's sister-in-law said to her, but Mary was extra gentle for the next few days.

A Double Buggy at Lahey's Creek

I
SPUDS, AND A WOMAN'S OBSTINACY

EVER since we were married it had been Mary's great ambition to have a buggy. The house or furniture didn't matter so much – out there in the Bush where we were – but, where there were no railways or coaches, and the roads were long, and mostly hot and dusty, a buggy was the great thing. I had a few pounds when we were married, and was going to get one then; but new buggies went high, and another party got hold of a second-hand one that I'd had my eye on, so Mary thought it over and at last she said, 'Never mind the buggy, Joe; get a sewing-machine and I'll be satisfied. I'll want the machine more than the buggy, for a while. Wait till we're better off.'

After that, whenever I took a contract – to put up a fence or woolshed, or sink a dam or something – Mary would say, 'You ought to knock a buggy out of this job, Joe'; but something always turned up – bad weather or sickness. Once I cut my foot with the adze and was laid up; and, another time, a dam I was making was washed away by a flood before I finished it. Then Mary would say, 'Ah, well – never mind, Joe. Wait till we are better off.' But she felt it hard the time I built a woolshed and didn't get paid for it, for we'd as good as settled about another second-hand buggy then.

I always had a fancy for carpentering, and was handy with tools. I made a spring-cart – body and wheels – in spare time, out of colonial hardwood, and got Little the blacksmith to do the ironwork: I painted the cart myself. It wasn't much lighter than one of the tip-drays I had, but it *was* a spring-cart, and Mary pretended to be satisfied with it: anyway, I didn't hear any more of the buggy for a while.

I sold that cart for fourteen pounds, to a Chinese gardener who wanted a strong cart to carry his vegetables round through the Bush. It was just before our first youngster came: I told Mary that I wanted the money in case of extra expense – and she didn't fret much at losing the cart. But the fact was that I was going to make another try for a buggy, as a present for Mary when the child was born. I thought of getting the turn-out while she was laid up, keeping it dark from her till she was on her feet again, and then showing her the buggy standing in the shed. But she had a bad time, and I had to have the doctor regularly, and get a proper nurse, and a lot of things extra; so the buggy idea was knocked on the head. I was set on it, too; I'd thought of how, when Mary was up and getting strong, I'd say one morning, 'Go round and have a look in the shed, Mary; I've got a few fowls for you,' or something like that – and follow her round to watch her eyes when she saw the buggy. I never told Mary about that – it wouldn't have done any good.

Later on I got some good timber – mostly scraps that were given to me – and made a light body for a spring-cart. Galletly, the coach-builder at Cudgegong, had got a dozen pairs of American hickory wheels up from Sydney, for light spring-carts, and he let me have a pair for cost price and carriage. I got him to iron the cart, and he put it through the paintshop for nothing. He sent it out, too, at the tail of Tom Tarrant's big van – to increase the surprise. We were swells then for a while; I heard no more of a buggy until after we'd been settled at Lahey's Creek for a couple of years.

I told you how I went into the carrying line, and took up a selection at Lahey's Creek – for a run for the horses and to grow a bit of feed – and shifted Mary and little Jim out there from Gulgong, with Mary's young scamp of a brother James to keep them company while I was on the road. The first year I did well enough carrying, but I never cared for it – it was too slow; and, besides, I was always anxious when I was away from home. The game was right enough for a single man – or a married one whose wife had got the nagging habit (as many Bushwomen have – God help 'em), and who wanted peace and quietness sometimes. Besides, other small carriers started (seeing me getting on); and Tom Tarrant, the coach-builder at Cudgegong, had another heavy spring-van built, and put it on the road, and he took a lot of the light stuff.

The second year I made a rise – out of 'spuds', of all the things in the world. It was Mary's idea. Down at the lower end of our selection – Mary called it 'the run' – was a shallow watercourse called Snake's Creek, dry most of the year, except for a muddy waterhole or two; and, just above the junction, where it ran into Lahey's Creek, was a low piece of good black-soil flat, on our side – about three acres. The flat was fairly clear when I came to the selection – save for a few logs that had been washed up there in some big 'old man' flood, way back in blackfellows' times: and one day when I had a spell at home, I got the horses and trace-chains and dragged the logs together – those that wouldn't split for fencing timber – and burnt them off. I had a notion to get the flat ploughed and make a lucerne-paddock of it. There was a good waterhole, under a clump of she-oak in the bend, and Mary used to take her stools and tubs and boiler down there in the spring-cart in hot weather, and wash the clothes under the shade of the trees – it was cooler, and saved carrying water to the house. And one evening after she'd done the washing she said to me:

'Look here, Joe; the farmers out here never seem to get a new idea: they don't seem to me ever to try and find out beforehand what the market is going to be like – they just go on farming the same old way, and putting in the same old crops year after year. They sow wheat, and, if it comes on anything like the thing, they reap and thresh it; if it doesn't they mow it for hay – and some of 'em don't have the brains to do that in time. Now, I was looking at that bit of flat you cleared, and it struck me that it wouldn't be a half-bad idea to get a bag of seed potatoes, and have the land ploughed – old Corny George would do it cheap – and get them put in at once. Potatoes have been dear all round for the last couple of years.'

I told her she was talking nonsense, that the ground was no good for potatoes, and the whole district was too dry. 'Everybody I know has tried it, one time or another, and made nothing of it,' I said.

'All the more reason why you should try it, Joe,' said Mary. 'Just try one crop. It might rain for weeks, and then you'll be sorry you didn't take my advice.'

'But I tell you the ground is not potato-ground,' I said.

'How do you know? You haven't sown any there yet.'

'But I've turned up the surface and looked at it. It's not rich enough, and too dry, I tell you. You need swampy, boggy ground for potatoes. Do you think I don't know land when I see it?'

'But you haven't *tried* to grow potatoes there yet, Joe. How do you know –'

I didn't listen to any more. Mary was obstinate when she got an idea into her head. It was no use arguing with her. All the time I'd be talking she'd just knit her forehead and go on thinking straight ahead, on the track she'd started – just as if I wasn't there – and it used to make me mad. She'd keep driving at me till I took her advice or lost my temper – I did both at the same time, mostly.

I took my pipe and went out to smoke and cool down.

A couple of days after the potato breeze, I started with the team down to Cudgegong for a load of fencing-wire I had to bring out; and after I'd kissed Mary good-bye, she said:

'Look here, Joe, if you bring out a bag of seed potatoes, James and I will slice them, and old Corny George down the creek would bring his plough up in the dray, and plough the ground for very little. We could put the potatoes in ourselves if the ground were only ploughed.'

I thought she'd forgotten all about it. There was no time to argue – I'd be sure to lose my temper, and then I'd either have to waste an hour comforting Mary, or go off in a 'huff', as the women call it, and be miserable for the trip. So I said I'd see about it. She gave me another hug and a kiss. 'Don't forget, Joe,' she said as I started. 'Think it over on the road.' I reckon she had the best of it that time.

About five miles along, just as I turned into the main road, I heard someone galloping after me, and I saw young James on his hack. I got a start, for I thought that something had gone wrong at home. I remember the first day I left Mary on the creek, for the first five or six miles I was half-a-dozen times on the point of turning back – only I thought she'd laugh at me.

'What is it, James?' I shouted, before he came up – but I saw he was grinning.

'Mary says to tell you not to forget to bring a hoe out with you.'

'You clear off home!' I said, 'or I'll lay the whip about your young hide; and don't come riding after me again as if the run was on fire.'

'Well, you needn't get shirty with me!' he said. '*I* don't want to have anything to do with a hoe.' And he rode off.

I *did* get thinking about those potatoes, though I hadn't meant to. I knew of an independent man in that district who'd made his money out of a crop of potatoes; but that was away back in the roaring Fifties – '54 – when spuds went up to twenty-eight shillings a hundredweight (in Sydney), on account of the gold rush. We might get good rain now, and, anyway, it wouldn't cost much to put the potatoes in. If they came on well, it would be a few pounds in my pocket; if the crop was a failure, I'd have a better show with Mary next time she was struck by an idea outside housekeeping, and have something to grumble about when I felt grumpy.

I got a couple of bags of potatoes – we could use those that were left over; and I got a small iron plough and harrow that Little the blacksmith had lying in his yard and let me have cheap – only about a pound more than I told Mary I gave for them. When I took advice I generally made the mistake of taking more than was offered, or adding notions of my own. It was vanity, I suppose. If the crop came on well I could claim the plough-and-harrow part of the idea, anyway. (It didn't strike me that if the crop failed Mary would have the plough and harrow against me, for old Corny would plough the ground for ten or fifteen shillings.) Anyway, I'd want a plough and harrow later on, and I might as well get it now; it would give James something to do.

I came out by the western road, by Guntawang, and up the creek home; and the first thing I saw was old Corny George ploughing the flat. And Mary was down on the bank superintending. She'd got James with the trace-chains and the spare horses, and had made him clear off every stick and bush where another furrow might be squeezed in. Old Corny looked pretty grumpy on it – he'd broken all his ploughshares but one, in the roots; and James didn't look much brighter. Mary had an old felt hat and a new pair of 'lastic-side boots of mine on, and the boots were covered with clay, for she'd been down hustling James to get a rotten old stump out of the way by the time old Corny came round with his next furrow.

'I thought I'd make the boots easy for you, Joe,' said Mary.

'It's all right, Mary,' I said, 'I'm not going to growl.' Those boots were a bone of contention between us; but she generally got them off before I got home.

Her face fell when she saw the plough and harrow in the wagon, but I said that would be all right – we'd want a plough anyway.

'I thought you wanted old Corny to plough the ground,' she said.

'I never said so.'

'But when I sent Jim after you about the hoe to put the spuds in, you didn't say you wouldn't bring it,' she said.

I had a few days at home, and entered into the spirit of the thing. When Corny was done, James and I cross-ploughed the land, and got a stump or two, a big log, and some scrub out of the way at the upper end and added nearly an acre, and ploughed that. James was all right at most Bushwork: he'd bullock so long as the novelty lasted; he liked ploughing or fencing, or any graft he could make a show at. He didn't care for grubbing out stumps, or splitting posts and rails. We sliced the potatoes of an evening – and there was trouble between Mary and James over cutting through the 'eyes'. There was no time for the hoe – and besides it wasn't a novelty to James – so I just ran furrows and they dropped the spuds in behind me, and I turned another furrow over them, and ran the harrow over the ground. I think I hilled those spuds, too, with furrows – or a crop of Indian corn I put in later on.

It rained heavens-hard for over a week: we had regular showers all through, and it was the finest crop of potatoes ever seen in the district. I believe at first Mary used to slip down at daybreak to see if the potatoes were up; and she'd write to me about them, on the road. I forget how many bags I got but the few who had grown potatoes in the district sent theirs to Sydney, and spuds went up to twelve and fifteen shillings a hundred-weight in that district. I made a few quid out of mine – and saved carriage too, for I could take them out on the wagon. Then Mary began to hear (through James) of a buggy that someone had for sale cheap, or a dogcart that somebody else wanted to get rid of – and let me know about it, in an off-hand way.

II
JOE WILSON'S LUCK

THERE was good grass on the selection all the year. I'd picked up a small lot – about twenty head – of half-starved steers for next to nothing, and turned them on the run; they came on wonderfully, and my brother-in-law (Mary's sister's husband), who was running a butchery at Gulgong, gave me a good price for them. His carts ran out twenty or thirty miles, to little bits of gold rushes that were going on at th' Home Rule, Happy

Valley, Guntawang, Tallawang, and Cooyal, and those places round there, and he was doing well.

Mary had heard of a light American wagonette, when the steers went – a tray-body arrangement, and she thought she'd do with that. 'It would be better than the buggy, Joe,' she said. 'There'd be more room for the children, and, besides, I could take butter and eggs to Gulgong, or Cobborah, when we get a few more cows.' Then James heard of a small flock of sheep that a selector – who was about starved off his selection out Talbragar way – wanted to get rid of. James reckoned he could get them for less than half-a-crown a head. We'd had a heavy shower of rain, that came over the ranges and didn't seem to go beyond our boundaries. Mary said, 'It's a pity to see all that grass going to waste, Joe. Better get those sheep and try your luck with them. Leave some money with me, and I'll send James over for them. Never mind about the buggy – we'll get that when we're on our feet.'

So James rode across to Talbragar and drove a hard bargain with that unfortunate selector, and brought the sheep home. There were about two hundred, wethers and ewes, and they were young and looked a good breed too, but so poor they could scarcely travel; they soon picked up, though. The drought was blazing all round and out back, and I think that my corner of the ridges was the only place where there was any grass to speak of. We had another shower or two, and the grass held out. Chaps began to talk of 'Joe Wilson's luck'.

I would have liked to shear those sheep; but I hadn't time to get a shed or anything ready – along towards Christmas there was a bit of a boom in the carrying line. Wethers in wool were going as high as thirteen to fifteen shillings at the Homebush yards at Sydney, so I arranged to truck the sheep down from the river by rail, with another small lot that was going, and I started James off with them. He took the west road, and down Guntawang way a big farmer who saw James with the sheep (and who was speculating, or adding to his stock, or took a fancy to the wool) offered James as much for them as he reckoned I'd get in Sydney, after paying the carriage and the agents and the auctioneer. James put the sheep in a paddock and rode back to me. He was all there where riding was concerned. I told him to let the sheep go. James made a Greener shot-gun, and got his saddle done up, out of that job.

I took up a couple more forty-acre blocks – one in James's name, to encourage him with the fencing. There was a good slice of land in an angle between the range and the creek, farther down, which everybody thought belonged to Wall, the squatter, but Mary got an idea, and went to the local land office, and found out that it was unoccupied Crown land, and so I took it up on pastoral lease, and got a few more sheep – I'd saved some of the best-looking ewes from the last lot.

One evening – I was going down next day for a load of fencing-wire for myself – Mary said:

'Joe! do you know that the Matthews have got a new double buggy?'

The Matthews were a big family of cockatoos, along up the main road, and I didn't think much of them. The sons were all 'bad-eggs', though the old woman and girls were right enough.

'Well, what of that?' I said. 'They're up to their neck in debt, and camping like blackfellows in a big bark humpy. They do well to go flashing round in a double buggy.'

'But that isn't what I was going to say,' said Mary. 'They want to sell their old single buggy, James says. I'm sure you could get it for six or seven pounds; and you could have it done up.'

'I wish James to the devil!' I said. 'Can't he find anything better to do than ride round after cock-and-bull yarns about buggies?'

'Well,' said Mary, 'it was James who got the steers and the sheep.'

Well, one word led to another, and we said things we didn't mean – but couldn't forget in a hurry. I remember I said something about Mary always dragging me back just when I was getting my head above water and struggling to make a home for her and the children; and that hurt her, and she spoke of 'homes' she'd had since she was married. And that cut me deep.

It was about the worst quarrel we had. When she began to cry I got my hat and went out and walked up and down by the creek. I hated anything that looked like injustice – I was so sensitive about it that it made me unjust sometimes. I tried to think I was right, but I couldn't – it wouldn't have made me feel any better if I could have thought so. I got thinking of Mary's first year on the selection and the life she'd had since we were married.

When I went in she'd cried herself to sleep. I bent over and, 'Mary,' I whispered.

She seemed to wake up.

'Joe – Joe!' she said.

'What is it, Mary?' I said.

'I'm pretty sure that old Spot's calf isn't in the pen. Make James go at once!'

Old Spot's last calf was two years old now; so Mary was talking in her sleep, and dreaming she was back in her first year.

We both laughed when I told her about it afterwards; but I didn't feel like laughing just then.

Later on in the night she called out in her sleep:

'Joe – Joe! Put that buggy in the shed, or the sun will blister the varnish!'

I wish I could say that that was the last time I ever spoke unkindly to Mary.

Next morning I got up early and fried the bacon and made the tea, and took Mary's breakfast in to her – like I used to do, sometimes, when we were first married. She didn't say anything – just pulled my head down and kissed me.

When I was ready to start, Mary said:

'You'd better take the spring-cart in behind the dray, and get the tyres cut and set. They're ready to drop off, and James has been wedging them up till he's tired of it. The last time I was out with the children I had to knock one of them back with a stone: there'll be an accident yet.'

So I lashed the shafts of the cart under the tail of the wagon and mean and ridiculous enough the cart looked, going along that way. It suggested a man stooping along handcuffed, with his arms held out and down in front of him.

It was dull weather, and the scrubs looked extra dreary and endless – and I got thinking of old things. Everything was going all right with me, but that didn't keep me from brooding sometimes – trying to hatch out stones, like an old hen we had at home. I think, taking it all round, I used to be happier when I was mostly hard up – and more generous. When I had ten pounds I was more likely to listen to a chap who said, 'Lend me a pound note, Joe,' than when I had fifty; *then* I fought shy of careless chaps – and lost mates that I wanted afterwards – and got the name of being mean. When I got a good cheque I'd be as miserable as a miser over the first ten pounds I spent; but when I got down to the last I'd buy things for the house. And now that I was getting on, I hated to spend a pound on anything. But then, the farther I got away from poverty the greater the fear I had of it – and, besides, there was always before us all the thought of the terrible drought, with blazing runs as bare and dusty as the road, and dead stock rotting every yard, all along the barren creeks.

I had a long yarn with Mary's sister and her husband that night in Gulgong, and it brightened me up. I had a fancy that that sort of a brother-in-law made a better mate than a nearer one; Tom Tarrant had one, and he said it was sympathy. But while we were yarning I couldn't help thinking of Mary, out there in the hut on the creek, with no one to talk to but the children, or James, who was sulky at home, or Black Mary or Black Jimmy (our black boy's father and mother), who weren't over-sentimental. Or, maybe, a selector's wife (the nearest was five miles away) who could talk only of two or three things – 'lambin' ' and 'shearin' ' and 'cookin' for the men', and what she said to her old man, and what he said to her – and her own ailments over and over again.

It's a wonder it didn't drive Mary mad! – I know I could never listen to that woman more than an hour. Mary's sister said:

'Now if Mary had a comfortable buggy, she could drive in with the children oftener. Then she wouldn't feel the loneliness so much.'

I said 'Good night' then and turned in. There was no getting away from that buggy. Whenever Mary's sister started hinting about a buggy, I reckoned it was a put-up job between them.

III
THE GHOST OF MARY'S SACRIFICE

WHEN I got to Cudgegong I stopped at Galletly's coach-shop to leave the cart. The Galletlys were good fellows: there were two brothers – one was a saddler and harness-maker. Big brown-bearded men – the biggest men in the district, 'twas said.

Their old man had died lately and left them some money; they had men, and only worked in their shops when they felt inclined, or there was a special work to do; they were both first-class tradesmen. I went into the painter's shop to have a look at a double buggy that Galletly had built for a man who couldn't pay cash for it when it was finished – and Galletly wouldn't trust him.

There it stood, behind a calico screen that the coach-painters used to keep out the dust when they were varnishing. It was a first-class piece of work – pole, shafts, cushions, whip, lamps, and all complete. If you only wanted to drive one horse you could take out the pole and put in the shafts, and there you were. There was a tilt over the front seat; if you only wanted the buggy to carry two, you could fold down the back seat, and there you had a handsome, roomy, single buggy. It would go near fifty pounds.

While I was looking at it, Bill Galletly came in and slapped me on the back.

'Now, there's a chance for you, Joe!' he said. 'I saw you rubbing your head round that buggy the last time you were in. You wouldn't get a better one in the colonies, and you won't see another like it in the district again in a hurry – for it doesn't pay to build 'em. Now you're a full-blown squatter, and it's time you took little Mary for a fly round in her own buggy now and then, instead of having her stuck out there in the scrub, or jolting through the dust in a cart like some old Mother Flourbag.'

He called her 'little Mary' because the Galletly family had known her when she was a girl.

I rubbed my head and looked at the buggy again. It was a great temptation.

'Look here, Joe,' said Bill Galletly in a quieter tone. 'I'll tell you what I'll do. I'll let *you* have the buggy. You can take it out and send along a bit of a cheque when you feel you can manage it, and the rest later on – a year will do, or even two years. You've had a hard pull, and I'm not likely to be hard up for money in a hurry.'

They were good fellows the Galletlys, but they knew their men. I happened to know that Bill Galletly wouldn't let the man he built the buggy for take it out of the shop without cash down, though he was a big-bug round there. But that didn't make it easier for me.

Just then Robert Galletly came into the shop. He was rather quieter than his brother, but the two were very much alike.

'Look here, Bob,' said Bill; 'here's a chance for you to get rid of your harness. Joe Wilson's going to take that buggy off my hands.'

Bob Galletly put his foot up on a saw-stool, took one hand out of his pocket, rested his elbow on his knee and his chin on the palm of his hand, and bunched up his big beard with his fingers, as he always did when he was thinking. Presently he took his foot down, put his hand back in his pocket, and said to me, 'Well, Joe, I've got a double set of harness made for the man who ordered that damned buggy, and if you like I'll let you have it. I suppose when Bill there has squeezed all he can out of you I'll stand a show of getting something. He's a regular Shylock, he is.'

I pushed my hat forward and rubbed the back of my head and stared at the buggy.

'Come across to the Royal, Joe,' said Bob.

But I knew that a beer would settle the business, so I said I'd get the wool up to the station first and think it over, and have a drink when I came back.

I thought it over on the way to the station, but it didn't seem good enough. I wanted to get some more sheep, and there was the new run to be fenced in, and the instalments on the selections. I wanted lots of things that I couldn't well do without. Then, again, the farther I got away from debt and hard-upedness the greater the horror I had of it. I had two horses that would do; but I'd have to get another later on, and altogether the buggy would run me nearer a hundred than fifty pounds. Supposing a dry season threw me back with that buggy on my hands. Besides, I wanted a spell. If I got the buggy it would only mean an extra turn of graft for me. No, I'd take Mary for a trip to Sydney, and she'd have to be satisfied with that.

I'd got it settled, and was just turning in through the big white gates to the goods-shed when young Black, the squatter, dashed past to the station in his big new wagonette, with his wife and a driver and a lot of portmanteaux and rugs and things. They were going to do the grand in Sydney over Christmas. Now it was young Black who was so shook after Mary when she was in service with the Blacks before the old man died, and if I hadn't come along – and if girls never cared for vagabonds – Mary would have been mistress of Haviland homestead, with servants to wait on her; and she was far better fitted for it than the one that was there. She would have been going to Sydney every holiday and putting up at the old Royal, with every comfort that a woman could ask for, and seeing a play every night. And I'd have been knocking around amongst the big stations out back, or maybe drinking myself to death at the shanties.

The Blacks didn't see me as I went by, ragged and dusty, and with an old, nearly black, cabbage-tree hat drawn over my eyes. I didn't care a damn for them, or any one else, at most times, but I had moods when I felt things.

One of Black's big wool-teams was just coming away from the shed, and the driver, a big, dark, rough fellow, with some foreign blood in him, didn't seem inclined to wheel his team an inch out of the middle of the road. I stopped my horses and waited. He looked at me and I looked at him – hard. Then he wheeled off, scowling, and swearing at his horses. I'd given him a hiding, six or seven years before, and he hadn't forgotten it. And I felt then as if I wouldn't mind trying to give someone a hiding.

The goods clerk must have thought that Joe Wilson was pretty grumpy that day. I was thinking of Mary, out there in the lonely hut on a barren creek in the Bush – for it was little better – with no one to speak to except a haggard, worn-out Bushwoman or two, that came to see her on Sunday. I thought of the hardships she went through in the first year – that I haven't told you about yet; of the time she was ill, and I away, and no one to understand; of the time she was alone with James and Jim sick; and of the loneliness she fought through out there. I thought of Mary, outside in the blazing heat, with an old print dress and a felt hat, and a pair of 'lastic-siders of mine on, doing the work of a station manager as well as that of a housewife and mother. And her cheeks were getting thin, and the colour was going: I thought of the gaunt, brick-brown, saw-file voiced, hopeless and spiritless Bushwomen I knew – and some of them not much older than Mary.

When I went back into the town, I had a drink with Bill Galletly at the Royal, and that settled the buggy; then Bob shouted, and I took the harness. Then I shouted, to wet the bargain. When I was going, Bob said, 'Send in that young scamp of a brother of Mary's with the horses: if the collars don't fit I'll fix up a pair of makeshifts, and alter the others.' I thought they both gripped my hand harder than usual, but that might have been the beer.

IV
THE BUGGY COMES HOME

I 'WHIPPED the cat' a bit, the first twenty miles or so, but then, I thought, what did it matter? What was the use of grinding to save money until we were too old to enjoy it. If we had to go down in the

world again, we might as well fall out of a buggy as out of a dray –
there'd be some talk about it, anyway, and perhaps a little sympathy.
When Mary had the buggy she wouldn't be tied down so much to that
wretched hole in the Bush; and the Sydney trips needn't be off either. I
could drive down to Wallerawang on the main line, where Mary had
some people, and leave the buggy and horses there, and take the train to
Sydney, or go right on, by the old coach road, over the Blue Mountains:
it would be a grand drive. I thought best to tell Mary's sister at Gulgong
about the buggy; I told her I'd keep it dark from Mary till the buggy
came home. She entered into the spirit of the thing, and said she'd give
the world to be able to go out with the buggy, if only to see Mary open
her eyes when she saw it; but she couldn't go, on account of a new baby
she had. I was rather glad she couldn't, for it would spoil the surprise a
little, I thought. I wanted that all to myself.

I got home about sunset next day, and, after tea, when I'd finished
telling Mary all the news, and a few lies as to why I didn't bring the cart
back, and one or two other things, I sat with James, out on a log of the
wood-heap, where we generally had our smokes and interviews, and
told him all about the buggy. He whistled, then he said:

'But what do you want to make it such a bushranging business for?
Why can't you tell Mary now? It will cheer her up. She's been pretty
miserable since you've been away this trip.'

'I want it to be a surprise,' I said.

'Well, I've got nothing to say against a surprise, out in a hole like this;
but it 'ud take a lot to surprise me. What am I to say to Mary about
taking the two horses in? I'll only want one to bring the cart out, and
she's sure to ask.'

'Tell her you're going to get yours shod.'

'But he had a set of slippers only the other day. She knows as much
about horses as we do. I don't mind telling a lie so long as a chap has
only got to tell a straight lie and be done with it. But Mary asks so many
questions.'

'Well, drive the other horse up the creek early, and pick him up as
you go.'

'Yes. And she'll want to know what I want with two bridles. But I'll
fix her – *you* needn't worry.'

'And, James,' I said, 'get a chamois leather and sponge – we'll want 'em anyway – and you might give the buggy a wash down in the creek, coming home. It's sure to be covered with dust.'

'Oh! – orlright.'

'And if you can, time yourself to get here in the cool of the evening, or just about sunset.'

'What for?'

I'd thought it would be better to have the buggy there in the cool of the evening, when Mary would have time to get excited and get over it – better than in the blazing hot morning, when the sun rose as hot as at noon, and we'd have the long broiling day before us.

'What do you want me to come at sunset for?' asked James. 'Do you want me to camp out in the scrub and turn up like a blooming sundowner?'

'Oh well,' I said, 'get here at midnight if you like.'

We didn't say anything for a while – just sat and puffed at our pipes. Then I said:

'Well, what are you thinking about?'

'I'm thinking it's time you got a new hat, the sun seems to get in through your old one too much,' and he got out of my reach and went to see about penning the calves. Before we turned in he said:

'Well, what am I to get out of the job, Joe?'

He had his eye on a double-barrel gun that Franca the gunsmith in Cudgegong had – one barrel shot, and the other rifle; so I said:

'How much does Franca want for that gun?'

'Five-ten; but I think he'd take my single barrel off it. Anyway, I can squeeze a couple of quid out of Phil Lambert for the single barrel.' (Phil was his bosom chum.)

'All right,' I said. 'Make the best bargain you can.'

He got his own breakfast and made an early start next morning, to get clear of any instructions or messages that Mary might have forgotten to give him overnight. He took his gun with him.

I'd always thought that a man was a fool who couldn't keep a secret from his wife – that there was something womanish about him. I found out. Those three days waiting for the buggy were about the longest I ever spent in my life. It made me scotty with everyone and everything; and poor Mary had to suffer for it. I put in the time patching up the harness and mending the stockyard and the roof, and, the third morning, I rode up the ridges to look for trees for fencing timber. I remember I hurried home that afternoon because I thought the buggy might get there before me.

At tea-time I got Mary on to the buggy business.

'What's the good of a single buggy to you, Mary?' I asked. 'There's only room for two, and what are you going to do with the children when we go out together?'

'We can put them on the floor at our feet, like other people do. I can always fold up a blanket or 'possum rug for them to sit on.'

But she didn't take half so much interest in buggy talk as she would have taken at any other time, when I didn't want her to. Women are aggravating that way. But the poor girl was tired and not very well, and both the children were cross. She did look knocked up.

'We'll give the buggy a rest, Joe,' she said. (I thought I heard it coming then.) 'It seems as far off as ever. I don't know why you want to harp on it to-day. Now, don't look so cross, Joe – I didn't mean to hurt you. We'll wait until we can get a double buggy, since you're so set on it. There'll be plenty of time when we're better off.'

After tea, when the youngsters were in bed, and she'd washed up, we sat outside on the edge of the veranda floor, Mary sewing, and I smoking and watching the track up the creek.

'Why don't you talk, Joe?' asked Mary. 'You scarcely ever speak to me now: it's like drawing blood out of a stone to get a word from you. What makes you so cross, Joe?'

'Well, I've got nothing to say.'

'But you should find something. Think of me – it's very miserable for me. Have you anything on your mind? Is there any new trouble? Better tell me, no matter what it is, and not go worrying and brooding and making both our lives miserable. If you never tell me anything, how can you expect me to understand?'

I said there was nothing the matter.

'But there must be, to make you so unbearable. Have you been drinking, Joe – or gambling?'

I asked her what she'd accuse me of next.

'And another thing I want to speak to you about,' she went on. 'Now, don't knit up your forehead like that, Joe, and get impatient –'

'Well, what is it?'

'I wish you wouldn't swear in the hearing of the children. Now, little

Jim to-day, he was trying to fix his little go-cart, and it wouldn't run right, and – and –'

'Well, what did he say?'

'He –' (she seemed a little hysterical, trying not to laugh) – 'he said, "Damn it!"'

I had to laugh. Mary tried to keep serious but it was no use.

'Never mind, old woman,' I said, putting an arm round her, for her mouth was trembling, and she was crying more than laughing. 'It won't be always like this. Just wait till we're a bit better off.'

Just then a black boy we had (I must tell you about him some other time) came sidling along by the wall, as if he were afraid somebody was going to hit him – poor little devil! I never did.

'What is it, Harry?' said Mary.

'Buggy comin', I bin thinkit.'

'Where?'

He pointed up the creek.

'Sure it's a buggy?'

'Yes, missus.'

'How many horses?'

'One – two.'

We knew that he could hear and see things long before we could. Mary went and perched on the wood-heap, and shaded her eyes – though the sun had gone – and peered through between the eternal grey trunks of the stunted trees on the flat across the creek. Presently she jumped down and came running in.

'There's someone coming in a buggy, Joe!' she cried, excitedly. 'And both my white table-cloths are rough dry. Harry! put two flat-irons down to the fire, quick, and put on some more wood. It's lucky I kept those new sheets packed away. Get up out of that, Joe! What are you sitting grinning like that for? Go and get on another shirt. Hurry – Why, it's only James – by himself.'

She stared at me, and I sat there, grinning like a fool.

'Joe!' she said. 'Whose buggy is that?'

'Well, I suppose it's yours,' I said.

She caught her breath, and stared at the buggy, and then at me again. James drove down out of sight into the crossing, and came up close to the house.

'Oh, Joe! what have you done?' cried Mary. 'Why, it's a new double buggy!' Then she rushed at me and hugged my head. 'Why didn't you tell me, Joe? You poor old boy! – and I've been nagging at you all day!' And she hugged me again.

James got down and started taking the horses out – as if it was an everyday occurrence. I saw the double-barrel gun sticking out from under the seat. He'd stopped to wash the buggy, and I suppose that's what made him grumpy. Mary stood on the veranda, with her eyes twice as big as usual, and breathing hard – taking the buggy in.

James skimmed the harness off, and the horses shook themselves and went down to the dam for a drink. 'You'd better look under the seats,' growled James, as he took his gun out with great care.

Mary dived for the buggy. There was a dozen of lemonade and ginger-beer in a candle-box from Galletly – James said that Galletly's men had a gallon of beer, and they cheered him, James (I suppose he meant they cheered the buggy), as he drove off; there was a 'little bit of ham' from Pat Murphy, the storekeeper at Home Rule, that he'd 'cured himself' – it was the biggest I ever saw; there were three loaves of baker's bread, a cake, and a dozen yards of something 'to make up for the children,' from Aunt Gertrude at Gulgong; there was a fresh-water cod, that long Dave Regan had caught the night before in the Macquarie River, and sent out packed in salt in a box; there was a holland suit for the black boy, with red braid to trim it; and there was a jar of preserved ginger, and some lollies (sweets) ('for the lil' boy'), and a rum-looking Chinese doll and a rattle ('for lil' girl') from Sun Tong Lee, our storekeeper at Gulgong – James was chummy with Sun Tong Lee, and got his powder and shot and caps there on tick when he was short of money. And James said that the people would have loaded the buggy with 'rubbish' if he'd waited. They all seemed glad to see Joe Wilson getting on – and these things did me good.

We got the things inside, and I don't think either of us knew what we were saying or doing for the next half-hour. Then James put his head in and said, in a very injured tone:

'What about my tea? I ain't had anything to speak of since I left Cudgegong. I want some grub.'

Then Mary pulled herself together.

'You'll have your tea directly,' she said. 'Pick up that harness at once, and hang it on the pegs in the skillion; and you, Joe, back that buggy under the end of the veranda, the dew will be on it presently – and we'll put wet bags up in front of it to-morrow, to keep the sun off. And James will have to go back to Cudgegong for the cart – we can't have that buggy to knock about in.'

'All right,' said James – 'anything! Only get me some grub.'

Mary fried the fish, in case it wouldn't keep till the morning, and rubbed over the table-cloths, now the irons were hot – James growling all the time – and got out some crockery she had packed away that had belonged to her mother, and set the table in a style that made James uncomfortable.

'I want some grub – not a blooming banquet!' he said. And he growled a lot because Mary wanted him to eat his fish without a knife, 'and that sort of tommy-rot.' When he'd finished he took his gun, and the black boy, and the dogs, and went out 'possum-shooting.

When we were alone Mary climbed into the buggy to try the seat, and made me get up alongside her. We hadn't had such a comfortable seat for years; but we soon got down, in case anyone came by, for we began to feel like a pair of fools up there.

Then we sat, side by side, on the edge of the veranda, and talked more than we'd done for years – and there was a good deal of 'Do you remember?' in it – and I think we got to understand each other better that night.

And at last Mary said, 'Do you know, Joe, why, I feel to-night just – just like I did the day we were married.'

And somehow I had that strange, shy sort of feeling too.

'WATER THEM GERANIUMS'

I
A LONELY TRACK

THE time Mary and I shifted out into the Bush from Gulgong to 'settle on the land' at Lahey's Creek.

I'd sold the two tip-drays that I used for tank-sinking and dam-making, and I took the traps out in the wagon on top of a small load of rations and horse-feed that I was taking to a sheep station out that way. Mary drove out in the spring-cart. You remember we left little Jim with his aunt in Gulgong till we got settled down. I'd sent James (Mary's brother) out the day before, on horseback, with two or three cows and some heifers and steers and calves we had, and I'd told him to clean up a bit, and make the hut as bright and cheerful as possible before Mary came.

We hadn't much in the way of furniture. There was the four-poster cedar bedstead that I bought before we were married, and Mary was rather proud of it: it had 'turned' posts and joints that bolted together. There was a plain hardwood table, that Mary called her 'ironing-table', upside down on top of the load, with the bedding and blankets between the legs; there were four of those common black kitchen-chairs – with apples painted on the hardboard backs – that we used for the parlour; there was a cheap batten sofa with arms at the ends and turned rails between the uprights of the arms (we were a little proud of the turned rails); and there was the camp-oven, and the three-legged pot, and pans and buckets, stuck about the load and hanging under the tail-board of the wagon.

There was the little Wilcox & Gibb's sewing-machine – my present to Mary when we were married (and what a present, looking back to it!). There was a cheap little rocking-chair, and a looking-glass and some pictures that were presents from Mary's friends and sister. She had her mantelshelf ornaments and crockery and nick-nacks packed away, in the linen and old clothes, in a big tub made of half a cask, and a box that had been Jim's cradle. The live stock was a cat in one box, and in another an old rooster, and three hens that formed cliques, two against one, turn about, as three of the same sex will do all over the world. I had my old cattle-dog, and of course a pup on the load – I always had a pup that I gave away, or sold and didn't get paid for, or had 'touched' (stolen) as soon as it was old enough. James had his three spidery, sneaking, thieving, cold-blooded kangaroo-dogs with him. I was taking out three months' provisions in the way of ration-sugar, tea, flour, and potatoes, &c.

I started early, and Mary caught up to me at Ryan's Crossing on Sandy Creek, where we boiled the billy and had some dinner.

Mary bustled about the camp and admired the scenery and talked too much, for her, and was extra cheerful, and kept her face turned from me as much as possible. I soon saw what was the matter. She'd been crying to herself coming along the road. I thought it was all on account of leaving little Jim behind for the first time. She told me that she couldn't make up her mind till the last moment to leave him, and that, a mile or two along the road, she'd have turned back for him, only that she knew her sister would laugh at her. She was always terribly anxious about the children.

We cheered each other up, and Mary drove with me the rest of the way to the creek, along the lonely branch track, across native apple-tree flats. It was a dreary, hopeless track. There was no horizon, nothing but the rough ashen trunks of the gnarled and stunted trees in all directions, little or no undergrowth, and the ground, save for the coarse, brownish tufts of dead grass, as bare as the road, for it was a dry season: there had been no rain for months, and I wondered what I should do with the cattle if there wasn't more grass on the creek.

In this sort of country a stranger might travel for miles without seeming to have moved, for all the difference there is in the scenery. The new tracks were 'blazed' – that is, slices of bark cut off from both sides of trees, within sight of each other, in a line, to mark the track until the horses and wheel marks made it plain. A smart Bushman, with a sharp tomahawk, can blaze a track as he rides. But a Bushman a little used to the country soon picks out differences amongst the trees, half unconsciously as it were, and so finds his way about.

Mary and I didn't talk much along this track – we couldn't have heard each other very well, anyway, for the 'clock-clock' of the wagon and the rattle of the cart over the hard lumpy ground. And I suppose we both began to feel pretty dismal as the shadows lengthened. I'd noticed lately that Mary and I had got out of the habit of talking to each other – noticed it in a vague sort of way that irritated me (as vague things will irritate one) when I thought of it. But then I thought, 'It won't last long – I'll make life brighter for her by and by.'

As we went along – and the track seemed endless – I got brooding, of course, back into the past. And I feel now, when it's too late, that Mary must have been thinking that way too. I thought of my early boyhood, of the hard life of 'grubbin'' and 'milkin'' and 'fencin'' and 'ploughin'' and 'ring-barkin',' &c., and all for nothing. The few months at the little bark school, with a teacher who couldn't spell. The cursed ambition or craving that tortured my soul as a boy – ambition or craving for – I didn't know what for! For something better and brighter, anyhow. And I made the life harder by reading at night.

It all passed before me as I followed on in the wagon, behind Mary in the spring-cart. I thought of these old things more than I thought of her. She had tried to help me to better things. And I tried too – I had the energy of half-a-dozen men when I saw a road clear before me, but shied at the first check. Then I brooded, or dreamed of making a home – that one might call a home – for Mary – some day. Ah, well! –

And what was Mary thinking about, along the lonely, changeless miles? I never thought of that. Of her kind, careless, gentleman father, perhaps. Of her girlhood. Of her homes – not the huts and camps she lived in with me. Of our future? – she used to plan a lot, and talk a good deal of our future – but not lately. These things didn't strike me at the time – I was so deep in my own brooding. Did she think now – did she begin to feel now that she had made a great mistake and thrown away her life, but must make the best of it? This might have roused me, had I thought of it. But whenever I thought Mary was getting indifferent towards me, I'd think, 'I'll soon win her back. We'll be sweet-hearts again – when things brighten up a bit.'

It's an awful thing to me, now I look back to it, to think how far apart we had grown, what strangers we were to each other. It seems, now, as though we had been sweethearts long years before, and had parted, and had never really met since.

The sun was going down when Mary called out:

'There's our place, Joe!'

She hadn't seen it before, and somehow it came new and with a shock to me, who had been out here several times. Ahead, through the trees to the right, was a dark green clump of she-oaks standing out of the creek, darker for the dead grey grass and blue-grey bush on the barren ridge in the background. Across the creek (it was only a deep, narrow gutter – a watercourse with a chain of waterholes after rain), across on the other bank, stood the hut, on a narrow flat between the spur and the creek, and a little higher than this side. The land was much better than on our old selection, and there was good soil along the creek on both sides: I expected a rush of selectors out here soon. A few acres round the hut was cleared and fenced in by a light two-rail fence of timber split from logs and saplings. The man who took up this selection left it because his wife died here.

It was a small oblong hut built of split slabs, and he had roofed it with shingles which he split in spare times. There was no veranda, but I built one later on. At the end of the house was a big slab-and-bark shed, bigger than the hut itself, with a kitchen, a skillion for tools, harness, and horsefeed, and a spare bedroom partitioned off with sheets of bark and old chaff-bags. The house itself was floored roughly, with cracks between the boards; there were cracks between the slabs all round – though he'd nailed strips of tin, from old kerosene-tins, over some of them; the partitioned-off bedroom was lined with old chaff-bags with newspapers pasted over them for wall-paper. There was no ceiling, calico or otherwise, and we could see the round pine rafters and battens, and the under ends of the shingles. But ceilings make a hut hot and harbour insects and reptiles – snakes sometimes. There was one small glass window in the 'dining-room' with three panes and a sheet of greased paper, and the rest were rough wooden shutters. There was a pretty good cow-yard and calf-pen, and – that was about all. There was no dam or tank (I made one later on); there was a water-cask, with the hoops falling off and the staves gaping, at the corner of the house, and spouting, made of lengths of bent tin, ran round the eaves. Water from a new shingle roof is wine-red for a year or two, and water from a stringy-bark roof is like tan-water for years. In dry weather the selector had got his house water from a cask sunk in the gravel at the bottom of the deepest waterhole in the creek. And the longer the drought lasted, the farther he had to go down the creek for his water, with a cask on a cart, and take his cows to drink, if he had any. Four, five, six, or seven miles – even ten miles to water is nothing in some places.

James hadn't found himself called upon to do more than milk old 'Spot' (the grandmother cow of our mob), pen the calf at night, make a fire in the kitchen, and sweep out the house with a bough. He helped me unharness and water and feed the horses, and then started to get the furniture off the wagon and into the house. James wasn't lazy – so long as one thing didn't last too long; but he was too uncomfortably practical and matter-of-fact for me. Mary and I had some tea in the kitchen. The kitchen was permanently furnished with a table of split slabs, adzed smooth on top, and supported by four stakes driven into the ground, a three-legged stool and a block of wood, and two long stools made of half-round slabs (sapling trunks split in halves) with auger-holes bored in the round side and sticks stuck into them for legs. The floor was of clay; the chimney of slabs and tin; the fire-place was about eight feet wide, lined with clay, and with a blackened pole across, with sooty chains and wire hooks on it for the pots.

Mary didn't seem able to eat. She sat on the three-legged stool near the fire, though it was warm weather, and kept her face turned from me. Mary was still pretty, but not the little dumpling she had been: she was thinner now. She had big dark hazel eyes that shone a little too much when she was pleased or excited. I thought at times that there was something very German about her expression; also something aristocratic about the turn of her nose, which nipped in at the nostrils when she spoke. There was nothing aristocratic about me. Mary was German in figure and walk. I used sometimes to call her 'Little Duchy' and 'Pigeon Toes.' She had a will of her own, as shown sometimes by the obstinate knit in her forehead between the eyes.

Mary sat still by the fire, and presently I saw her chin tremble.

'What is it, Mary?'

She turned her face farther from me. I felt tired, disappointed, and irritated – suffering from a reaction.

'Now, what is it, Mary?' I asked; 'I'm sick of this sort of thing. Haven't you got everything you wanted? You've had your own way. What's the matter with you now?'

'You know very well, Joe.'

'But I *don't* know,' I said. I knew too well.

She said nothing.

'Look here, Mary,' I said, putting my hand on her shoulder, 'don't go on like that; tell me what's the matter.'

'It's only this,' she said suddenly, 'I can't stand this life here; it will kill me!'

I had a pannikin of tea in my hand, and I banged it down on the table.

'This is more than a man can stand!' I shouted. 'You know very well that it was you that dragged me out here. You run me on to this. Why weren't you content to stay in Gulgong?'

'And what sort of a place was Gulgong, Joe?' asked Mary quietly.

(I thought even then in a flash what sort of a place Gulgong was. A wretched remnant of a town on an abandoned goldfield. One street, each side of the dusty main road; three or four one-storey square brick cottages with hip-roofs of galvanised-iron that glared in the heat – four rooms and a passage – the police station, bank-manager's and school-master's cottages. Half-a-dozen tumble-down weather-board shanties – the three pubs, the two stores, and the post office. The town tailing off into weather-board boxes with tin tops, and old bark huts – relics of the digging days – propped up by many rotting poles. The men, when at home, mostly asleep or droning over their pipes or hanging about the veranda-posts of the pubs, saying, ' 'Ullo, Bill!' or ' 'Ullo, Jim!' – or sometimes drunk. The women, mostly hags, who blackened each other's and girls' characters with their tongues, and criticised the aris-tocracy's washing hung out on the line: 'And the colour of the clothes! Does that woman wash her clothes at all? or only soak 'em and hang 'em out?' – that was Gulgong.)

'Well, why didn't you come to Sydney, as I wanted you to?' I asked Mary.

'You know very well, Joe,' said Mary quietly.

(I knew very well, but the knowledge only maddened me. I had had an idea of getting a billet in one of the big wool-stores – I was a fair wool expert – but Mary was afraid of the drink. I could keep well away from it so long as I worked hard in the Bush. I had gone to Sydney twice since I met Mary, once before we were married, and she forgave me when I came back; and once afterwards. I got a billet there then, and was going to send for her in a month. After eight weeks she raised the money somehow and came to Sydney and brought me home. I got pretty down that time.)

'But Mary,' I said, 'it would have been different this time. You would have been with me. I can take a glass now or leave it alone.'

'As long as you take a glass there is danger,' she said.

'Well, what did you want to advise me to come out here for, if you can't stand it? Why didn't you stay where you were?' I asked.

'Well,' she said, 'why weren't you more decided?'

I'd sat down, but I jumped to my feet then.

'Good God!' I shouted, 'this is more than any man can stand. I'll chuck it all up! I'm damned well sick and tired of the whole thing.'

'So am I, Joe,' said Mary wearily.

We quarrelled badly then – that first hour in our new home. I know now whose fault it was.

I got my hat and went out and started to walk down the creek. I didn't feel bitter against Mary – I had spoken too cruelly to her to feel that way. Looking back, I could see plainly that if I had taken her advice all through, instead of now and again, things would have been all right with me. I had come away and left her crying in the hut, and James telling her, in a brotherly way, that it was all her fault. The trouble was that I never liked to 'give in' or go half-way to make it up – not half-way – it was all the way or nothing with our natures.

'If I don't make a stand now,' I'd say, 'I'll never be master. I gave up the reins when I got married, and I'll have to get them back again.'

What women some men are! But the time came, and not many years after, when I stood by the bed where Mary lay, white and still; and, amongst other things, I kept saying, 'I'll give in, Mary – I'll give in,' and then I'd laugh. They thought I was raving mad, and took me from the room. But that time was to come.

As I walked down the creek track in the moonlight the question rang in my ears again, as it had done when I first caught sight of the house that evening:

'Why did I bring her here?'

I was not fit to 'go on the land'. The place was only fit for some stolid German, or Scotsman, or even Englishman and his wife, who had no ambition but to bullock and make a farm of the place. I had only drifted here through carelessness, brooding, and discontent.

I walked on and on till I was more than half-way to the only neighbours – a wretched selector's family, about four miles down the creek – and I thought I'd go on to the house and see if they had any fresh meat.

A mile or two farther I saw the loom of the bark hut they lived in, on a patchy clearing in the scrub, and heard the voice of the selector's wife – I had seen her several times: she was a gaunt, haggard Bushwoman, and I supposed the reason why she hadn't gone mad through hardship and loneliness was that she hadn't either the brains or the memory to go farther than she could see through the trunks of the 'apple-trees'.

'You, An-nay!' (Annie.)

'Ye-es' (from somewhere in the gloom).

'Didn't I tell yer to water them geraniums!'

'Well, didn't I?'

'Don't tell lies or I'll break yer young back!'

'I did, I tell yer – the water won't soak inter the ashes.'

Geraniums were the only flowers I saw grow in the drought out there. I remembered this woman had a few dirty grey-green leaves behind some sticks against the bark wall near the door; and in spite of the sticks the fowls used to get in and scratch beds under the geraniums and scratch dust over them, and ashes were thrown there – with an idea of helping the flowers, I suppose; and greasy dish-water, when fresh water was scarce – till you might as well try to water a dish of fat.

Then the woman's voice again:

'You, Tom-may!' (Tommy.)

Silence, save for an echo on the ridge.

'Y-o-u T-o-m-*may!*'

'Y-e-s!' shrill shriek from across the creek.

'Didn't I tell you to ride up to them new people and see if they want any meat or anythink?' in one long screech.

'Well – I karn't find the horse.'

'Well – find – it – first – think – in – the – morning – and – don't –

forgit – to – tell – Mrs – Wi'son – that – mother'll – be – up – as – soon – as – she – can.'

I didn't feel like going to the woman's house that night. I felt – and the thought came like a whipstroke on my heart – that this was what Mary would come to if I left her here.

I turned and started to walk home, fast. I'd made up my mind. I'd take Mary straight back to Gulgong in the morning – I forgot about the load I had to take to the sheep station. I'd say, 'Look here, Girlie' (that's what I used to call her), 'we'll leave this wretched life; we'll leave the Bush for ever. We'll go to Sydney, and I'll be a man! and work my way up.' And I'd sell wagon, horses, and all, and go.

When I got to the hut it was lighted up. Mary had the only kerosene lamp, a slush-lamp, and two tallow candles going. She had got both rooms washed out – to James's disgust, for he had to move the furniture and boxes about. She had a lot of things unpacked on the table; she had laid clean newspapers on the mantelshelf – a slab on two pegs over the fireplace – and put the little wooden clock in the centre and some of the ornaments on each side, and was tacking a strip of vandyked American oilcloth round the rough edge of the slab.

'How does that look, Joe? We'll soon get things shipshape.'

I kissed her, but she had her mouth full of tacks. I went out in the kitchen, drank a pint of cold tea, and sat down.

Somehow I didn't feel satisfied with the way things had gone.

II
'PAST CARIN''

NEXT morning things looked a lot brighter. Things always look brighter in the morning – more so in the Australian Bush, I should think, than in most other places. It is when the sun goes down on the dark bed of the lonely Bush, and the sunset flashes like a sea of fire and then fades, and then glows out again, like a bank of coals, and then burns away to ashes – it is then that old things come home to one. And strange, new-old things too, that haunt and depress you terribly, and that you can't understand. I often think how, at sunset, the past must come home to a new-chum black sheep, sent out to Australia and drifted into the Bush. I used to think that they couldn't have much brains, or the loneliness would drive them mad.

I'd decided to let James take the team for a trip or two. He could drive all right; he was a better business man, and no doubt would manage better than me – as long as the novelty lasted; and I'd stay at home for a week or so, till Mary got used to the place, or I could get a girl from somewhere to come and stay with her. The first weeks or few months of loneliness are the worst, as a rule, I believe, as they say the first weeks in jail are – I was never there. I know it's so with tramping or hard graft: the first day or two are twice as hard as any of the rest. But, for my part, I could never get used to loneliness and dullness; the last days used to be the worst with me: then I'd have to make a move, or drink. When you've been too much and too long alone in a lonely place, you begin to do queer things, and think queer thoughts – provided you have any imagination at all. You'll sometimes sit of an evening and watch the lonely track, by the hour, for a horseman or a cart or someone that's never likely to come that way – someone, or a stranger, that you can't and don't really expect to see. I think that most men who have been alone in the Bush for any length of time – and married couples too – are more or less mad. With married couples it is generally the husband who is painfully shy and awkward when strangers come. The woman seems to stand the loneliness better, and can hold her own with strangers, as a rule. It's only afterwards, and looking back, that you see how queer you got. Shepherds and boundary-riders, who are alone for months, *must* have their periodical spree, at the nearest shanty, else they'd go raving mad. Drink is the only break in the awful monotony, and the yearly or half-yearly spree is the only thing they've got to look forward to: it keeps their minds fixed on something definite ahead.

But Mary kept her head pretty well through the first months of loneliness. *Weeks* rather, I should say, for it wasn't as bad as it might have been farther up-country: there was generally someone came of a Sunday afternoon – a spring-cart with a couple of women, or maybe a family – or a lanky shy bush native or two on lanky shy horses. On a quiet Sunday, after I'd brought Jim home, Mary would dress him and herself – just the same as if we were in town – and make me get up on one end and put on a collar and take her and Jim for a walk along the creek. She said she wanted to keep me civilised. She tried to make a gentleman of me for years, but gave it up gradually.

Well. It was the first morning on the creek: I was greasing the wagon-wheels, and James out after the horse, and Mary hanging out clothes, in an old print dress and a big ugly white hood, when I heard her being hailed as 'Hi, missus!' from the front sliprails.

It was a boy on horseback. He was a light-haired, very much freckled boy of fourteen or fifteen, with a small head, but with limbs, especially his bare sun-blotched shanks, that might have belonged to a grown man. He had a good face and frank grey eyes. An old, nearly black cabbage-tree hat rested on the butts of his ears, turning them out at right angles from his head, and rather dirty sprouts they were. He wore a dirty torn Crimean shirt; and a pair of men's moleskin trousers rolled up above the knees, with a wide waistband gathered under a greenhide belt. I noticed, later on, that, even when he wore trousers short enough for him, he always rolled 'em up above the knees when on horseback, for some reason of his own: to suggest leggings, perhaps, for he had them rolled up in all weathers, and he wouldn't have bothered to save them from the sweat of the horse, even if that horse ever sweated.

He was seated astride a three-bushel bag thrown across the ridge-pole of a big grey horse, with a coffin-shaped head, and built astern something after the style of a roughly put up hip-roofed box-bark humpy. His colour was like old box-bark, too, a dirty bluish-grey; and, one time, when I saw his rump looming out of the scrub, I really thought it was some old shepherd's hut that I hadn't noticed there before. When he cantered it was like the humpy starting off on its corner-posts.

'Are you Mrs Wilson?' asked the boy.

'Yes,' said Mary.

'Well, mother told me to ride acrost and see if you wanted anythink. We killed lars' night, and I fetched a piece er cow.'

'Piece of *what*?' asked Mary.

He grinned, and handed a sugar-bag across the rail with something heavy in the bottom of it, that nearly jerked Mary's arm out when she took it. It was a piece of beef, that looked as if it had been cut off with a wood-axe, but it was fresh and clean.

'Oh, I'm so glad!' cried Mary. She was always impulsive, save to me sometimes. 'I was just wondering where we were going to get any fresh meat. How kind of your mother! Tell her I'm very much obliged to her indeed.' And she felt behind her for a poor little purse she had. 'And now – how much did your mother say it would be?'

The boy blinked at her, and scratched his head.

'How much will it be,' he repeated, puzzled. 'Oh – how much does it weigh I-s'pose-yer-mean. Well, it ain't been weighed at all – we ain't got no scales. A butcher does all that sort of thing. We just kills it, and cooks it, and eats it – and goes by guess. What won't keep we salts down in the cask. I reckon it weighs about a ton by the weight of it if yer wanter know. Mother thought that if she sent any more it would go bad before you could scoff it. I can't see –'

'Yes, yes,' said Mary, getting confused. 'But what I want to know is, how do you manage when you sell it?'

He glared at her, and scratched his head. 'Sell it? Why, we only goes halves in a steer with someone, or sells steers to the butcher – or maybe some meat to a party of fencers or surveyors, or tank-sinkers, or them sorter people –"

'Yes, yes; but what I want to know is, how much am I to send your mother for this?'

'How much what?'

'Money, of course, you stupid boy,' said Mary. 'You seem a very stupid boy.'

Then he saw what she was driving at. He began to fling his heels convulsively against the sides of his horse, jerking his body backward and forward at the same time, as if to wind up and start some clock-work machinery inside the horse, that made it go, and seemed to need repairing or oiling.

'We ain't that sorter people, missus,' he said. 'We don't sell meat to new people that come to settle here.' Then, jerking his thumb contemptuously towards the ridges, 'Go over ter Wall's if yer wanter buy meat; they sell meat ter strangers.' (Wall was the big squatter over the ridges.)

'Oh!' said Mary, 'I'm *so* sorry. Thank your mother for me. She *is* kind.'

'Oh, that's nothink. She said to tell yer she'll be up as soon as she can. She'd have come up yisterday evening – she thought yer'd feel lonely comin' new to a place like this – but she couldn't git up.'

The machinery inside the old horse showed signs of starting. You almost heard the wooden joints *creak* as he lurched forward, like an old propped-up humpy when the rotting props give way; but at the sound of Mary's voice he settled back on his foundations again. It must have been a very poor selection that couldn't afford a better spare horse than that.

'Reach me that lump er wood, will yer, missus?' said the boy, and he pointed to one of my 'spreads' (for the team-chains) that lay inside the fence. 'I'll fling it back again over the fence when I git this ole cow started.'

'But wait a minute – I've forgotten your mother's name,' said Mary.

He grabbed at his thatch impatiently. 'Me mother – oh!– the old woman's name's Mrs Spicer. (Git up, karn't yer!)' He twisted himself round, and brought the stretcher down on one of the horse's 'points' (and he had many) with a crack that must have jarred his wrist.

'Do you go to school?' asked Mary. There was a three-days-a-week school over the ridges at Wall's station.

'No!' he jerked out, keeping his legs going. 'Me – why I'm going on fur fifteen. The last teacher at Wall's finished me. I'm going to Queensland next month drovin'.' (Queensland border was over three hundred miles away.)

'Finished you? How?' asked Mary.

'Me edgercation, of course! How do yer expect me to start this horse when yer keep talkin'?'

He split the 'spread' over the horse's point, threw the pieces over the fence, and was off, his elbows and legs flinging wildly, and the old sawstool lumbering along the road like an old working bullock trying a canter. That horse wasn't a trotter.

And next month he *did* start for Queensland. He was a younger son and a surplus boy on a wretched, poverty-stricken selection; and as there was 'northin' doin'' in the district, his father (in a burst of fatherly kindness, I suppose) made him a present of the old horse and a new pair of blucher boots, and I gave him an old saddle and a coat, and he started for the Never-Never country.

And I'll bet he got there. But I'm doubtful if the old horse did.

Mary gave the boy five shillings, and I don't think he had anything more except a clean shirt and an extra pair of white cotton socks.

'Spicer's farm' was a big bark humpy on a patchy clearing in the native apple-tree scrub. The clearing was fenced in by a light 'dog-legged' fence (a fence of sapling poles resting on forks and X-shaped uprights), and the dusty ground round the house was almost entirely covered with cattle-dung. There was no attempt at cultivation when I came to live on the creek; but there were old furrow-marks amongst the stumps of another shapeless patch in the scrub near the hut. There was a wretched sapling cow-yard and calf-pen, and a cow-bail with one sheet of bark over it for shelter. There was no dairy to be seen, and I suppose the milk was set in one of the two skillion rooms, or lean-to's behind the hut – the other was 'the boys' bedroom'. The Spicers kept a few cows and steers, and had thirty or forty sheep. Mrs Spicer used to drive down the creek once a week, in her rickety old spring-cart, to Cobborah, with butter and eggs. The hut was nearly as bare inside as it was out – just a frame of 'round-timber' (sapling poles) covered with bark. The furniture was permanent (unless you rooted it up), like in our kitchen: a rough slab table on stakes driven into the ground, and seats made the same way. Mary told me afterwards that the beds in the bag-and-bark partitioned-off room ('mother's bedroom') were simply poles laid side by side on cross-pieces supported by stakes driven into the ground, with straw mattresses and some worn-out bed-clothes. Mrs Spicer had an old patchwork quilt, in rags, and the remains of a white one, and Mary said it was pitiful to see how these things would be spread over the beds – to hide them as much as possible – when she went down there. A packing-case, with something like an old print skirt draped round it, and a cracked looking-glass (without a frame) on top, was the dressing-table. There were a couple of gin-cases for a wardrobe. The boys' beds were three-bushel bags stretched between poles fastened to uprights. The floor was the original surface, tramped hard, worn uneven with much sweeping, and with puddles in rainy weather where the roof leaked. Mrs Spicer used to stand old tins, dishes, and buckets under as many of the leaks as she could. The saucepans, kettles and boilers were old kerosene-tins and billies. They used kerosene-tins, too, cut longways in halves, for setting the milk in. The plates and cups were of tin; there were two or three cups without saucers, and a crockery plate or two – also two mugs, cracked, and without handles, one with 'For a Good Boy' and the other with 'For a Good Girl' on it; but all these were kept on the mantelshelf for ornament and for company. They were the only ornaments in the house, save a little wooden clock that hadn't gone for years. Mrs Spicer had a superstition that she had 'some things packed away from the children'.

The pictures were cut from old copies of the *Illustrated Sydney News* and pasted on to the bark. I remember this, because I remembered, long ago, the Spencers, who were our neighbours when I was a boy, had the walls of their bedroom covered with illustrations of the American Civil War, cut from illustrated London papers, and I used to 'sneak' into 'mother's bedroom' with Fred Spencer whenever we got a chance, and gloat over the prints. I gave him the blade of a pocket-knife once, for taking me in there.

I saw very little of Spicer. He was a big, dark, dark-haired and whiskered man. I had an idea that he wasn't a selector at all, only a 'dummy' for the squatter of the Cobborah run. You see, selectors were allowed to take up land on runs, or pastoral leases. The squatters kept them off as much as possible, by all manner of dodges and paltry persecution. The squatter would get as much freehold as he could afford, 'select' as much land as the law allowed one man to take up, and then employ dummies (dummy selectors) to take up bits of land that he fancied about his run, and hold them for him.

Spicer seemed gloomy and unsociable. He was seldom at home. He was generally supposed to be away shearin', or fencin', or workin' on somebody's station. It turned out that the last six months he was away it was on the evidence of a cask of beef and a hide with the brand cut out, found in his camp on a fencing contract up-country, and which he and his mates couldn't account for satisfactorily, while the squatter could. Then the family lived mostly on bread and honey, or bread and treacle, or bread and dripping, and tea. Every ounce of butter and every egg was needed for the market, to keep them in flour, tea, and sugar. Mary found that out, but couldn't help them much – except by 'stuffing' the children with bread and meat or bread and jam whenever they came to our place – for Mrs Spicer was proud with the pride that lies down in the end and turns its face to the wall and dies.

Once, when Mary asked Annie, the eldest girl at home, if she was hungry, she denied it – but she looked it. A ragged mite she had with her explained things. The little fellow said:

'Mother told Annie not to say we was hungry if yer asked; but if yer give us anythink to eat, we was to take it an' say thenk yer, Mrs Wilson.'

'I wouldn't 'a' told yer a lie; but I thought Jimmy would split on me, Mrs Wilson,' said Annie. 'Thenk yer, Mrs Wilson.'

She was not a big woman. She was gaunt and flat-chested, and her face was 'burnt to a brick', as they say out there. She had brown eyes, nearly red, and a little wild-looking at times, and a sharp face – ground sharp by hardship – the cheeks drawn in. She had an expression like – well, like a woman who had been very curious and suspicious at one time, and wanted to know everybody's business and hear everything, and had lost all her curiosity, without losing the expression or the quick suspicious movements of the head. I don't suppose you understand. I can't explain it any other way. She was not more than forty.

I remember the first morning I saw her. I was going up the creek to look at the selection for the first time, and called at the hut to see if she had a bit of fresh mutton, as I had none and was sick of 'corned beef'.

'Yes – of – course,' she said, in a sharp nasty tone, as if to say, 'Is there anything more you want while the shop's open?' I'd met just the same sort of woman years before while I was carrying swag between the shearing-sheds in the awful scrubs out west of the Darling River, so I didn't turn on my heels and walk away. I waited for her to speak again.

'Come – inside,' she said, 'and sit down. I see you've got the wagon outside. I s'pose your name's Wilson, ain't it? You're thinkin' about takin' on Harry Marshfield's selection up the creek, so I heard. Wait till I fry you a chop, and boil the billy.'

Her voice sounded, more than anything else, like a voice coming out of a phonograph – I heard one in Sydney the other day – and not like a voice coming out of her. But sometimes when she got outside her everyday life on this selection she spoke in a sort of – in a sort of lost groping-in-the-dark kind of voice.

She didn't talk much this time – just spoke in a mechanical way of the drought, and the hard times, 'an' butter 'n' eggs bein' down, an' her husban' an' eldest son bein' away, an' that makin' it so hard for her.'

I don't know how many children she had. I never got a chance to count them, for they were nearly all small, and shy as piccaninnies, and used to run and hide when anybody came. They were mostly nearly as black as piccaninnies too. She must have averaged a baby a year for years – and God only knows how she got over her confinements! Once, they said, she only had a black gin with her. She had an elder boy and girl, but she seldom spoke of them. The girl, 'Liza', was 'in service in Sydney'. I'm afraid I knew what that meant. The elder son was 'away'. He had been a bit of a favourite round there, it seemed.

Someone might ask her, 'How's your son Jack, Mrs Spicer?' or, 'Heard of Jack lately? and where is he now?'

'Oh, he's somewheres up-country,' she'd say in the 'groping' voice, or 'He's drovin' in Queenslan',' or 'Shearin' on the Darlin' the last time I heerd from him. We ain't had a line from him since – le's see – since Chris'mas 'fore last.'

And she'd turn her haggard eyes in a helpless, hopeless sort of way towards the west – towards 'up-country' and 'Out-Back'.

The eldest girl at home was nine or ten, with a little old face and lines across her forehead: she had an older expression than her mother. Tommy went to Queensland, as I told you. The eldest son at home, Bill (older than Tommy), was 'a bit wild'.

I've passed the place in smothering hot mornings in December, when the droppings about the cow-yard had crumpled to dust that rose in the warm, sickly, sunrise wind, and seen that woman at work in the cow-yard, 'bailing up' and leg-roping cows, milking, or hauling at a rope round the neck of a half-grown calf that was too strong for her (and she was tough as fencing-wire), or humping great buckets of sour milk to the pigs or the 'poddies' (hand-fed calves) in the pen. I'd get off the horse and give her a hand sometimes with a young steer, or a cranky old cow that wouldn't 'bail-up' and threatened her with her horns. She'd say:

'Thenk yer, Mr Wilson. Do yer think we're ever goin' to have any rain?'

I've ridden past the place on bitter black rainy mornings in June or July, and seen her trudging abut the yard – that was ankle-deep in black liquid filth – with an old pair of blucher boots on, and an old coat of her husband's, or maybe a three-bushel bag over her shoulders. I've seen her climbing on the roof by means of the water-cask at the corner, and trying to stop a leak by shoving a piece of tin in under the bark. And when I'd fixed the leak:

'Thenk yer, Mr Wilson. This drop of rain's a blessin'! Come in and have a dry at the fire and I'll make yer a cup of tea.' And, if I was in a hurry, 'Come in, man alive! Come in! and dry yerself a bit till the rain holds up. Yer can't go home like this! Yer'll git yer death o' cold.'

I've even seen her, in the terrible drought, climbing she-oaks and apple-trees by a makeshift ladder, and awkwardly lopping off boughs to feed the starving cattle.

'Jist tryin' ter keep the milkers alive till the rain comes.'

They said that when the pleuro-pneumonia was in the district and amongst her cattle she bled and physicked them herself, and fed those that were down with slices of half-ripe pumpkins (from a crop that had failed).

'An' one day,' she told Mary, 'there was a big barren heifer (that we called Queen Elizabeth) that was down with the ploorer. She'd been down for four days and hadn't moved, when one mornin' I dumped some wheaten chaff – we had a few bags that Spicer brought home – I dumped it in front of her nose, an' – would yer b'lieve me, Mrs Wilson? – she stumbled onter her feet an' chased me all the way to the house! I had to pick up me skirts an' run! Wasn't it redic'lus?'

They had a sense of the ridiculous, most of those poor sundried Bushwomen. I fancy that that helped save them from madness.

'We lost nearly all our milkers,' she told Mary. 'I remember one day Tommy came running to the house and screamed: 'Marther! [mother] there's another milker down with the ploorer!' Jist as if it was great news. Well, Mrs Wilson, I was dead-beat, an' I giv' in. I jist sat down to have a good cry, and felt for my han'kerchief – it *was* a rag of a han'kerchief, full of holes (all me others was in the wash). Without seein' what I was doin' I put my finger through the hole in the han'kerchief an' me thumb through the other, and poked me fingers into me eyes, instead of wipin' them. Then I had to laugh.'

There's a story that once, when the Bush, or rather grass, fires were out all along the creek on Spicer's side, Wall's station-hands were up above our place, trying to keep the fire back from the boundary, and towards the evening one of the men happened to think of the Spicers: they saw smoke down that way. Spicer was away from home, and they had a small crop of wheat, nearly ripe, on the selection.

'My God! that poor devil of a woman will be burnt out, if she ain't already!' shouted young Billy Wall. 'Come along, three or four of you chaps' – it was shearing-time, and there were plenty of men on the station.

They raced down the creek to Spicer's, and were just in time to save the wheat. She had her sleeves tucked up, and was beating out the burning grass with a bough. She'd been at it for an hour, and was as black as a gin, they said. She only said when they'd turned the fire: 'Thenk yer! Wait an' I'll make some tea.'

After tea the first Sunday she came to see us, Mary asked:

'Don't you feel lonely, Mrs Spicer, when your husband goes away?'

'Well – no, Mrs Wilson,' she said in the groping sort of voice. 'I uster, once. I remember, when we lived on the Cudgegong River – we lived in a brick house then – the first time Spicer had to go away from home I nearly fretted my eyes out. And he was only goin' shearin' for a month. I muster bin a fool; but then we were only jist married a little while. He's been away drovin' in Queenslan' as long as eighteen months at a time since then. But' (her voice seemed to grope in the dark more than ever) 'I don't mind – I somehow seem to have got past carin'. Besides – besides, Spicer was a very different man then to what he is now. He's got so moody and gloomy at home, he hardly ever speaks.'

Mary sat silent for a minute thinking. Then Mrs Spicer roused herself:

'Oh, I don't know what I'm talkin' about! You mustn't take any notice of me, Mrs Wilson – I don't often go on like this. I do believe I'm gittin' a bit ratty at times. It must be the heat and the dullness.'

But once or twice afterwards she referred to a time 'when Spicer was a different man to what he was now.'

I walked home with her a piece along the creek. She said nothing for a long time, and seemed to be thinking in a puzzled way. Then she said suddenly:

'What-did-you-bring-her-here-for? She's only a girl.'

'I beg pardon, Mrs Spicer.'

'Oh, I don't know what I'm talkin' about! I b'lieve I'm gettin' ratty. You mustn't take any notice of me, Mr Wilson.'

She wasn't much company for Mary; and often, when she had a child with her, she'd start taking notice of the baby while Mary was talking, which used to exasperate Mary. But poor Mrs Spicer couldn't help it, and she seemed to hear all the same.

Her great trouble was that she 'couldn't git no reg-lar schoolin' for the children.'

'I learns 'em at home as much as I can. But I don't git a minute to call me own; an' I'm ginerally that dead-beat at night that I'm fit for nothink.'

Mary had some of the children up now and then later on, and taught them a little. When she first offered to do so, Mrs Spicer laid hold of the handiest youngster and said:

'There – do you hear that? Mrs Wilson is goin' to teach yer, an' it's more than yer deserve!' the youngster had been 'cryin'' over something). 'Now, go up an' say 'Thenk yer, Mrs Wilson.' And if yer ain't good, and don't do as she tells yer, I'll break every bone in yer young body!'

The poor little devil stammered something, and escaped.

The children were sent by turns over to Wall's to Sunday-school. When Tommy was at home he had a new pair of elastic-side boots, and there was no end of rows about them in the family – for the mother made him lend them to his sister Annie, to go to Sunday-school in her turn. There were only about three pairs of anyway decent boots in the family, and these were saved for great occasions. The children were always as clean and tidy as possible when they came to our place.

And I think the saddest and most pathetic sight on the face of God's earth is the children of very poor people made to appear well: the broken worn-out boots polished or greased, the blackened (inked) pieces of string for laces; the clean patched pinafores over the wretched threadbare frocks. Behind the little row of children hand-in-hand – and no matter where they are – I always see the worn face of the mother.

Towards the end of the first year on the selection our little girl came. I'd sent Mary to Gulgong for four months that time, and when she came back with the baby Mrs Spicer used to come up pretty often. She came up several times when Mary was ill, to lend a hand. She wouldn't sit down and condole with Mary, or waste her time asking questions, or talking about the time when she was ill herself. She'd take off her hat – a shapeless little lump of black straw she wore for visiting – give her hair a quick brush back with the palms of her hands, roll up her sleeves, and set to work to 'tidy up'. She seemed to take most pleasure in sorting out our children's clothes, and dressing them. Perhaps she used to dress her own like that in the days when Spicer was a different man from what he was now. She seemed interested in the fashion-plates of some women's journals we had, and used to study them with an interest that puzzled me, for she was not likely to go in for fashion. She never talked of her early girlhood; but Mary, from some things she noticed, was inclined to think that Mrs Spicer had been fairly well brought up. For instance, Dr Balanfantie, from Cudgegong, came out to see Wall's wife, and drove up the creek to our place on his way back to see how Mary and the baby were getting on. Mary got out some crockery and some table-napkins that she had packed away for occasions like this; and she said that the way Mrs Spicer handled the things, and helped set the table (though she did it in a mechanical sort of way) convinced her that she had been used to table-napkins at one time in her life.

Sometimes, after a long pause in the conversation, Mrs Spicer would say suddenly:

'Oh, I don't think I'll come up next week, Mrs Wilson.'

'Why, Mrs Spicer?'

'Because the visits doesn't do me any good. I git the dismals afterwards.'

'Why, Mrs Spicer? What on earth do you mean?'

'Oh, I-don't-know-what-I'm-talkin'-about. You mustn't take any notice of me.' And she'd put on her hat, kiss the children – and Mary too, sometimes, as if she mistook her for a child – and go.

Mary thought her a little mad at times. But I seemed to understand.

Once, when Mrs Spicer was sick, Mary went down to her, and down again next day. As she was coming away the second time Mrs Spicer said:

'I wish you wouldn't come down any more till I'm on my feet, Mrs Wilson. The children can do for me.'

'Why, Mrs Spicer?'

'Well, the place is in such a muck, and it hurts me.'

We were the aristocrats of Lahey's Creek. Whenever we drove down on Sunday afternoon to see Mrs Spicer, and as soon as we got near enough for them to hear the rattle of the cart, we'd see the children running to the house as fast as they could split, and hear them screaming:

'Oh, marther! Here comes Mr and Mrs Wilson in their spring-cart.'

And we'd see her bustle round, and two or three fowls fly out the front door, and she'd lay hold of a broom (made of a bound bunch of 'broom-stuff' – coarse reedy grass or bush from the ridges – with a stick stuck in it) and flick out the floor, with a flick or two round in front of the door perhaps. The floor nearly always needed at least one lick of the broom on account of the fowls. Or she'd catch a youngster and scrub his face with a wet end of a cloudy towel or twist the towel round her finger and dig out his ears – as if she was anxious to have him hear every word that was going to be said.

No matter what state the house would be in she'd always say, 'I was jist expectin' yer, Mrs Wilson.' And she was original in that, anyway.

She had an old patched and darned white table-cloth that she used to spread on the table when we were there, as a matter of course ('The others is in the wash, so you must excuse this, Mrs Wilson'), but I saw by the eyes of the children that the cloth was rather a wonderful thing for them. 'I must really git some more knives and forks next time I'm in Cobborah,' she'd say. 'The children break an' lose 'em till I'm ashamed ter ask Christians ter sit down ter the table.'

She had many Bush yarns, some of them very funny, some of them rather ghastly, but all interesting, and with a grim sort of humour about them. But the effect was often spoilt by her screaming at the children to 'Drive out them fowls, karn't yer,' or 'Take yer maulies [hands] outer the sugar,' or 'Don't touch Mrs Wilson's baby with them dirty maulies,' or 'Don't stand starin' at Mrs Wilson with yer mouth an' ears in that vulgar way.'

Poor woman! she seemed everlastingly nagging at the children. It was a habit, but they didn't seem to mind. Most Bushwomen get the nagging habit. I remember one, who had the prettiest, dearest, sweetest, most willing, and affectionate little girl I think I ever saw, and she nagged that child from daylight till dark – and after it. Taking it all round, I think that the nagging habit in a mother is often worse on ordinary children, and more deadly on sensitive youngsters, than the drinking habit in a father.

One of the yarns Mrs Spicer told us was about a squatter she knew who used to go wrong in his head every now and again, and try to commit suicide. Once, when the station-hand, who was watching him, had his eye off him for a minute, he hanged himself to a beam in the stable. The men ran in and found him hanging and kicking. 'They let him hang for a while,' said Mrs Spicer, 'till he went black in the face and stopped kicking. Then they cut him down and threw a bucket of water over him.'

'Why! what on earth did they let the man hang for?' asked Mary.

'To give him a good bellyful of it: they thought it would cure him of tryin' to hang himself again.'

'Well, that's the coolest thing I ever heard of,' said Mary.

'That's jist what the magistrate said, Mrs Wilson,' said Mrs Spicer.

'One morning,' said Mrs Spicer, 'Spicer had gone off on his horse somewhere, and I was alone with the children, when a man came to the door and said:

' "For God's sake, woman, give me a drink!"

'Lord only knows where he came from! He was dressed like a new chum, his clothes was good, but he looked as if he'd been sleepin' in them in the Bush for a month. He was very shaky. I had some coffee that mornin', so I gave him some in a pint-pot; he drank it, and then he stood on his head till he tumbled over, and then he stood up on his feet and said, "Thenk yer, mum."

'I was so surprised that I didn't know what to say, so I jist said, "Would you like some more coffee!"

' "Yes, thenk yer," he said – "about two quarts."

'I nearly filled the pint-pot, and he drank it and stood on his head as long as he could, and when he got right end up he said, "Thenk yer, mum – it's a fine day," and then he walked off. He had two saddle-straps in his hands.'

'Why, what did he stand on his head for?' asked Mary.

'To wash it up and down, I suppose, to get twice as much taste of the coffee. He had no hat. I sent Tommy across to Wall's to tell them that there was a man wanderin' about the bush in the horrors of drink, and to get someone to ride for the police. But they were too late, for he hanged himself that night.'

'O Lord!' cried Mary.

'Yes, right close to here, jist down the creek where the track to Wall's branches off. Tommy found him while he was out after the cows. Hangin' to the branch of a tree with two saddle-straps.'

Mary stared at her, speechless.

'Tommy came home yellin' with fright. I sent him over to Wall's at once. After breakfast, the minute my eyes was off them, the children slipped away and went down there. They came back screamin' at the tops of their voices. I did give it to them. I reckon they won't want ter see a dead body again in a hurry. Every time I'd mention it they'd huddle together, or ketch hold of me skirts and howl.

' "Yer'll go agen when I tell yer not to," I'd say.

' "Oh no, mother," they'd howl.

' "Yer wanted ter see a man hangin'," I said.

' "Oh, don't, mother! Don't talk about it."

' "Yer wouldn't be satisfied till yer see it," I'd say; "yer had to see it or burst. Yer satisfied now, ain't yer?"

' "Oh, don't, mother!"

' "Yer run all the way there, I s'pose?"

' "Don't, mother!"

' "But yer run faster back, didn't yer?"

' "Oh, don't, mother."

'But,' said Mrs Spicer, in conclusion, 'I'd been down to see it myself before they was up.'

'And ain't you afraid to live alone here, after all these horrible things?' asked Mary.

'Well, no; I don't mind. I seem to have got past carin' for anythink now. I felt it a little when Tommy went away – the first time I felt anythink for years. But I'm over that now.'

'Haven't you got any friends in the district, Mrs Spicer?'

'Oh yes. There's me married sister near Cobborah, and a married brother near Dubbo; he's got a station. They wanted to take me an' the children between them, or take some of the younger children. But I couldn't bring my mind to break up the home. I want to keep the children together as much as possible. There's enough of them gone, God knows. But it's a comfort to know that there's someone to see to them if anythink happens me.'

One day – I was on my way home with the team that day – Annie Spicer came running up the creek in terrible trouble.

'Oh, Mrs Wilson! something terribl's happened at home! A trooper' (mounted policeman – they called them 'mounted troopers' out there), 'a trooper's come and took Billy!' Billy was the eldest son at home.

'What?'

'It's true, Mrs Wilson.'

'What for? What did the policeman say?'

'He – he – he said, "I – I'm very sorry, Mrs Spicer; but – I – I want William."'

It turned out that William was wanted on account of a horse missed from Wall's station and sold down-country.

'An' mother took on awful,' sobbed Annie; 'an' now she'll only sit stock-still an' stare in front of her, and won't take no notice of any of us. Oh! it's awful, Mrs Wilson. The policeman said he'd tell Aunt Emma' (Mrs Spicer's sister at Cobborah), 'and send her out. But I had to come to you, an' I've run all the way.'

James put the horse to the cart and drove Mary down.

Mary told me all about it when I came home.

'I found her just as Annie said; but she broke down and cried in my arms. Oh, Joe! it was awful. She didn't cry like a woman. I heard a man at Haviland cry at his brother's funeral, and it was just like that. She came round a bit after a while. Her sister's with her now . . . Oh, Joe! you must take me away from the Bush.'

Later on Mary said:

'How the oaks are sighing to-night, Joe!'

Next morning I rode across to Wall's station and tackled the old man; but he was a hard man, and wouldn't listen to me – in fact, he ordered me off his station. I was a selector and that was enough for him. But young Billy Wall rode after me.

'Look here, Joe!' he said, 'it's a blanky shame. All for the sake of a horse! As if that poor devil of a woman hasn't got enough to put up with already! I wouldn't do it for twenty horses. *I'll* tackle the boss, and if he won't listen to me, I'll walk off the run for the last time, if I have to carry my swag.'

Billy Wall managed it. The charge was withdrawn, and we got young Billy Spicer off up-country.

But poor Mrs Spicer was never the same after that. She seldom came up to our place unless Mary dragged her, so to speak; and then she would talk of nothing but her last trouble, till her visits were painful to look forward to.

'If it only could have been kep' quiet – for the sake of the other children; they are all I think of now. I tried to bring 'em all up decent, but I s'pose it was my fault, somehow. It's the disgrace that's killin' me – I can't bear it.'

I was at home one Sunday with Mary, and a jolly bush-girl named Maggie Charlsworth, who rode over sometimes from Wall's station (I must tell you about her some other time; James was 'shook after her'), and we got talkin' about Mrs Spicer. Maggie was very warm about old Wall.

high tempered

'I expected Mrs Spicer up to-day,' said Mary. 'She seems better lately.'

'Why!' cried Maggie Charlsworth, 'if that ain't Annie coming running up along the creek. Something's the matter!'

We all jumped up and ran out.

'What is it, Annie?' cried Mary.

'Oh, Mrs Wilson! Mother's asleep, and we can't wake her!'

'What?'

'It's – it's the truth, Mrs Wilson.'

'How long has she been asleep?'

'Since lars' night.'

'My God!' cried Mary, '*since last night*?'

'No, Mrs Wilson, not all the time; she woke wonst, about daylight this mornin'. She called me and said she didn't feel well, and I'd have to manage the milkin'.'

'Was that all she said?'

'No. She said not to go for you; and she said to feed the pigs and calves; and she said to be sure and water them geraniums.'

Mary wanted to go, but I wouldn't let her. James and I saddled our horses and rode down the creek.

Mrs Spicer looked very little different from what she did when I last saw her alive. It was some time before we could believe that she was dead. But she was 'past carin'' right enough.

JOE WILSON'S COURTSHIP

THERE are many times in this world when a healthy boy is happy. When he is put into knickerbockers, for instance, and 'comes a man to-day', as my little Jim used to say. When they're cooking something at home that he likes. When the 'sandy blight' or measles breaks out amongst the children, or the teacher or his wife falls dangerously ill – or dies, it doesn't matter which – 'and there ain't no school.' When a boy is naked and in his natural state for a warm climate like Australia, with three or four of his schoolmates, under the shade of the creek-oaks in the bend where there's a good clear pool with a sandy bottom. When his father buys him a gun, and he starts out after kangaroos or 'possums. When he gets a horse, saddle, and bridle, of his own. When he has his arm in splints or a stitch in his head – he's proud then, the proudest boy in the district.

I wasn't a healthy-minded, average boy; I reckon I was born for a poet by mistake, and grew up to be a Bushman, and didn't know what was the matter with me – or the world – but that's got nothing to do with it.

There are times when a man is happy. When he finds out that the girl loves him. When he's just married. When he's a lawful father for the first time, and everything's going on all right: some men make fools of themselves then – I know I did. I'm happy to-night because I'm out of debt and can see clear ahead, and because I haven't been easy for a long time.

But I think that the happiest time in a man's life is when he's courting a girl and finds out for sure that she loves him, and hasn't a thought for anyone else. Make the most of your courting days, you young chaps, and keep them clean, for they're about the only days when there's a chance of poetry and beauty coming into this life. Make the best of them, and you'll never regret it the longest day you live. They're the days that the wife will look back to, anyway, in the brightest of times as well as in the blackest, and there shouldn't be anything in those days that might hurt her when she looks back. Make the most of your courting days, you young chaps, for they will never come again.

A married man knows all about it – after a while: he sees the woman world through the eyes of his wife; he knows what an extra moment's pressure of the hand means, and, if he has had a hard life, and is inclined to be cynical, the knowledge does him no good. It leads him into awful messes sometimes, for a married man, if he's inclined that way, has three times the chance with a woman that a single man has – because the married man knows. He is privileged; he can guess pretty closely what a woman means when she says something else; he knows just how far he can go; he can go farther in five minutes towards coming to the point with a woman than an innocent young man dares go in three weeks. Above all, the married man is more decided with women; he takes them and things for granted. In short he is – well, he is a married man. And, when he knows all this, how much better or happier is he for it? Mark Twain says that he lost all the beauty of the river when he saw it with a pilot's eye – and there you have it.

But it's all new to a young chap, provided he hasn't been a young blackguard. It's all wonderful, new, and strange to him. He's a different man. He finds that he never knew anything about women. He sees none of woman's little ways and tricks in his girl. He is in heaven one day and down near the other place the next; and that's the sort of thing that makes life interesting. He takes his new world for granted. And, when she says she'll be his wife – !

Make the most of your courting days, you young chaps, for they've got a lot of influence on your married life afterwards – a lot more than you'd think. Make the best of them, for they'll never come any more, unless we do our courting over again in another world. If we do, I'll make the most of mine.

But, looking back, I didn't do so badly after all. I never told you about the days I courted Mary. The more I look back the more I come to think that I made the most of them, and if I had no more to regret in married life than I have in my courting days, I wouldn't walk to and fro in the room, or up and down the yard in the dark sometimes, or lie awake some nights thinking . . . Ah, well!

I was between twenty-one and thirty then: birthdays had never been any use to me, and I'd left off counting them. You don't take much stock in birthdays in the Bush. I'd knocked about the country for a few years, shearing and fencing and droving a little, and wasting my life without getting anything for it. I drank now and then, and made a fool of myself. I was reckoned 'wild'; but I only drank because I felt less sensitive, and the world seemed a lot saner and better and kinder when I had a few drinks: I loved my fellow-man then and felt nearer to him. It's better to be thought 'wild' than to be considered eccentric or ratty. Now, my old mate, Jack Barnes, drank – as far as I could see – first because he'd inherited the gambling habit from his father along with his father's luck; he'd the habit of being cheated and losing very bad, and when he lost he drank. Till drink got a hold on him. Jack was sentimental too, but in a different way. I was sentimental about other people – more fool I! – whereas Jack was sentimental about himself. Before he was married, and when he was recovering from a spree, he'd write rhymes about 'Only a boy, drunk by the roadside,' and that sort of thing; and he'd call 'em poetry, and talk about signing them and sending them to the *Town and Country Journal*. But he generally tore them up when he got better. The Bush is breeding a race of poets, and I don't know what the country will come to in the end.

Well. It was after Jack and I had been out shearing at Beenaway Shed in the big scrubs. Jack was living in the little farming town of Solong, and I was hanging round. Black, the squatter, wanted some fencing done and a new stable built, or buggy and harness-house, at his place at Haviland, a few miles out of Solong. Jack and I were good Bush carpenters, so we took the job to keep us going till something else turned up. 'Better than doing nothing,' said Jack.

'There's a nice little girl in service at Black's,' he said. 'She's more like an adopted daughter, in fact, than a servant. She's a real good little girl, and good-looking into the bargain. I hear that young Black is sweet on her, but they say she won't have anything to do with him. I know a lot of chaps that have tried for her, but they've never had any luck. She's a regular little dumpling, and I like dumplings. They call her 'Possum. You ought to try a bear up in that direction, Joe.'

I was always shy with women – except perhaps some that I should have fought shy of; but Jack wasn't – he was afraid of no woman, good, bad, or indifferent. I haven't time to explain why, but somehow, whenever a girl took any notice of me I took it for granted that she was only playing with me, and felt nasty about it. I made one or two mistakes, but – ah well!

'My wife knows little 'Possum,' said Jack. 'I'll get her to ask her out to our place, and let you know.'

I reckoned that he wouldn't get me there then, and made a note to be on the watch for tricks. I had a hopeless little love-story behind me, of course. I suppose most married men can look back to their lost love; few marry the first flame. Many a married man looks back and thinks it was damned lucky that he didn't get the girl he couldn't have. Jack had been my successful rival, only he didn't know it – I don't think his wife knew it either. I used to think her the prettiest and sweetest little girl in the district.

But Jack was mighty keen on fixing me up with the little girl at Haviland. He seemed to take it for granted that I was going to fall in love with her at first sight. He took too many things for granted as far as I was concerned, and got me into awful tangles sometimes.

'You let me alone, and I'll fix you up, Joe,' he said, as we rode up to the station. 'I'll make it all right with the girl. You're rather a good-looking chap. You've got the sort of eyes that take with girls, only you don't know it; you haven't got the go. If I had your eyes along with my other attractions, I'd be in trouble on account of a woman about once a week.'

'For God's sake shut up, Jack,' I said.

Do you remember the first glimpse you got of your wife? Perhaps not in England, where so many couples grow up together from childhood; but it's different in Australia, where you may hail from two thousand miles away from where your wife was born, and yet she may be a countrywoman of yours, and a countrywoman in ideas and politics too. I remember the first glimpse I got of Mary.

It was a two-storey brick house with wide balconies and verandas all round, and a double row of pines down to the front gate. Parallel at the back was an old slab-and-shingle place, one room deep, and about eight rooms long, with a row of skillions at the back: the place was used for kitchen, laundry and servants' rooms, &c. This was the old homestead before the new house was built. There was a wide, old-fashioned, brick-floored veranda in front, with an open end; there was ivy climbing up the veranda-post on one side and a baby-rose on the other, and a grape-vine near the chimney. We rode up to the end of the veranda, and Jack called to see if there was anyone at home, and Mary came trotting out; so it was in the frame of vines that I first saw her.

More than once since then I've had a fancy to wonder whether the rose-bush killed the grape-vine or the ivy smothered 'em both in the end. I used to have a vague idea of riding that way some day to see. You do get strange fancies at odd times.

Jack asked her if the boss was in. He did all the talking. I saw a little girl, rather plump, with a complexion like a New England or Blue Mountain girl, or a girl from Tasmania, or from Gippsland in Victoria. Red and white girls were very scarce in the Solong district. She had the biggest and brightest eyes I'd seen round there, dark hazel eyes, as I found out afterwards, and bright as a 'possum's. No wonder they called her 'Possum. I forgot at once that Mrs Jack Barnes was the prettiest girl in the district. I felt a sort of comfortable satisfaction in the fact that I was on horseback; most Bushmen look better on horseback. It was a black filly, a fresh young thing, and she seemed as shy of girls as I was myself. I noticed Mary glanced in my direction once or twice to see if she knew me; but, when she looked, the filly took all my attention. Mary trotted in to tell old Black he was wanted, and after Jack had seen him, and arranged to start work next day, we started back to Solong.

I expected Jack to ask me what I thought of Mary – but he didn't. He squinted at me sideways once or twice, and didn't say anything for a long time, and then he started talking of other things. I began to feel wild at him. He seemed so damnably satisfied with the way things were going. He seemed to reckon that I was a gone case now; but, as he didn't say so, I had no way of getting at him. I felt sure he'd go home and tell his wife that Joe Wilson was properly gone on little 'Possum at Haviland. That was all Jack's way.

Next morning we started to work. We were to build the buggy-house at the back near the end of the old house, but first we had to take down a rotten old place that might have been the original hut in the Bush before the old house was built. There was a window in it, opposite the laundry window in the old place, and the first thing I did was to take out the sash. I'd noticed Jack yarning with 'Possum before he started work.

While I was at work at the window he called me round to the other end of the hut to help him lift a grindstone out of the way; and when we'd done it, he took the tip of my ear between his fingers and thumb and stretched it and whispered into it:

'Don't hurry with that window, Joe; the strips are hardwood and hard to get off – you'll have to take the sash out very carefully so as not to break the glass.' Then he stretched my ear a little more and put his mouth closer:

'Make a looking-glass of that window, Joe,' he said.

I was used to Jack, and when I went back to the window I started to puzzle out what he meant, and presently I saw it by chance.

That window reflected the laundry window: the room was dark inside, and there was a good clear reflection; and presently I saw Mary come to the laundry window and stand with her hands behind her back, thoughtfully watching me. The laundry window had an old-fashioned hinged sash, and I like that sort of window – there's more romance about it, I think. There was a thick dark-green ivy all round the window, and Mary looked prettier than a picture. I squared up my shoulders and put my heels together, and put as much style as I could into the work. I couldn't have turned round to save my life.

Presently Jack came round, and Mary disappeared.

'Well?' he whispered.

'You're a fool, Jack,' I said. 'She's only interested in the old house being pulled down.'

'That's all right,' he said. 'I've been keeping an eye on the business round the corner, and she ain't interested when *I'm* round this end.'

'You seem mighty interested in the business,' I said.

'Yes,' said Jack. 'This sort of thing just suits a man of my rank in times of peace.'

'What made you think of the window?' I asked.

'Oh, that's as simple as striking matches. I'm up to all those dodges. Why, where there wasn't a window, I've fixed up a piece of looking-glass to see if a girl was taking any notice of me when she thought I wasn't looking.'

He went away, and presently Mary was at the window again, and this time she had a tray with cups of tea and a plate of cake and bread-and-butter. I was prising off the strips that held the sash, very carefully, and my heart suddenly commenced to gallop, without any reference to me. I'd never felt like that before, except once or twice. It was just as if I'd swallowed some clock-work arrangement, unconsciously, and it had started to go, without warning. I reckon it was all on account of that blarsted Jack working me up. He had a quiet way of working you up to a thing that made you want to hit him sometimes – after you'd made an ass of yourself.

I didn't hear Mary at first. I hoped Jack would come round and help me out of the fix, but he didn't.

'Mr – Mr Wilson!' said Mary. She had a sweet voice.

I turned around.

'I thought you and Mr Barnes might like a cup of tea.'

'Oh, thank you!' I said, and I made a dive for the window, as if hurry would help it. I trod on an old cask-hoop; it sprang up and dinted my shin and I stumbled – and that didn't help matters much.

'Oh! did you hurt yourself, Mr Wilson? cried Mary.

'Hurt myself! Oh no, not at all, thank you,' I blurted out. 'It takes more than that to hurt me.'

I was about the reddest shy lanky fool of a Bushman that ever was taken at a disadvantage on foot, and when I took the tray my hands shook so that a lot of the tea was spilt into the saucers. I embarrassed her too, like the damned fool I was, till she must have been as red as I was, and it's a wonder we didn't spill the whole lot between us. I got away from the window in as much of a hurry as if Jack had cut his leg with a chisel and fainted, and I was running with whisky for him. I blundered round to where he was, feeling like a man feels when he has just made an ass of himself in public. The memory of that sort of thing hurts you worse and makes you jerk your head more impatiently than the thought of a past crime would, I think.

I pulled myself together when I got to where Jack was.

'Here, Jack!' I said. 'I've struck something all right; here's some tea and brownie – we'll hang out here all right.'

Jack took a cup of tea and a piece of cake and sat down to enjoy it, just as if he'd paid for it and ordered it to be sent out about that time.

He was silent for a while, with the sort of silence that always made me wild at him. Presently he said, as if he'd just thought of it:

'That's a very pretty little girl, 'Possum, isn't she, Joe? Do you notice how she dresses? – always fresh and trim. But she's got on her best bib-and-tucker to-day, and a pinafore with frills to it. And it's ironing-day, too. It can't be on your account. If it was Saturday or Sunday afternoon, or some holiday, I could understand it. But perhaps one of her admirers is going to take her to the church bazaar in Solong to-night. That's what it is.'

He gave me time to think over that.

'But yet she seems interested in you, Joe,' he said. 'Why didn't you offer to take her to the bazaar instead of letting another chap get in ahead of you? You miss all your chances, Joe.'

Then a thought struck me. I ought to have known Jack well enough to have thought of it before.

'Look here, Jack,' I said. 'What have you been saying to that girl about me?'

'Oh, not much,' said Jack. 'There isn't much to say about you.'

'What did you tell her?'

'Oh, nothing in particular. She'd heard all about you before.'

'She hadn't heard much good, I suppose,' I said.

'Well, that's true, as far as I could make out. But you've only got yourself to blame. I didn't have the breeding and rearing of you. I smoothed over matters with her as much as I could.'

'What did you tell her?' I said. 'That's what I want to know.'

'Well, to tell the truth, I didn't tell her anything much. I only answered questions.'

'And what questions did she ask?'

'Well, in the first place, she asked if your name wasn't Joe Wilson; and I said it was, as far as I knew. Then she said she heard that you wrote poetry, and I had to admit that that was true.'

'Look here, Jack,' I said, 'I've two minds to punch your head.'

'And she asked me if it was true that you were wild,' said Jack, 'and I said you was, a bit. She said it seemed a pity. She asked me if it was true that you drank, and I drew a long face and said that I was sorry to say it was true. She asked me if you had any friends, and I said none that I knew of, except me. I said that you'd lost all your friends; they stuck to you as long as they could, but they had to give you best, one after the other.'

'What next?'

'She asked me if you were delicate, and I said no, you were as tough as fencing-wire. She said you looked rather pale and thin, and asked me if you'd had an illness lately. And I said no – it was all on account of the wild, dissipated life you'd led. She said it was a pity you hadn't a mother or a sister to look after you – it was a pity that something couldn't be done for you, and I said it was, but I was afraid that nothing could be done. I told her that I was doing all I could to keep you straight.'

I knew enough of Jack to know that most of this was true. And so she only pitied me after all. I felt as if I'd been courting her for six months and she'd thrown me over – but I didn't know anything about women yet.

'Did you tell her I was in jail?' I growled.

'No, by gum! I forgot that. But never mind, I'll fix that up all right. I'll tell her that you got two years' hard for horse-stealing. That ought to make her interested in you, if she isn't already.'

We smoked a while.

'And was that all she said?' I asked.

'Who? – Oh! 'Possum,' said Jack, rousing himself. 'Well – no; let me think – We got chatting of other things – you know a married man's privileged, and can say a lot more to a girl than a single man can. I got talking nonsense about sweethearts, and one thing led to another till at last she said, 'I suppose Mr Wilson's got a sweetheart, Mr Barnes?'

'And what did you say?' I growled.

'Oh, I told her that you were a holy terror amongst the girls,' said Jack. 'You'd better take back that tray, Joe, and let us get to work.'

I wouldn't take back the tray – but that didn't mend matters, for Jack took it back himself.

I didn't see Mary's reflection in the window again, so I took the window out. I reckoned that she was just a big-hearted, impulsive little thing, as many Australian girls are, and I reckoned that I was a fool for thinking for a moment that she might give me a second thought, except by way of kindness. Why! young Black and half a dozen better men than me were sweet on her, and young Black was to get his father's station and the money – or rather his mother's money, for she held the stuff (she kept it close, too, by all accounts). Young Black was away at the time, and his mother was dead against him about Mary, but that didn't make any difference, as far as I could see. I reckoned that it was only just going to be a hopeless, heart-breaking, stand-far-off-and-worship affair, as far as I was concerned – like my first love affair, that I haven't told you about yet. I was tired of being pitied by good girls. You see, I didn't know women then. If I had known, I think I might have made more than one mess of my life.

Jack rode home to Solong every night. I was staying at a pub some distance out of town, between Solong and Haviland. There were three or four wet days, and we didn't get on with the work. I fought shy of Mary till one day she was hanging out clothes and the line broke. It was the old-style sixpenny clothes-line. The clothes were all down, but it was clean grass, so it didn't matter much. I looked at Jack.

'Go and help her, you capital idiot!' he said, and I made the plunge.

'Oh, thank you, Mr Wilson!' said Mary, when I came to help. She had the broken end of the line, and was trying to hold some of the clothes off the ground, as if she could pull it an inch with the heavy wet sheets and table-cloths and things on it, or as if it would do any good if she did. But that's the way with women – especially little women – some of 'em would try to pull a store bullock if they got the end of the rope on the right side of the fence. I took the line from Mary, and accidentally touched her soft, plump little hand as I did so: it sent a thrill right through me. She seemed a lot cooler than I was.

Now, in cases like this, especially if you lose your head a bit, you get hold of the loose end of the rope that's hanging from the post with one hand, and the end of the line with the clothes on with the other, and try to pull 'em far enough together to make a knot. And that's about all you do for the present, except look like a fool. Then I took off the post end, spliced the line, took it over the fork, and pulled, while Mary helped me with the prop. I thought Jack might have come and taken the prop from her, but he didn't; he just went on with his work as if nothing was happening inside the horizon.

She'd got the line about two-thirds full of clothes; it was a bit short now, so she had to jump and catch it with one hand and hold it down while she pegged a sheet she'd thrown over. I'd made the plunge now, so I volunteered to help her. I held down the line while she threw the things over and pegged out. As we got near the post and higher I straightened out some ends and pegged myself. Bushmen are handy at most things. We laughed, and now and again Mary would say, 'No, that's not the way, Mr Wilson; that's not right; the sheet isn't far enough over; wait till I fix it.' I'd a reckless idea once of holding her up while she pegged, and I was glad afterwards that I hadn't made such a fool of myself.

'There's only a few more things in the basket, Miss Brand,' I said. 'You can't reach – I'll fix 'em up.'

She seemed to give a little gasp.

'Oh, those things are not ready yet,' she said, 'they're not rinsed,' and she grabbed the basket and held it away from me. The things looked the same to me as the rest on the line; they looked rinsed enough and blued too. I reckoned that she didn't want me to take the trouble, or thought that I mightn't like to be seen hanging out clothes, and was only doing it out of kindness.

'Oh, it's no trouble,' I said, 'let me hang 'em out. I like it. I've hung out clothes at home on a windy day,' and I made a reach into the basket. But she flushed red, with temper I thought, and snatched the basket away.

'Excuse me, Mr Wilson,' she said, 'but those things are not ready yet!' and she marched into the wash-house.

'Ah well! you've got a little temper of your own,' I thought to myself.

When I told Jack, he said that I'd made another fool of myself. He said I'd both disappointed and offended her. He said that my line was to stand off a bit and be serious and melancholy in the background.

That evening when we'd started home, we stopped some time yarning with a chap we met at the gate; and I happened to look back and saw Mary hanging out the rest of the things – she thought that we were out of sight. Then I understood why those things weren't ready while we were round.

For the next day or two Mary didn't take the slightest notice of me, and I kept out of her way. Jack said I'd disillusioned her – and hurt her dignity – which was a thousand times worse. He said I'd spoilt the thing altogether. He said that she'd got an idea that I was shy and poetic, and I'd only shown myself the usual sort of Bush-whacker.

I noticed her talking and chatting with other fellows once or twice, and it made me miserable. I got drunk two evenings running, and then, as it appeared afterwards, Mary consulted Jack, and at last she said to him, when we were together:

'Do you play draughts, Mr Barnes?'

'No,' said Jack.

'Do you, Mr Wilson?' she asked, suddenly turning her big bright eyes on me, and speaking to me for the first time since last washing-day.

'Yes,' I said, 'I do a little.' Then there was a silence, and I had to say something else.

'Do you play draughts, Miss Brand?' I asked.

'Yes,' she said, 'but I can't get anyone to play with me here of an evening, the men are generally playing cards or reading.' Then she said, 'It's very dull these long winter evenings when you've got nothing to do. Young Mr Black used to play draughts, but he's away.'

I saw Jack winking at me urgently.

'I'll play a game with you, if you like,' I said, 'but I ain't much of a player.'

'Oh, thank you, Mr Wilson! When shall you have an evening to spare?'

We fixed it for that same evening. We got chummy over the draughts. I had a suspicion even then that it was a put-up job to keep me away from the pub.

Perhaps she found a way of giving a hint to old Black without committing herself. Women have ways – or perhaps Jack did it. Anyway, next day the Boss came round and said to me:

'Look here, Joe, you've got no occasion to stay at the pub. Bring along your blankets and camp in one of the spare rooms of the old house. You can have your tucker here.'

He was a good sort, was Black the squatter: a squatter of the old school, who'd shared the early hardships with his men, and couldn't see why he should not shake hands and have a smoke and a yarn over old times with any of his old station-hands that happened to come along. But he'd married an Englishwoman after the hardships were over, and she'd never got any Australian notions.

Next day I found one of the skillion rooms scrubbed out and a bed fixed up for me. I'm not sure to this day who did it, but I supposed that good-natured old Black had given one of the women a hint. After tea I had a yarn with Mary, sitting on a log of the wood-heap. I don't remember exactly how we came to be there, or who sat down first. There was about two feet between us. We got very chummy and confidential. She told me about her childhood and her father.

He'd been an old mate of Black's, a younger son of a well-to-do

English family (with blue blood in it, I believe), and sent out to Australia with a thousand pounds to make his way, as many younger sons are, with more or less. They think they're hard done by; they blue their thousand pounds in Melbourne or Sydney, and they don't make any more nowadays, for the Roarin' Days have been dead these thirty years. I wish I'd had a thousand pounds to start on!

Mary's mother was the daughter of a German immigrant, who selected up there in the old days. She had a will of her own as far as I could understand, and bossed the home till the day of her death. Mary's father made money, and lost it, and drank – and died. Mary remembered him sitting on the veranda one evening with his hand on her head, and singing a German song (the 'Lorelei', I think it was) softly, as if to himself. Next day he stayed in bed, and the children were kept out of the room; and, when he died, the children were adopted round (there was a little money coming from England).

Mary told me all about her girlhood. She went first to live with a sort of cousin in town, in a house where they took cards in on a tray, and then she came to live with Mrs Black, who took a fancy to her at first. I'd had no boyhood to speak of, so I gave her some of my ideas on what the world ought to be, and she seemed interested.

Next day there were sheets on my bed, and I felt pretty cocky until I remembered that I'd told her I had no one to care for me; then I suspected pity again.

But next evening we remembered that both our fathers and mothers were dead, and discovered that we had no friends except Jack and old Black, and things went on very satisfactorily.

And next day there was a little table in my room with a crocheted cover and a looking-glass.

I noticed the other girls began to act mysterious and giggle when I was round, but Mary didn't seem aware of it.

We got very chummy. Mary wasn't comfortable at Haviland. Old Black was very fond of her and always took her part, but she wanted to be independent. She had a great idea of going to Sydney and getting into the hospital as a nurse. She had friends in Sydney, but she had no money. There was a little money coming to her when she was twenty-one – a few pounds – and she was going to try and get it before that time.

'Look here, Miss Brand,' I said, after we'd watched the moon rise.

'I'll lend you the money. I've got plenty – more than I know what to do with.'

But I saw I'd hurt her. She sat up very straight for a while, looking before her; then she said it was time to go in, and said, 'Good night, Mr Wilson.'

I reckoned I'd done it that time; but Mary told me afterwards that she was only hurt because it struck her that what she said about money might have been taken for a hint. She didn't understand me yet, and I didn't know human nature. I didn't say anything to Jack – in fact, about this time I left off telling him about things. He didn't seem hurt; he worked hard and seemed happy.

I really meant what I said to Mary about the money. It was pure good nature. I'd be a happier man now, I think, and a richer man perhaps, if I'd never grown more selfish than I was that night on the wood-heap with Mary. I felt a great sympathy for her – but I got to love her. I went through all the ups and downs of it. One day I was having tea in the kitchen, and Mary and another girl, named Sarah, reached me a clean plate at the same time: I took Sarah's because she was first, and Mary seemed very nasty about it, and that gave me great hopes. But all next evening she played draughts with a drover that she'd chummed up with. I pretended to be interested in Sarah's talk, but it didn't seem to work.

A few days later a Sydney jackeroo visited the station. He had a good pea-rifle, and one afternoon he started to teach Mary to shoot at a target. They seemed to get very chummy. I had a nice time for three or four days, I can tell you. I was worse than a wall-eyed bullock with the pleuro. The other chaps had a shot out of the rifle. Mary called 'Mr Wilson' to have a shot, and I made a worse fool of myself by sulking. If it hadn't been a blooming jackeroo I wouldn't have minded so much.

Next evening the jackeroo and one or two other chaps and the girls went out 'possum shooting. Mary went. I could have gone, but I didn't. I mooched round all the evening like an orphan bandicoot on a burnt ridge, and then I went up to the pub and filled myself up with beer, and damned the world, and came home and went to bed. I think that evening was the only time I ever wrote poetry down on a piece of paper. I got so miserable that I enjoyed it.

I felt better next morning, and reckoned I was cured. I ran against Mary accidentally, and had to say something.

'How did you enjoy yourself yesterday evening, Miss Brand?' I asked.

'Oh, very well, thank you, Mr Wilson,' she said. Then she asked, 'How did you enjoy yourself, Mr Wilson?'

I puzzled over that afterwards, but couldn't make anything out of it. Perhaps she only said it for the sake of saying something. But about this time my handkerchiefs and collars disappeared from the room and turned up washed and ironed, and laid tidily on my table. I used to keep an eye out, but could never catch anybody near my room. I straightened up, and kept my room a bit tidy, and when my handkerchief got too dirty, and I was ashamed of letting it go to the wash, I'd slip down to the river after dark and wash it out, and dry it next day, and rub it up to look as if it hadn't been washed, and leave it on my table. I felt so full of hope and joy that I worked twice as hard as Jack, till one morning he remarked casually:

'I see you've made a new mash, Joe. I saw the half-caste cook tidying up your room this morning and taking your collars and things to the wash-house.'

I felt very much off colour all the rest of the day, and I had such a bad night of it that I made up my mind next morning to look the hopelessness square in the face and live the thing down.

It was the evening before Anniversary Day. Jack and I had put in a good day's work to get the job finished, and Jack was having a smoke and a yarn with the chaps before he started home. We sat on an old log along by the fence at the back of the house. There was Jimmy Nowlett the bullock-driver, and long Dave Regan the drover, and Jim Bullock the fencer, and one or two others. Mary and the station girls and one or two visitors were sitting under the old veranda. The jackeroo was there too, so I felt happy. It was the girls who used to bring the chaps hanging round. They were getting up a dance party for Anniversary night. Along in the evening another chap came riding up to the station: he was a big shearer, a dark, handsome fellow, who looked like a gipsy; it was reckoned that there was foreign blood in him. He went by the name of Romany. He was supposed to be shook after Mary too. He had the nastiest temper and the best violin in the district, and the chaps put up with him a lot because they wanted him to play at Bush dances. The moon had risen over Pine Ridge, but it was dusky where we were. We saw Romany loom up, riding in from the gate; he rode round the end of the coach-house and across towards where we were – I suppose he was going to tie up his horse at the fence; but about half-way across the grass he disappeared. It struck me that there was something peculiar about the way he got down, and I heard a sound like a horse stumbling.

'What the hell's Romany trying to do?' said Jimmy Nowlett. 'He couldn't have fell off his horse – or else he's drunk.'

A couple of chaps got up and went to see. Then there was that waiting, mysterious silence that comes when something happens in the dark, and nobody knows what it is. I went over, and the thing dawned on me. I'd stretched a wire clothes-line across there during the day and had forgotten all about it for the moment. Romany had no idea of the line and, as he rode up, it caught him on a level with his elbows, and scraped him off his horse. He was sitting on the grass, swearing in a surprised voice, and the horse looked surprised too. Romany wasn't hurt, but the sudden shock had spoilt his temper. He wanted to know who'd put up that bloody line. He came over and sat on the log. The chaps smoked a while.

'What did you git down so sudden for, Romany?' asked Jim Bullock, presently. 'Did you hurt yerself on the pommel?'

'Why didn't you ask the horse to go round?' asked Dave Regan.

'I'd only like to know who put up that bleeding wire!' growled Romany.

'Well,' said Jimmy Nowlett, 'if we'd put up a sign to beware of the line you couldn't have seen it in the dark.'

'Unless it was a transparency with a candle behind it,' said Dave Regan. 'But why didn't you get down on one end, Romany, instead of all along? It wouldn't have jolted yer so much.'

All this with the Bush drawl, and between the puffs of their pipes. But I didn't take any interest in it. I was brooding over Mary and the jackeroo.

'I've heard of men getting down over their horse's head,' said Dave presently, in a reflective sort of way – 'In fact, I've done it myself – but I never saw a man get off backwards over his horse's rump.'

But they saw that Romany was getting nasty, and they wanted him to play the fiddle next night, so they dropped it.

Mary was singing an old song. I always thought she had a sweet voice, and I'd have enjoyed it if that damned jackeroo hadn't been listening too. We listened in silence until she'd finished.

'That gal's got a nice voice,' said Jimmy Nowlett.

'Nice voice!' snarled Romany, who'd been waiting for a chance to be nasty. 'Why, I've heard a tom-cat sing better.'

I moved, and Jack, he was sitting next me, nudged me to keep quiet. The chaps didn't like Romany's talk about 'Possum at all. They were all fond of her: she wasn't a pet or tomboy, for she wasn't built that way, but they were fond of her in such a way that they didn't like to hear anything said about her. They said nothing for a while, but it meant a lot. Perhaps the single men didn't care to speak for fear that it would be said that they were gone on Mary. But presently Jimmy Nowlett gave a big puff at his pipe and spoke:

'I suppose you got bit, too, in that quarter, Romany?'

'Oh, she tried it on, but it didn't go,' said Romany. 'I've met her sort before. She's setting her cap at that jackeroo now. Some girls will run after anything with trousers on,' and he stood up.

Jack Barnes must have felt what was coming, for he grabbed my arm, and whispered, 'Sit still, Joe, damn you! He's too good for you!' But I was on my feet and facing Romany as if a giant hand had reached down and wrenched me off the log and set me there.

'You're a damned crawler, Romany!' I said.

Little Jimmy Nowlett was between us, and the other fellows round us before a blow got home. 'Hold on, you damned fools!' they said. 'Keep quiet till we get away from the house!' There was a little clear flat down by the river and plenty of light there, so we decided to go down there and have it out.

Now I never was a fighting man; I'd never learnt to use my hands. I scarcely knew how to put them up. Jack often wanted to teach me, but I wouldn't bother about it. He'd say, 'You'll get into a fight some day, Joe, or out of one, and shame me'; but I hadn't the patience to learn. He'd wanted me to take lessons at the station after work, but he used to get excited, and I didn't want Mary to see him knocking me about. Before he was married, Jack was always getting into fights – he generally tackled a better man and got a hiding; but he didn't seem to care so long as he made a good show – though he used to explain the thing away from a scientific point of view for weeks after. To tell the truth, I had a horror of fighting; I had a horror of being marked about the face;

I think I'd sooner stand off and fight a man with revolvers than fight him with fists; and then I think I would say, last thing, 'Don't shoot me in the face!' Then again I hated the idea of hitting a man. It seemed brutal to me. I was too sensitive and sentimental, and that was what the matter was. Jack seemed very serious on it as we walked down to the river, and he couldn't help hanging out blue lights.

'Why didn't you let me teach you to use your hands?' he said. 'The only chance now is that Romany can't fight after all. If you'd waited a minute I'd have been at him.' We were a bit behind the rest, and Jack started giving me points about lefts and rights, and 'half-arms', and that sort of thing. 'He's left-handed, and that's the worst of it,' said Jack. 'You must only make as good a show as you can, and one of us will take him on afterwards.'

But I just heard him and that was all. It was to be my first fight since I was a boy, but somehow I felt cool about it – sort of dulled. If the chaps had known all they would have set me down as a cur. I thought of that, but it didn't make any difference with me then; I knew it was a thing they couldn't understand. I knew I was reckoned pretty soft. But I knew one thing that they didn't know. I knew that it was going to be a fight to a finish, one way or the other. I had more brains and imagination than the rest put together, and I suppose that that was the real cause of most of my trouble. I kept saying to myself, 'You'll have to go through with it now, Joe, old man! It's the turning point of your life.' If I won the fight, I'd set to work and win Mary; if I lost, I'd leave the district for ever. A man thinks a lot in a flash sometimes; I used to get excited over little things, because of the very paltriness of them, but I was mostly cool in a crisis – Jack was the reverse. I looked ahead: I wouldn't be able to marry a girl who could look back and remember when her husband was beaten by another man – no matter what sort of brute the other man was.

I never in my life felt so cool about a thing. Jack kept whispering instructions, and showing with his hands, up to the last moment, but it was all lost on me.

Looking back, I think there was a bit of romance about it: Mary singing under the vines to amuse a jackeroo dude, and a coward going down to the river in the moonlight to fight for her.

It was very quiet in the little moonlit flat by the river. We took off our coats and were ready. There was no swearing or barracking. It seemed an understood thing with the men that if I went out first round Jack would fight Romany; and if Jack knocked him out somebody else would fight Jack to square matters. Jim Bullock wouldn't mind obliging for one; he was a mate of Jack's, but he didn't mind who he fought so long as it was for the sake of fair play – or 'peace and quietness,' as he said. Jim was very good-natured. He backed Romany, and of course Jack backed me.

As far as I could see, all Romany knew about fighting was to jerk one arm up in front of his face and duck his head by way of a feint, and then rush and lunge out. But he had the weight and strength and length of reach, and my first lesson was a very short one. I went down early in the round. But it did me good; the blow and the look I'd seen in Romany's eyes knocked all the sentiment out of me. Jack said nothing – he seemed to regard it as a hopeless job from the first. Next round I tried to remember some things Jack had told me, and made a better show, but I went down in the end.

I felt Jack breathing quick and trembling as he lifted me up.

'How are you, Joe?' he whispered.

'I'm all right,' I said.

'It's all right,' whispered Jack in a voice as if I was going to be hanged, but it would soon be all over. 'He can't use his hands much more than you can – take your time, Joe – try to remember something I told you, for God's sake!'

When two men fight who don't know how to use their hands, they stand a show of knocking each other about a lot. I got some awful thumps, but mostly on the body. Jimmy Nowlett began to get excited and jump round – he was an excitable little fellow.

'Fight! you — !' he yelled. 'Why don't you fight? That ain't fightin'. Fight, and don't try to murder each other. Use your crimson hands or, by God, I'll chip you! Fight, or I'll blanky well bullock-whip the pair of you'; then his language got awful. They said we went like windmills, and that nearly every one of the blows we made was enough to kill a bullock if it had got home. Jimmy stopped us once, but they held him back.

Presently I went down pretty flat, but the blow was well up on the head, and didn't matter much – I had a good thick skull. And I had one good eye yet.

'For God's sake, hit him!' whispered Jack – he was trembling like a leaf. 'Don't mind what I told you. I wish I was fighting him myself! Get a blow home, for God's sake! Make a good show this round and I'll stop the fight.'

That showed how little even Jack, my old mate, understood me.

I had the Bushman up in me now, and wasn't going to be beaten while I could think. I was wonderfully cool, and learning to fight. There's nothing like a fight to teach a man. I was thinking fast, and learning more in three seconds than Jack's sparring could have taught me in three weeks. People think that blows hurt in a fight, but they don't – not till afterwards. I fancy that a fighting man, if he isn't altogether an animal, suffers more mentally than he does physically.

While I was getting my wind I could hear through the moonlight and still air the sound of Mary's voice singing up at the house. I thought hard into the future, even as I fought. The fight only seemed something that was passing.

I was on my feet again and at it, and presently I lunged out and felt such a jar on my arm that I thought it was telescoped. I thought I'd put out my wrist and elbow. And Romany was lying on the broad of his back.

I heard Jack draw three breaths of relief in one. He said nothing as he straightened me up, but I could feel his heart beating. He said afterwards that he didn't speak because he thought a word might spoil it.

I went down again, but Jack told me afterwards that he *felt* I was all right when he lifted me.

Then Romany went down, then we fell together, and the chaps separated us. I got another knock-down blow in, and was beginning to enjoy the novelty of it, when Romany staggered and limped.

'I've done,' he said. 'I've twisted my ankle.' He'd caught his heel against a tuft of grass.

'Shake hands,' yelled Jimmy Nowlett.

I stepped forward, but Romany took his coat, and limped to his horse.

'If yer don't shake hands with Wilson, I'll lam yer,' howled Jimmy; but Jack told him to let the man alone, and Romany got on his horse somehow and rode off.

I saw Jim Bullock stoop and pick up something from the grass, and heard him swear in surprise. There was some whispering, and presently Jim said:

'If I thought that, I'd kill him.'

'What is it?' asked Jack.

Jim held up a butcher's knife. It was common for a man to carry a butcher's knife in a sheath fastened to his belt.

'Why did you let your man fight with a butcher's knife in his belt?' asked Jimmy Nowlett.

But the knife could easily have fallen out when Romany fell, and we decided it that way.

'Any way,' said Jimmy Nowlett, 'if he'd stuck Joe in hot blood before us all it wouldn't be so bad as if he sneaked up and stuck him in the back in the dark. But you'd best keep an eye over yer shoulder for a year or two, Joe. That chap's got Eye-talian blood in him somewhere. And now the best thing you chaps can do is to keep your mouth shut and keep all this dark from the gals.'

Jack hurried me on ahead. He seemed to act queer, and when I glanced at him I could have sworn that there was water in his eyes. I said that Jack had no sentiment except for himself, but I forgot, and I'm sorry I said it.

'What's up, Jack?' I asked.

'Nothing,' said Jack.

'What's up, you old fool?' I said.

'Nothing,' said Jack, 'except that I'm damned proud of you, Joe, you old ass!' and he put his arm round my shoulders and gave me a shake. 'I didn't know it was in you, Joe – I wouldn't have said it before, or listened to any other man say it, but I didn't think you had the pluck – God's truth, I didn't. Come along and get your face fixed up.'

We got into my room quietly, and Jack got a dish of water, and told one of the chaps to sneak a piece of fresh beef from somewhere.

Jack was as proud as a dog with a tin tail as he fussed round me. He fixed up my face in the best style he knew, and he knew a good many – he'd been mended himself so often.

While he was at work we heard a sudden hush and a scraping of feet amongst the chaps that Jack had kicked out of the room, and a girl's voice whispered. 'Is he hurt? Tell me. I want to know – I might be able to help.'

It made my heart jump, I can tell you. Jack went out at once, and there was some whispering. When he came back he seemed wild.

'What is it, Jack?' I asked.

'Oh, nothing,' he said, 'only that damned slut of a half-caste cook overheard some of those blanky fools arguing as to how Romany's knife got out of the sheath, and she's put a nice yarn round amongst the girls. There's a regular bobbery, but it's all right now, Jimmy Nowlett's telling 'em lies at a great rate.'

Presently there was another hush outside, and a saucer with vinegar and brown paper was handed in.

One of the chaps brought some beer and whisky from the pub, and we had a quiet little time in my room. Jack wanted to stay all night, but I reminded him that his little wife was waiting for him in Solong, so he said he'd be round early in the morning, and went home.

I felt the reaction pretty bad. I didn't feel proud of the affair at all. I thought it was a low brutal business all round. Romany was a quiet chap after all, and the chaps had no right to chyack him. Perhaps he'd had a hard life, and carried a big swag of trouble that we didn't know anything about. He seemed a lonely man. I'd gone through enough myself to teach me not to judge men. I made up my mind to tell him how I felt about the matter next time we met. Perhaps I made my usual mistake of bothering about 'feelings' in another party that hadn't any feelings at all – perhaps I didn't; but it's generally best to chance it on the kind side in a case like this. Altogether I felt as if I'd made another fool of myself, and been a weak coward. I drank the rest of the beer and went to sleep.

About daylight I woke and heard Jack's horse on the gravel. He came round the back of the buggy-shed and up to my door, and then, suddenly, a girl screamed out. I pulled on my trousers and 'lastic-side boots and hurried out. It was Mary herself, dressed, and sitting on an old stone step at the back of the kitchen with her face in her hands, and Jack was off his horse and stooping by her side with his hand on her shoulder. She kept saying, 'I thought you were — ! I thought you were — !' I didn't catch the name. An old single-barrel muzzle-loader shotgun was lying in the grass at her feet. It was the gun they used to keep loaded and hanging in straps in a room off the kitchen ready for a shot at a cunning old hawk that they called ' 'Tarnal Death,' and that used to be always after the chickens.

When Mary lifted her face it was as white as notepaper and her eyes seemed to grow wilder when she caught sight of me.

'Oh, you did frighten me, Mr Barnes,' she gasped. Then she gave a little ghost of a laugh and stood up, and some colour came back.

'Oh, I'm a little fool!' she said quickly. 'I thought I heard old 'Tarnal Death at the chickens, and I thought it would be a great thing if I got the gun and brought him down; so I got up and dressed quietly so as not to wake Sarah. And then you came round the corner and frightened me. I don't know what you must think of me, Mr Barnes.'

'Never mind,' said Jack. 'You go and have a sleep, or you won't be able to dance to-night. Never mind the gun – I'll put that away.' And he steered her round to the door of her room off the brick veranda where she slept with one of the other girls.

'Well, that's a rum start!' I said.

'Yes, it is,' said Jack; 'it's very funny. Well, how's your face this morning, Joe?'

He seemed a lot more serious than usual.

We were hard at work all the morning cleaning out the big wool-shed and getting it ready for the dance, hanging hoops for the candles, and making seats, &c. I kept out of sight of the girls as much as I could. One side of my face was a sight, and the other wasn't too classical. I felt as if I had been stung by a swarm of bees.

'You're a fresh, sweet-scented beauty now, and no mistake, Joe,' said Jimmy Nowlett – he was going to play the accordion that night. 'You ought to fetch the girls now, Joe. But never mind, your face'll go down in about three weeks.' My lower jaw is crooked yet; but that fight straightened my nose, that had been knocked crooked when I was a boy – so I didn't lose much beauty by it.

When we'd done in the shed, Jack took me aside and said:

'Look here, Joe; if you won't come to the dance to-night – and I can't say you'd ornament it – I tell you what you'll do. You get little Mary away on the quiet and take her out for a stroll – and act like a man. The job's finished now, and you won't get another chance like this.'

'But how am I to get her out?' I said.

'Never you mind. You be mooching round down by the big pepper-mint-tree near the river-gate, say about half-past ten.'

'What good'll that do?'

'Never you mind. You just do as you're told, that's all you've got to do,' said Jack, and he went home to get dressed and bring his wife.

After the dancing started that night I had a peep in once or twice. The first time I saw Mary dancing with Jack, and looking serious; and the second time she was dancing with the blarsted jackeroo dude, and looking excited and happy. I noticed that some of the girls, that I could see sitting on a stool along the opposite wall, whispered, and gave Mary black looks as the jackeroo swung her past. It struck me pretty forcibly that I should have taken fighting lessons from him instead of from poor Romany. I went away and walked about four miles down the river road, getting out of the way into the Bush whenever I saw any chap riding along. I thought of poor Romany and wondered where he was, and thought that there wasn't much to choose between us as far as happiness was concerned. Perhaps he was walking by himself in the Bush, and feeling like I did. I wished I could shake hands with him.

But somehow, about half-past ten, I drifted back to the river sliprails and leant over them, in the shadow of the peppermint-tree, looking at the rows of river-willows in the moonlight. I didn't expect anything, in spite of what Jack said.

I didn't like the idea of hanging myself: I'd been with a party who found a man hanging in the Bush, and it was no place for a woman round where he was. And I'd helped drag two bodies out of the Cudgegong River in a flood, and they weren't sleeping beauties. I thought it was a pity that a chap couldn't lie down on a grassy bank in a graceful position in the moonlight and die just by thinking of it – and die with his eyes and mouth shut. But then I remembered that I wouldn't make a beautiful corpse, any way it went, with the face I had on me.

I was just getting comfortably miserable when I heard a step behind me, and my heart gave a jump. And I gave a start, too.

'Oh, is that you, Mr Wilson?' said a timid little voice.

'Yes,' I said. 'Is that you, Mary?'

And she said yes. It was the first time I called her Mary, but she did not seem to notice it.

'Did I frighten you?' I asked.

'No – yes – just a little,' she said. 'I didn't know there was any one – ' then she stopped.

'Why aren't you dancing?' I asked her.

'Oh, I'm tired,' she said. 'It was too hot in the wool-shed. I thought

I'd like to come out, and get my head cool and be quiet a little while.'

'Yes,' I said. 'It must be hot in the wool-shed.'

She stood looking out over the willows. Presently she said: 'It must be very dull for you, Mr Wilson – you must feel lonely. Mr Barnes said – ' Then she gave a little gasp and stopped – as if she was just going to put her foot in it.

'How beautiful the moonlight looks on the willows!' she said.

'Yes,' I said, 'doesn't it? Supposing we have a stroll by the river.'

'Oh, thank you, Mr Wilson. I'd like it very much.'

I didn't notice it then, but, now I come to think of it, it was a beautiful scene: there was a horse-shoe of high blue hills round behind the house, with the river running round under the slopes, and in front was a rounded hill covered with pines, and pine ridges, and a soft blue peak away over the ridges ever so far in the distance.

I had a handkerchief over the worst of my face, and kept the best side turned to her. We walked down by the river, and didn't say anything for a good while. I was thinking hard. We came to a white smooth log in a quiet place out of sight of the house.

'Suppose we sit down for a while, Mary,' I said.

'If you like, Mr Wilson,' she said.

There was about a foot of log between us.

'What a beautiful night!' she said.

'Yes,' I said, 'isn't it?'

Presently she said, 'I suppose you know I'm going away next month, Mr Wilson?'

I felt suddenly empty. 'No,' I said, 'I didn't know that.'

'Yes,' she said, 'I thought you knew. I'm going to try to get into the hospital to be trained for a nurse, and if that doesn't come off I'll get a place as assistant public-school teacher.'

We didn't say anything for a good while.

'I suppose you won't be sorry to go, Miss Brand?' I said.

'I – I don't know,' she said. 'Everybody's been so kind to me here.'

She sat looking straight before her, and I fancied her eyes glistened. I put my arm round her shoulders, but she didn't seem to notice it. In fact, I scarcely noticed it myself at the time.

'So you think you'll be sorry to go away?' I said.

'Yes, Mr Wilson. I suppose I'll fret for a while. It's been my home, you know.'

I pressed my hand on her shoulder, just a little, so she couldn't pretend not to know it was there. But she didn't seem to notice.

'Ah, well,' I said. 'I suppose I'll be on the wallaby again next week.'

'Will you, Mr Wilson?' she said. Her voice seemed very soft.

I slipped my arm round her waist, under her arm. My heart was going like clockwork now.

Presently she said:

'Don't you think it's time to go back now, Mr Wilson?'

'Oh, there's plenty of time!' I said. I shifted up, and put my arm further round, and held her closer. She sat straight up, looking right in front of her, but she began to breathe hard.

'Mary,' I said.

'Yes,' she said.

'Call me Joe,' I said.

'I – I don't like to,' she said. 'I don't think it would be right.'

So I just turned her face round and kissed her. She clung to me and cried.

'What is it, Mary?' I said.

She only held me tighter and cried.

'What is it, Mary?' I said. 'Ain't you well? Ain't you happy?'

'Yes, Joe,' she said, 'I'm very happy.' Then she said, 'Oh, your poor face! Can't I do anything for it?'

'No,' I said. 'That's all right. My face doesn't hurt me a bit now.'

But she didn't seem right.

'What is it, Mary?' I said. 'Are you tired? You didn't sleep last night – ' Then I got an inspiration.

'Mary,' I said. 'what were you doing out with the gun this morning?'

And after some coaxing it all came out, a bit hysterical.

'I couldn't sleep – I was frightened. Oh! I had such a terrible dream about you, Joe! I thought Romany came back and got into your room and stabbed you with his knife. I got up and dressed, and about daybreak I heard a horse at the gate; then I got the gun down from the wall – and – and Mr Barnes came round the corner and frightened me. He's something like Romany, you know.'

Then I got as much of her as I could into my arms.

And, oh, but wasn't I happy walking home with Mary that night! She was too little for me to put my arm round her waist, so I put it round her shoulder, and that felt just as good. I remember I asked her who'd cleaned up my room and washed my things, but she wouldn't tell.

She wouldn't go back to the dance yet; she said she'd go into her room and rest a while. There was no one near the old veranda; and when she stood on the end of the floor she was just on a level with my shoulder.

'Mary,' I whispered, 'put your arms round my neck and kiss me.'

She put her arms round my neck, but she didn't kiss me; she only hid her face.

'Kiss me, Mary!' I said.

'I – I don't like to,' she whispered.

'Why not, Mary?'

Then I felt her crying or laughing, or half-crying and half-laughing. I'm not sure to this day which it was.

'Why won't you kiss me, Mary? Don't you love me?'

'Because,' she said, 'because – because I – I don't – I don't think it's right for – for a girl to – to kiss a man unless she's going to be his wife.'

Then it dawned on me! I'd forgot all about proposing.

'Mary,' I said, 'would you marry a chap like me?'

And that was all right.

Next morning Mary cleared out my room and sorted out my things, and didn't take the slightest notice of the other girls' astonishment.

But she made me promise to speak to old Black, and I did the same evening. I found him sitting on the log by the fence, having a yarn on the quiet with an old Bushman; and when the old Bushman got up and went away, I sat down.

'Well, Joe,' said Black, 'I see somebody's been spoiling your face for the dance.' And after a bit he said, 'Well, Joe, what is it? Do you want another job? If you do, you'll have to ask Mrs Black, or Bob' (Bob was his eldest son); 'they're managing the station for me now, you know.' He could be bitter sometimes in his quiet way.

'No,' I said; 'it's not that, Boss.'

'Well, what is it, Joe?'

'I – well, the fact is, I want little Mary.'

He puffed at his pipe for a long time, then I thought he spoke.

'What did you say, Boss?' I said.

'Nothing, Joe,' he said. 'I was going to say a lot, but it wouldn't be any use. My father used to say a lot to me before I was married.'

I waited a good while for him to speak.

'Well, Boss,' I said, 'what about Mary?'

'Oh! I suppose that's all right, Joe,' he said. 'I – I beg your pardon. I got thinking of the days when I was courting Mrs Black.'

TELLING MRS BAKER

Most Bushmen who hadn't 'known Bob Baker to speak to', had 'heard tell of him'. He'd been a squatter, not many years before, on the Macquarie River in New South Wales, and had made money in the good seasons, and had gone in for horse-racing and racehorse-breeding, and long trips to Sydney, where he put up at swell hotels and went the pace. So after a pretty severe drought, when the sheep died by thousands on his runs, Bob Baker went under, and the bank took over his station and put a manager in charge.

He'd been a jolly, open-handed, popular man, which means that he'd been a selfish man as far as his wife and children were concerned, for they had to suffer for it in the end. Such generosity is often born of vanity, or moral cowardice, or both mixed. It's very nice to hear the chaps sing 'For he's a jolly good fellow', but you've mostly got to pay for it twice – first in company, and afterwards alone. I once heard the chaps singing that I was a jolly good fellow, when I was leaving a place and they were giving me a send-off. It thrilled me, and brought a warm gush to my eyes; but, all the same, I wished I had half the money I'd lent them, and spent on 'em, and I wished I'd used the time I'd wasted to be a jolly good fellow.

When I first met Bob Baker he was a boss-drover on the great north-western route, and his wife lived at the township of Solong on the Sydney side. He was going north to new country round by the Gulf of Carpentaria with a big mob of cattle, on a two years' trip; and I and my mate, Andy M'Culloch, engaged to go with him. We wanted to have a look at the Gulf Country.

After we had crossed the Queensland border it seemed to me that the

Boss was too fond of going into wayside shanties and town pubs. Andy had been with him on another trip, and he told me that the Boss was only going this way lately. Andy knew Mrs Baker well, and seemed to think a deal of her. 'She's a good little woman,' said Andy. 'One of the right stuff. I worked on their station for a while when I was a nipper, and I know. She was always a damned sight too good for the Boss, but she believed in him. When I was coming away this time she says to me, 'Look here, Andy, I am afraid Robert is drinking again. Now I want you to look after him for me, as much as you can – you seem to have as much influence with him as anyone. I want you to promise me that you'll never have a drink with him.'

'And I promised,' said Andy, 'and I'll keep my word.' Andy was a chap who could keep his word, and nothing else. And, no matter how the Boss persuaded, or sneered, or swore at him, Andy would never drink with him.

It got worse and worse: the Boss would ride on ahead and get drunk at a shanty, and sometimes he'd be days behind us; and when he'd catch up to us his temper would be just about as much as we could stand. At last he went on a howling spree at Mulgatown, about a hundred and fifty miles north of the border, and, what was worse, he got in tow with a flash barmaid there – one of those girls who are engaged, by the publicans up-country, as baits for chequemen.

He went mad over that girl. He drew an advance cheque from the stock-owner's agent there, and knocked that down; then he raised some more money somehow, and spent that – mostly on the girl.

We did all we could. Andy got him along the track for a couple of stages, and just when we thought he was all right, he slipped us in the night and went back.

We had two other men with us, but had the devil's own bother on account of the cattle. It was a mixed-up job all round. You see it was all big runs round there, and we had to keep the bullocks moving along the route all the time, or else get into trouble for trespass. The agent wasn't going to go to the expense of putting the cattle in a paddock until the Boss sobered up; there was very little grass on the route or the travel-ling-stock reserves or camps, so we had to keep travelling for grass.

The world might wobble and all the banks go bung, but the cattle have to go through – that's the law of the stock-routes. So the agent wired to the owners, and, when he got their reply, he sacked the Boss and sent the cattle on in charge of another man. The new Boss was a drover coming south after a trip; he had his two brothers with him, so he didn't want me and Andy; but anyway, we were full up of this trip, so we arranged, between the agent and the new Boss, to get most of the wages due to us – the Boss had drawn some of our stuff and spent it.

We could have started on the back track at once, but, drunk or sober, mad or sane, good or bad, it isn't Bush religion to desert a mate in a hole; and the Boss was a mate of ours; so we stuck to him.

We camped on the creek, outside the town, and kept him in the camp with us as much as possible, and did all we could for him.

'How could I face his wife if I went home without him?' asked Andy, 'or any of his old mates?'

The Boss got himself turned out of the pub where the barmaid was, and then he'd hang round the other pubs, and get drink somehow, and fight, and get knocked about. He was an awful object by this time, wild-eyed and gaunt, and he hadn't washed or shaved for days.

Andy got the constable in charge of the police station to lock him up for a night, but it only made him worse: we took him back to the camp next morning, and while our eyes were off him for a few minutes he slipped away into the scrub, stripped himself naked, and started to hang himself to a leaning tree with a piece of clothes-line rope. We got to him just in time.

Then Andy wired to the Boss's brother Ned, who was fighting the drought, the rabbit-pest, and the banks, on a small station back on the border. Andy reckoned it was about time to do something.

Perhaps the Boss hadn't been quite right in his head before he started drinking – he had acted queer sometimes, now we came to think of it; maybe he'd got a touch of sunstroke or got brooding over his troubles – anyway he died in the horrors within the week.

His brother Ned turned up on the last day, and Bob thought he was the devil, and grappled with him. It took the three of us to hold the Boss down sometimes.

Sometimes, towards the end, he'd be sensible for a few minutes and talk about his 'poor wife and children'; and immediately afterwards he'd fall a-cursing me, and Andy, and Ned, and calling us devils. He cursed everything; he cursed his wife and children, and yelled that they were dragging him down to hell. He died raving mad. It was the worst case of death in the horrors of drink that I ever saw or heard of in the Bush.

Ned saw to the funeral: it was very hot weather, and men have to be buried quick who die out there in the hot weather – especially men who die in the state the Boss was in. Then Ned went to the public-house where the barmaid was and called the landlord out. It was a desperate fight: the publican was a big man, and a bit of a fighting man; but Ned was one of those quiet, simple-minded chaps who will carry a thing through to death when they make up their minds. He gave that publican nearly as good a thrashing as he deserved. The constable in charge of the station backed Ned, while another policeman picked up the publican. Sounds queer to you city people, doesn't it?

Next morning we three started south. We stayed a couple of days at Ned Baker's station on the border, and then started on our three-hundred-mile ride down-country. The weather was still very hot, so we decided to travel at night for a while, and left Ned's place at dusk. He parted from us at the homestead gate. He gave Andy a small packet, done up in canvas, for Mrs Baker, which Andy told me contained Bob's pocket-book, letters, and papers. We looked back, after we'd gone a piece along the dusty road, and saw Ned still standing by the gate; and a very lonely figure he looked. Ned was a bachelor. 'Poor old Ned,' said Andy to me. 'He was in love with Mrs Bob Baker before she got married, but she picked the wrong man – girls mostly do. Ned and Bob were together on the Macquarie, but Ned left when his brother married, and he's been up in these God-forsaken scrubs ever since. Look, I want to tell you something, Jack: Ned has written to Mrs Bob to tell her that Bob died of fever, and everything was done for him that could be done, and that he died easy – and all that sort of thing. Ned sent her some money, and she is to think it was the money due to Bob when he died. Now I'll have to go and see her when we get to Solong; there's no getting out of it, I'll have to face her – and you'll have to come with me.'

'Damned if I will!' I said.

'But you'll have to,' said Andy. 'You'll have to stick to me; you're surely not crawler enough to desert a mate in a case like this? I'll have to lie like hell – I'll have to lie as I never lied to a woman before; and you'll have to back me and corroborate every lie.'

I'd never seen Andy show so much emotion.

'There's plenty of time to fix up a good yarn,' said Andy. He said no more about Mrs Baker, and we only mentioned the Boss's name casually, until we were within about a day's ride of Solong; then Andy told me the yarn he'd made up about the Boss's death.

'And I want you to listen, Jack,' he said, 'and remember every word – and if you can fix up a better yarn you can tell me afterwards. Now it was like this: the Boss wasn't too well when he crossed the border. He complained of pains in his back and head and a stinging pain in the back of his neck, and he had dysentery bad – but that doesn't matter; it's lucky I ain't supposed to tell a woman all the symptoms. The Boss stuck to the job as long as he could, but we managed the cattle and made it as easy as we could for him. He'd just take it easy, and ride on from camp to camp, and rest. One night I rode to a town off the route (or you did, if you like) and got some medicine for him; that made him better for a while, but at last, a day or two this side of Mulgatown, he had to give up. A squatter there drove him into town in his buggy and put him up at the best hotel. The publican knew the Boss and did all he could for him – put him in the best room and wired for another doctor. We wired for Ned as soon as we saw how bad the Boss was, and Ned rode night and day and got there three days before the Boss died. The Boss was a bit off his head some of the time with the fever, but was calm and quiet towards the end and died easy. He talked a lot about his wife and children, and told us to tell the wife not to fret but to cheer up for the children's sake. How does that sound?'

I'd been thinking while I listened, and an idea struck me.

'Why not let her know the truth?' I asked. 'She's sure to hear of it sooner or later; and if she knew he was only a selfish, drunken black-guard she might get over it all the sooner.'

'You don't know women, Jack,' said Andy quietly. 'And, anyway, even if she is a sensible woman, we've got a dead mate to consider as well as a living woman.'

'But she's sure to hear the truth sooner or later,' I said. 'The Boss was so well known.'

'And that's just the reason why the truth might be kept from her,' said Andy. 'If he wasn't well known – and nobody could help liking him, after all, when he was straight – if he wasn't so well known the truth might leak out unawares. She won't know if I can help it, or at least not yet a while. If I see any chaps that come from the North, I'll put them up to it. I'll tell M'Grath, the publican at Solong, too: he's a straight man – he'll keep his ears open and warn chaps. One of Mrs Baker's sisters is staying with her, and I'll give her a hint so that she can warn off any women that might get hold of a yarn. Besides, Mrs Baker is sure to go and live in Sydney, where all her people are – she was a Sydney girl; and she's not likely to meet anyone there that will tell her the truth. I can tell her that it was the last wish of the Boss that she should shift to Sydney.'

We smoked and thought a while, and by-and-by Andy had what he called a 'happy thought'. He went to his saddle-bags and got out the small canvas packet that Ned had given him: it was sewn up with packing-thread, and Andy ripped it open with his pocket-knife.

'What are you doing, Andy?' I asked.

'Ned's an innocent old fool, as far as sin is concerned,' said Andy. 'I guess he hasn't looked through the Boss's letters, and I'm just going to see that there's nothing here that will make liars of us.'

He looked through the letters and papers by the light of the fire. There were some letters from Mrs Baker to her husband, also a portrait of her and the children; these Andy put aside. But there were other letters from barmaids and women who were not fit to be seen in the same street with the Boss's wife; and there were portraits – one or two flash ones. There were two letters from other men's wives too.

'And one of those men, at least, was an old mate of his!' said Andy, in a tone of disgust.

He threw the lot into the fire; then he went through the Boss's pocket-book and tore out some leaves that had notes and addresses on them, and burnt them too. Then he sewed up the packet again and put it away in his saddle-bag.

'Such is life!' said Andy, with a yawn that might have been half a sigh.

We rode into Solong early in the day, turned our horses out in a paddock, and put up at M'Grath's pub until such time as we made up our minds as to what we'd do or where we'd go. We had an idea of waiting until the shearing season started and then making Out-Back to the big sheds.

Neither of us was in a hurry to go and face Mrs Baker. 'We'll go after dinner,' said Andy at first; then after dinner we had a drink, and felt sleepy – we weren't used to big dinners of roast-beef and vegetables and pudding, and, besides, it was drowsy weather – so we decided to have a snooze and then go. When we woke up it was late in the afternoon, so we thought we'd put it off until after tea. 'It wouldn't be manners to walk in while they're at tea,' said Andy – 'it would look as if we only came for some grub.'

But while we were at tea a little girl came with a message that Mrs Baker wanted to see us, and would be very much obliged if we'd call up as soon as possible. You see, in those small towns you can't move without the thing getting round inside of half an hour.

'We'll have to face the music now!' said Andy, 'and no get out of it.' He seemed to hang back more than I did. There was another pub opposite where Mrs Baker lived, and when we got up the street a bit I said to Andy:

'Suppose we go and have another drink first, Andy? We might be kept in there an hour or two.'

'You don't want another drink,' said Andy, rather short. 'Why, you seem to be going the same way as the Boss!' But it was Andy who edged off towards the pub, when we got near Mrs Baker's place. 'All right!' he said. 'Come on! We'll have this other drink, since you want it so bad.'

We had the drink, then we buttoned up our coats and started across the road – we'd bought new shirts and collars, and spruced up a bit. Halfway across Andy grabbed my arm and asked:

'How do you feel now, Jack?'

'Oh, *I'm* all right,' I said.

'For God's sake,' said Andy, 'don't put your foot in it and make a mess of it.'

'I won't, if you don't.'

Mrs Baker's cottage was a little weather-board box affair back in a garden. When we went in through the gate Andy gripped my arm again and whispered:

'For God's sake, stick to me now, Jack!'

'I'll stick all right,' I said – 'you've been having too much beer, Andy.'

I had seen Mrs Baker before, and remembered her as a cheerful, contented sort of woman, bustling about the house and getting the Boss's shirts and things ready when we started North. Just the sort of woman that is contented with housework and the children, and with nothing particular about her in the way of brains. But now she sat by the fire looking like the ghost of herself. I wouldn't have recognised her at first. I never saw such a change in a woman, and it came like a shock to me.

Her sister let us in, and after a first glance at Mrs Baker I had eyes for the sister and no one else. She was a Sydney girl, about twenty-four or twenty-five, and fresh and fair – not like the sun-browned women we were used to see. She was a pretty, bright-eyed girl, and seemed quick to understand, and very sympathetic. She had been educated, Andy had told me, and wrote stories for the Sydney *Bulletin* and other Sydney papers. She had her hair done and was dressed in the city style, and that took us back a bit at first.

'It's very good of you to come,' said Mrs Baker in a weak, weary voice, when we first went in, 'I heard you were in town.'

'We were just coming when we got your message,' said Andy. 'We'd have come before, only we had to see to the horses.'

'It's very kind of you, I'm sure,' said Mrs Baker.

They wanted us to have tea, but we said we'd just had it. Then Miss Standish (the sister) wanted us to have tea and cake; but we didn't feel as if we could handle cups and saucers and pieces of cake successfully just then.

There was something the matter with one of the children in a back room, and the sister went to see to it. Mrs Baker cried a little quietly.

'You mustn't mind me,' she said. 'I'll be all right presently, and then I want you to tell me all about poor Bob. It's seeing you, that saw the last of him, that set me off.'

Andy and I sat stiff and straight, on two chairs against the wall, and held our hats tight, and stared at a picture of Wellington meeting Blücher on the opposite wall. I thought it was lucky that that picture was there.

The child was calling 'mumma,' and Mrs Baker went in to it, and her sister came out. 'Best tell her all about it and get it over,' she whispered to Andy. 'She'll never be content until she hears all about poor Bob from someone who was with him when he died. Let me take your hats. Make yourselves comfortable.'

She took the hats and put them on the sewing-machine. I wished she'd let us keep them, for now we had nothing to hold on to, and nothing to do with our hands; and as for being comfortable, we were just about as comfortable as two cats on wet bricks.

When Mrs Baker came into the room she brought little Bobby Baker, about four years old; he wanted to see Andy. He ran to Andy at once, and Andy took him up on his knee. He was a pretty child, but he reminded me too much of his father.

'I'm so glad you've come, Andy!' said Bobby.

'Are you, Bobby?'

'Yes. I wants to ask you about daddy. You saw him go away, didn't you?' and he fixed his great wondering eyes on Andy's face.

'Yes,' said Andy.

'He went up among the stars, didn't he?'

'Yes,' said Andy.

'And he isn't coming back to Bobby any more?'

'No,' said Andy. 'But Bobby's going to him by-and-by.'

Mrs Baker had been leaning back in her chair, resting her head on her hand, tears glistening in her eyes; now she began to sob, and her sister took her out of the room.

Andy looked miserable. 'I wish to God I was off this job!' he whispered to me.

'Is that the girl that writes the stories?' I asked.

'Yes,' he said, staring at me in a hopeless sort of way, 'and poems too.'

'Is Bobby going up amongst the stars?' asked Bobby.

'Yes,' said Andy – 'if Bobby's good.'

'And auntie?'

'Yes.'

'And mumma?'

'Yes.'

'Are you going, Andy?'

'Yes,' said Andy, hopelessly.

'Did you see daddy go up amongst the stars, Andy?'

'Yes,' said Andy, 'I saw him go up.'

'And he isn't coming down again any more?'

'No,' said Andy.

'Why isn't he?'

'Because he's going to wait up there for you and mumma, Bobby.'

There was a long pause, and then Bobby asked:

'Are you going to give me a shilling, Andy?' with the same expression of innocent wonder in his eyes.

Andy slipped half-a-crown into his hand. 'Auntie' came in and told him he'd see Andy in the morning and took him away to bed, after he'd kissed us both solemnly; and presently she and Mrs Baker settled down to hear Andy's story.

'Brace up now, Jack, and keep your wits about you,' whispered Andy to me just before they came in.

'Poor Bob's brother Ned wrote to me,' said Mrs Baker, 'but he scarcely told me anything. Ned's a good fellow, but he's very simple, and never thinks of anything.'

Andy told her about the Boss not being well after he crossed the border.

'I knew he was not well,' said Mrs Baker, 'before he left. I didn't want him to go. I tried hard to persuade him not to go this trip. I had a feeling that I oughtn't to let him go. But he'd never think of anything but me and the children. He promised he'd give up droving after this trip, and get something to do near home. The life was too much for him – riding in all weathers and camping out in the rain, and living like a dog. But he was never content at home. It was all for the sake of me and the children. He wanted to make money and start on a station again. I shouldn't have let him go. He only thought of me and the children! Oh! my poor, dear, kind, dead husband!' She broke down again and sobbed, and her sister comforted her, while Andy and I stared at Wellington meeting Blücher on the field at Waterloo. I thought the artist had heaped up the dead a bit extra, and I thought that I wouldn't like to be trod on by horses even if I was dead.

'Don't you mind,' said Miss Standish, 'she'll be all right presently,' and she handed us the *Illustrated Sydney Journal*. This was a great relief – we bumped our heads over the pictures.

Mrs Baker made Andy go on again, and he told her how the Boss broke down near Mulgatown. Mrs Baker was opposite him and Miss Standish opposite me. Both of them kept their eyes on Andy's face: he sat, with his hair straight up like a brush as usual, and kept his big innocent grey eyes fixed on Mrs Baker's face all the time he was speaking. I watched Miss Standish. I thought she was the prettiest girl I'd ever seen; it was a bad case of love at first sight, but she was far and away above me, and the case was hopeless. I began to feel pretty miserable, and to think back into the past; I just heard Andy droning away by my side.

'So we fixed him up comfortable in the wagonette with the blankets and coats and things,' Andy was saying, 'and the squatter started into Mulgatown ... It was about thirty miles, Jack, wasn't it?' he asked, turning suddenly to me. He always looked so innocent that there were times when I itched to knock him down.

'More like thirty-five,' I said, waking up.

Miss Standish fixed her eyes on me, and I had another look at Wellington and Blücher.

'They were all very good and kind to the Boss,' said Andy. 'They thought a lot of him up there. Everybody was fond of him.'

'I know it,' said Mrs Baker. 'Nobody could help liking him. He was one of the kindest men that ever lived.'

'Tanner, the publican, couldn't have been kinder to his own brother,' said Andy. 'The local doctor was a decent chap, but he was only a young fellow, and Tanner hadn't much faith in him, so he wired for an older doctor at Mackintyre, and he even sent out fresh horses to meet the doctor's buggy. Everything was done that could be done, I assure you, Mrs Baker.'

'I believe it,' said Mrs Baker. 'And you don't know how it relieves me to hear it. And did the publican do all this at his own expense?'

'He wouldn't take a penny, Mrs Baker.'

'He must have been a good true man. I wish I could thank him.'

'Oh, Ned thanked him for you,' said Andy, though without meaning more than he said.

'I wouldn't have fancied that Ned would have thought of that,' said Mrs Baker. 'When I first heard of my poor husband's death, I thought perhaps he'd been drinking again – that worried me a bit.'

'He never touched a drop after he left Solong, I can assure you, Mrs Baker,' said Andy quickly.

Now I noticed that Miss Standish seemed surprised or puzzled, once or twice, while Andy was speaking, and leaned forward to listen to him; then she leaned back in her chair and clasped her hands behind her head and looked at him, with half-shut eyes, in a way I didn't like. Once or twice she looked at me as if she was going to ask me a question, but I always looked away quick and stared at Blücher and Wellington, or into the empty fire-place, till I felt her eyes were off me. Then she asked Andy a question or two, in all innocence I believe now, but it scared him, and at last he watched his chance and winked at her sharp. Then she gave a little gasp and shut up like a steel trap.

The sick child in the bedroom coughed and cried again. Mrs Baker went to it. We three sat like a deaf-and-dumb institution, Andy and I staring all over the place: presently Miss Standish excused herself, and went out of the room after her sister. She looked hard at Andy as she left the room, but he kept his eyes away.

'Brace up now, Jack,' whispered Andy to me, 'the worst is coming.'

When they came in again Mrs Baker made Andy go on with his story.

'He – he died very quietly,' said Andy, hitching round, and resting his elbows on his knees, and looking into the fire-place so as to have his face away from the light. Miss Standish put her arm round her sister. 'He died very easy,' said Andy. 'He was a bit off his head at times, but that was while the fever was on him. He didn't suffer much towards the end – I don't think he suffered at all . . . He talked a lot about you and the children.' (Andy was speaking very softly now.) 'He said that you were not to fret, but to cheer up for the children's sake . . . It was the biggest funeral ever seen round there.'

Mrs Baker was crying softly. Andy got the packet half-out of his pocket, but shoved it back again.

'The only thing that hurts me now,' said Mrs Baker presently, 'is to think of my poor husband buried out there in the lonely Bush, so far from home. It's – cruel!' and she was sobbing again.

'Oh, that's all right, Mrs Baker,' said Andy, losing his head a little. 'Ned will see to that. Ned is going to arrange to have him brought down and buried in Sydney.' Which was about the first thing Andy had told her that evening that wasn't a lie. Ned had said he would do it as soon as he sold his wool.

'It's very kind indeed of Ned,' sobbed Mrs Baker. 'I'd never have dreamed he was so kind-hearted and thoughtful. I misjudged him all along. And that is all you have to tell me about poor Robert?'

'Yes,' said Andy – then one of his 'happy thoughts' struck him. 'Except that he hoped you'd shift to Sydney, Mrs Baker, where you've got friends and relations. He thought it would be better for you and the children. He told me to tell you that.'

'He was thoughtful up to the end,' said Mrs Baker. 'It was just like poor Robert – always thinking of me and the children. We are going to Sydney next week.'

Andy looked relieved. We talked a little more, and Miss Standish wanted to make coffee for us, but we had to go and see to our horses. We got up and bumped against each other, and got each other's hats, and promised Mrs Baker we'd come again.

'Thank you very much for coming,' she said, shaking hands with us. 'I feel so much better now. You don't know how much you have relieved me. Now, mind, you have promised to come and see me again for the last time.'

Andy caught her sister's eye and jerked his head towards the door to let her know he wanted to speak to her outside.

'Good-bye, Mrs Baker,' he said, holding on to her hand. 'And don't you fret. You've – you've got the children yet. It's – it's all for the best; and, besides, the Boss said you wasn't to fret.' And he blundered out after me and Miss Standish.

She came out to the gate with us, and Andy gave her the packet.

'I want you to give that to her,' he said: 'it's his letters and papers. I hadn't the heart to give it to her, somehow.'

'Tell me, Mr M'Culloch,' she said. 'You've kept something back – you haven't told her the truth. It would be better and safer for me to know. Was it an accident – or the drink?'

'It was the drink,' said Andy. 'I was going to tell you – I thought it would be best to tell you. I had made up my mind to do it, but, some-how, I couldn't have done it if you hadn't asked me.'

'Tell me all,' she said. 'It would be better for me to know.'

'Come a little farther away from the house,' said Andy. She came along the fence a piece with us, and Andy told her as much of the truth as he could.

'I'll hurry her off to Sydney,' she said. 'We can get away this week as well as next.' Then she stood for a minute before us, breathing quickly, her hands behind her back and her eyes shining in the moonlight. She looked splendid.

'I want to thank you for her sake,' she said quickly. 'You are good men! I like the Bushmen! They are grand men – they are noble. I'll probably never see either of you again, so it doesn't matter,' and she put her white hand on Andy's shoulder and kissed him fair and square on the mouth. 'And you, too!' she said to me. I was taller than Andy, and had to stoop. 'Good-bye!' she said, and ran to the gate and in, waving her hand to us. We lifted our hats again and turned down the road.

I don't think it did either of us any harm.

VI

A CHILD IN THE DARK, AND A FOREIGN FATHER

A Child in the Dark, and
a Foreign Father

NEW Year's Eve! A hot night in midsummer in the drought. It was so dark – with a smothering darkness – that even the low loom of the scrub-covered ridges, close at hand across the creek, was not to be seen. The sky was not clouded for rain, but with drought haze and the smoke of distant bush fires.

Down the hard road to the crossing at Pipeclay Creek sounded the footsteps of a man. Not the crunching steps of an English labourer, clod-hopping contentedly home; these sounded more like the footsteps of one pacing steadily to and fro, and thinking steadily and hopelessly – sorting out the past. Only the steps went on. A glimmer of white mole-skin trousers and a suggestion of light-coloured tweed jacket, now and again, as if in the glimmer of a faint ghost light in the darkness.

The road ran along by the foot of a line of low ridges, or spurs, and, as he passed the gullies or gaps, he felt a breath of hotter air, like blasts from a furnace in the suffocating atmosphere. He followed a two-railed fence for a short distance, and turned in at a white batten gate. It seemed lighter now. There was a house, or, rather, a hut suggested, with whitewashed slab walls and a bark roof. He walked quietly round to the door of a detached kitchen, opened it softly, went in, and struck a match. A candle stood, stuck in a blot of its own grease, on one end of the dresser. He lit the candle and looked round.

The walls of the kitchen were of split slabs, the roof box-bark, the floor clay, and there was a large, clay-lined fireplace, the sides a dirty brown, and the back black. It had evidently never been whitewashed. There was a bed of about a week's ashes, and above it, suspended by a blackened hook and chain from a grimy crossbar, hung a black bucket full of warm water. The man got a fork, explored the bucket, and found what he expected: a piece of raw corned beef in water which had gone off the boil before the meat had been heated through.

The kitchen was furnished with a pine table, a well-made flour bin, and a neat safe and side-board, or dresser – evidently the work of a carpenter. The top of the safe was dirty – covered with crumbs and grease and tea stains. On one corner lay a school exercise book, with a stone ink-bottle and a pen beside it. The book was open at a page written in the form of verse, in a woman's hand, and headed:

'MISUNDERSTOOD'

He took the edges of the book between his fingers and thumbs, and made to tear it, but, the cover being tough, and resisting the first savage tug, he altered his mind, and put the book down. Then he turned to the table. There was a jumble of dirty crockery on one end, and on the other, set on a sheet of stained newspaper, the remains of a meal – a junk of badly-hacked bread, a basin of dripping (with the fat over the edges), and a tin of treacle. The treacle had run down the sides of the tin on to the paper. Knives, heavy with treacle, lay glued to the paper. There was a dish with some water, a rag, and a cup or two in it – evidently an attempt to wash up.

The man took up a cup and pressed it hard between his palms, until it broke. Then he felt relieved. He gathered the fragments in one hand, took the candle, and stumbled out to where there was a dustheap. Kicking a hole in the ashes, he dropped in the bits of broken crockery, and covered them. Then his anger blazed again. He walked quickly to the back door of the house, thrust the door open, and flung in, but a child's voice said from the dark:

'Is that you, father? Don't tread on me, father.'

The room was nearly as bare as the kitchen. There was a table, covered with cheap American oilcloth, and, on the other side, a sofa on which a straw mattress, a cloudy blanket, and a pillow without a slip had been thrown in a heap. On the floor, between the sofa and the table, lay a boy – child almost – on a similar mattress, with a cover of coarse sacking, and a bundle of dirty clothes for a pillow. A pale, thin-faced, dark-eyed boy.

'What are you doing here, sonny?' asked the father.

'Mother's bad again with her head. She says to tell you to come in quiet, and sleep on the sofa to-night. I started to wash up and clean up the kitchen, father, but I got sick.'

'Why, what is the matter with you, sonny?' His voice quickened, and he held the candle down to the child's face.

'Oh, nothing much, father. I felt sick, but I feel better now.'

'What have you been eating?'

'Nothing that I know of; I think it was the hot weather, father.'

The father spread the mattress, blew out the candle, and lay down in his clothes. After a while the boy began to toss restlessly.

'Oh, it's too hot, father,' he said. 'I'm smothering.'

The father got up, lit the candle, took a corner of the newspaper-covered 'scrim' lining that screened the cracks of the slab wall, and tore it away; then he propped open the door with a chair.

'Oh, that's better already, father,' said the boy.

The hut was three rooms long and one deep, with a veranda in front and a skillion harness and tool room, about half the length, behind. The father opened the door of the next room softly, and propped that open too. There was another boy on the sofa, younger than the first, but healthy and sturdy-looking. He had nothing on him but a very dirty shirt. A patchwork quilt was slipping from under him, and most of it was on the floor; the boy and the pillow were nearly off, too.

The father fixed him as comfortably as possible and put some chairs by the sofa to keep him from rolling off. He noticed that somebody had started to scrub this room, and left it. He listened at the door of the third room for a few moments to the breathing within; then he opened it gently and walked in. There was an old-fashioned four-poster cedar bedstead, a chest of drawers, and a baby's cradle made out of a gin-case. The woman was fast asleep. She was a big, strong, and healthy-looking woman with dark hair and strong, square features. There was a plate, a knife and fork, and egg-shells and a cup and saucer on the top of the chest of drawers; also two candles, one stuck in a mustard tin, and one in a pickle bottle, and a copy of *Ardath*.

He stepped out into the skillion and lifted some harness on to its pegs from chaff-bags in the corner. Coming in again, he nearly stumbled over a bucket half-full of dirty water on the floor, with a scrubbing-brush, some wet rags, and half a bar of yellow soap beside it. He put these things in the bucket, and carried it out. As he passed through the first room the sick boy said:

'I couldn't lift the saddle of the harness on to the peg, father. I had to leave the scrubbing to make some tea and cook some eggs for mother, and put baby to bed, and then I felt too bad to go on with the scrubbing – and I forgot about the bucket.'

'Did the baby have any tea, sonny?'

'Yes. I made her bread and milk, and she ate a big plateful. The calves are in the pen all right, and I fixed the gate. And I brought a load of wood this morning, father, before mother took bad.'

'You should not have done that. I told you not to. I could have done that on Sunday. Now, are you sure you didn't lift a log into the cart that was too heavy for you?'

'Quite sure, father. Oh, I'm plenty strong enough to put a load of wood on the cart.'

The father lay on his back on the sofa, with his hands behind his head, for a few minutes.

'Aren't you tired, father?' asked the boy.

'No, sonny, not very tired; you must try and go to sleep now,' and he reached across the table for the candle and blew it out.

Presently the baby cried, and in a moment the mother's voice was heard.

'Nils! Nils! Are you there, Nils?'

'Yes, Emma.'

'Then for God's sake come and take this child away before she drives me mad! My head's splitting!'

The father went in to the child and presently returned for a cup of water.

'She only wanted a drink,' the boy heard him say to the mother.

'Well, didn't I tell you she wanted a drink? I've been calling for the last half-hour, with that child screaming and not a soul to come near me, and me lying here helpless all day and not a wink of sleep for two nights.'

'But, Emma, you were asleep when I came in.'

'How can you tell such infernal lies? I –. To think I'm chained to a man who can't say a word of truth! God help me! To have to lie night after night in the same bed with a liar!'

The child in the first room lay quaking with terror, dreading one of those cruel and shameful scenes which had made a hell of his childhood.

'Hush, Emma!' the man kept saying. 'Do be reasonable. Think of the children. They'll hear us.'

'I don't care if they do. They'll know soon enough, God knows! I wish I was under the turf!'

'Emma, do be reasonable.'

'Reasonable! I – '

The child was crying again. The father came back to the first room, got something from his pocket, and took it in.

'Nils! are you quite mad, or do you want to drive me mad? Don't give the child that rattle! You must be either mad or a brute, and my nerves in this state. Haven't you got the slightest consideration for – .'

'It's not a rattle, Emma, it's a doll.'

'There you go again! Flinging your money away on rubbish that'll be on the dustheap to-morrow, and your poor wife slaving her fingernails off for you in this wretched hole, and not a decent rag to her back. Me, your clever wife that ought to be – . Light those candles, and bring me a wet towel for my head. I must read now, and try and compose my nerves, if I can.'

When the father returned to the first room, the boy was sitting up in bed, looking deathly white.

'Why! what's the matter, sonny?' said the father, bending over him, and putting a hand to his back.

'Nothing, father. I'll be all right directly. Don't you worry, father.'

'Where do you feel bad, sonny?'

'In my head and stomach, father; but I'll be all right d'rectly. I've often been that way.'

In a minute or two he was worse.

'For God's sake, Nils, take that boy into the kitchen, or somewhere,' cried the woman, 'or I'll go mad! It's enough to kill a horse. Do you *want* to drive me into a lunatic asylum?'

'Do you feel better now, sonny?' asked the father.

'Yes, ever so much better, father,' said the boy, white and weak. 'I'll be all right in a minute, father.'

'You had best sleep on the sofa to-night, sonny. It's cooler there.'

'No, father, I'd rather stay here; it's much cooler now.'

The father fixed the bed as comfortably as he could, and, despite the boy's protest, put his own pillow under his head. Then he made a fire in the kitchen, and hung the kettle and a big billy of water over it. He was haunted by recollections of convulsions amongst the children while they were teething. He took off his boots, and was about to lie down again when the mother called:

'Nils! Nils! Have you made a fire?'

'Yes, Emma.'

'Then for God's sake make me a cup of tea. I must have it after all this.'

He hurried up the kettle – she calling every few minutes to know if 'that kettle was boiling over yet'. He took her a cup of tea, and then a second. She said the tea was slush, and as sweet as syrup, and called for more, and hot water.

'How do you feel now, sonny?' he asked, as he lay down on the sofa once more.

'Much better, father. You can put out the light now if you like.'

The father blew out the candle, and settled back again, still dressed, save for his coat, and presently the small, weak hand sought the hard, strong, horny, knotted one; and so they lay, as was customary with them. After a while the father leaned over a little and whispered:

'Asleep, sonny?'

'No, father.'

'Feel bad again?'

'No, father.'

Pause.

'What are you thinking about, sonny?'

'Nothing, father.'

'But what is it? What are you worrying about? Tell me.'

'Nothing, father, only – it'll be a good while yet before I grow up to be a man, won't it, father?'

The father lay silent and troubled for a few moments.

'Why do you ask me that question to-night, sonny? I thought you'd done with all that. You were always asking me that question when you were a child. You're getting too old for those foolish fancies now. Why have you always had such a horror of growing up to be a man?'

'I don't know, father. I always had funny thoughts – you know, father. I used to think that I'd been a child once before, and grew up to be a man, and grew old and died.'

'You're not well to-night, sonny – that's what's the matter. You're queer, sonny; it's a touch of sun – that's all. Now, try to go to sleep. You'll grow up to be a man, in spite of laying awake worrying about it. If you do, you'll be a man all the sooner.'

Suddenly the mother called out:

'Can't you be quiet? What do you mean by talking at this hour of the night? Am I never to get another wink of sleep? Shut those doors, Nils, for God's sake, if you don't want to drive me mad – and make that boy hold his tongue!'

The father closed the doors.

'Better try to go to sleep now, sonny,' he whispered, as he lay down again.

The father waited for some time, then, moving very softly, he lit the candle at the kitchen fire, put it where it shouldn't light the boy's face, and watched him. And the child knew he was watching him, and pretended to sleep, and, so pretending, he slept. And the old year died as many old years had died.

The father was up at about four o'clock – he worked at his trade in a farming town about five miles away, and was struggling to make a farm and a home between jobs. He cooked bacon for breakfast, washed up the dishes and tidied the kitchen, gave the boys some bread and bacon fat, of which they were very fond, and told the eldest to take a cup of tea and some bread and milk to his mother and the baby when they woke.

The boy milked the three cows, set the milk, and heard his mother calling:

'Nils! Nils!'

'Yes, mother.'

'Why didn't you answer when I called you? I've been calling here for the last three hours. Is your father gone out?'

'Yes, mother.'

'Thank God! It's a relief to be rid of his everlasting growling. Bring me a cup of tea and the *Australian Journal*, and take this child and dress her; she should have been up hours ago.'

And so the New Year began.

Notes and Sources

IN the following notes, the details of the first publication of each story are listed, together with the source of the text used in this volume. Some of the stories were revised for book publication, and substantial changes have been noted. Interesting information on Lawson's texts is to be found in Colin Roderick, *Henry Lawson: Commentaries on his Prose Writings*, Sydney, Angus and Robertson, 1984. The editions from which the stories in *The Penguin Lawson* come are:

While the Billy Boils, Sydney, Angus and Robertson, 1896.
On the Track, Sydney, Angus and Robertson, 1900.
The Country I Come From, Edinburgh and London, Blackwood, 1901.
Joe Wilson and His Mates, Edinburgh and London, Blackwood, 1901.
Triangles of Life, Melbourne, Standard Publishing Company, 1913.

Small errors in the original texts have been corrected, and a few minor changes have been made in spelling, punctuation and capitalisation, but Lawson's use of an initial capital for 'bush' in stories written from 1900 on has been preserved.

Lawson's *Complete Works*, in two volumes compiled and edited by Leonard Cronin, were published in Sydney by Lansdowne in 1984. The Memorial Edition of Lawson's writing, seven volumes edited by Colin Roderick, was published in Sydney by Angus and Robertson (1967–1972).

The Drover's Wife   First published: *Bulletin*, 23 July 1892. Source: *The Country I Come From*.

The Bush Undertaker First published: *The Antipodean*, 1892, under the title, 'Christmas in the Far West; or, The Bush Undertaker'. Colin Roderick, who discusses the textual changes made by Lawson and his editors in subsequent reprintings, points out that in the original the grave which the old man digs up is described as 'the supposed blackfellow's grave, about which the old man had some doubts' (see his *Henry Lawson: Commentaries on his Prose Writings*, p. 27). Source: *The Country I Come From*.

In a Dry Season First published: *Bulletin*, 5 November 1892. Lawson had gone 'out back' to Bourke, which was the rail terminus for north-western New South Wales, in September 1892, and was working as a house-painter and station rouseabout in the district when he wrote this account of the journey. Roderick gives details of editorial emendations by Lawson. Source: *While the Billy Boils*.

The Union Buries Its Dead First published: *Truth*, 16 April 1893, under the title, 'A Bushman's Funeral: A Sketch from Life'. In 1902 Lawson wrote: ' "The Union Buries Its Dead" is simply an unornimented (*sic*) description of a funeral I took part in Bourk (*sic*) N.S.W. – it is true in *every* detail – even to the paragraph *re* the drowning of a man named Tyson having appeared in a Sydney Daily.' (Letter to Edward Garnett, '27th (or 28th) Feb 1902'). William Wood, writing from Paraguay in 1931, recalled knowing Lawson during his stay in Bourke: 'I was present, with other Union officials, at the funeral described by Henry in "The Union Buries its Dead" and still remember many of the incidents which he so humorously described ... The cemetery was a good step from town and many of the mourners developed a strong thirst long before the first pub. was met on the way back.' ('To the Memory of Henry Lawson', MS note, Mitchell Library.) James Tyson (1819–1898), a squatter, was reputed to be the wealthiest and meanest man in the whole continent. Source: *The Country I Come From*.

Hungerford First published: *Bulletin*, 16 December 1893. Lawson's tramp – 140 miles – from Bourke to Hungerford on the Queensland border left him 'a beaten man'. In 'this God-forgotten town' he resolved to walk back to Bourke, and somehow to return to Sydney 'never to face the bush again' (quotations are from a letter to his aunt, Emma Brooks, 16 January 1893). In the naming of the old man, *Bulletin* readers would have recognised the allusion to Paterson's 'Clancy of the Overflow' and would have recalled the verse controversy between Lawson and Paterson in the journal the previous year (see Lawson's 'Up the Country' and 'The City Bushman', and Paterson's 'In Defence of the Bush'). Source: *While the Billy Boils*.

'Rats'   First published: *Bulletin*, 3 June 1893. The story was included in Lawson's first book, *Short Stories in Prose and Verse*, 1894, with an additional final paragraph (subsequently deleted in *While the Billy Boils* and later reprintings):

And late that evening a little withered old man with no corks round his hat and with a humorous twinkle instead of a wild glare in his eyes called at a wayside shanty, had several drinks, and entertained the chaps with a yarn about the way in which he had 'had' three 'blanky fellows' for some tucker and 'half a caser' by pretending to be 'barmy'.

Source: *While the Billy Boils*.

An Old Mate of Your Father's   First published: *Worker*, 24 June 1893. Colin Roderick has drawn attention to the phrase, 'Fifty-Niners', which he considers to be a typesetter's error. In the original periodical version the text read, 'These two old "50" miners', the allusion apparently being to 1850, the year before the gold rush began in New South Wales. Source: *The Country I Come From*.

Mitchell: A Character Sketch   First published: *Bulletin*, 15 April 1893. Source: *While the Billy Boils*.

On the Edge of a Plain   First published: *Bulletin*, 6 May 1893. Source: *While the Billy Boils*.

'Some Day'   First published: *Worker*, 22 July 1893, under the title 'A Swagman's Love Story'. As Colin Roderick has pointed out, in the version of the story originally published the character was called 'Marsters'. Source: *While the Billy Boils*.

Our Pipes First published: *Bulletin*, 11 May 1895. Source: *While the Billy Boils*.

Bill the Ventriloquial Rooster First published: *Bulletin*, 22 October 1898. In Section IV of his 'A Fragment of Autobiography' (written 1903–6) Lawson describes the actual events from his childhood on which the yarn is based. Source: *On the Track*.

The Geological Spieler First published and source: *While the Billy Boils*. According to Lawson, Steelman was a New Zealander, a 'commercial traveller' whose family were unaware that he was a confidence man. Lawson worked for a time as a labourer in a gang on a telegraph line in the South Island of New Zealand, during a seven-month stay extending from November 1893 to July 1894. The first Steelman story appeared in the *Bulletin*, 19 January 1895.

The Iron-bark Chip First published and source: *On the Track*. Roderick points out that in Lawson's manuscript there was a further sentence at the end of the story: 'But when the rain held they went to work with easy consciences – as comfortable as if the inspector *had* taken the chip'.

The Loaded Dog First published and source: *Joe Wilson and His Mates*.

Brighten's Sister-in-law First published: *Blackwood's Magazine*, November 1900. When originally published, the story lacked the last two paragraphs of the version printed here: they are a slightly edited version of a passage that was part of 'Past Carin'' when it was published in *Blackwood's Magazine* six months later, and were apparently intended to strengthen the impression of a Joe Wilson series in the periodical. The revision was made when Lawson prepared the stories for book publication. The basic situation of the story was used by Lawson in a ballad, 'Brighten's Sister-in-law: or, The Carrier's Story' which was published in the *Town and Country Journal*, 21 December 1889. Source: *Joe Wilson and His Mates*.

A Double Buggy at Lahey's Creek First published: *Blackwood's Magazine*, February 1901. Source: *Joe Wilson and His Mates*.

'**Water Them Geraniums**' First published: *Joe Wilson and His Mates* ('Past Carin'' had been published separately in *Blackwood's Magazine*, May 1901). A poem by Lawson, entitled 'Past Carin'', appeared in the *Australian Magazine*, 30 May 1899. Source: *Joe Wilson and His Mates*.

Joe Wilson's Courtship First published and source: *Joe Wilson and His Mates*. This Joe Wilson story was written later than the others, but when they were collected in book form they were printed in the following order: 'Joe Wilson's Courtship', 'Brighten's Sister-in-law', ' "Water Them Geraniums" ', 'A Double Buggy at Lahey's Creek'. After the fourth story the following note was added:

THE WRITER WANTS TO SAY A WORD

In writing the first sketch of the Joe Wilson series, which happened to be 'Brighten's Sister-in-law', I had an idea of making Joe Wilson a strong character. Whether he is or not, the reader must judge. It seems to me that the man's natural sentimental selfishness, good-nature, 'softness', or weakness – call it which you like – developed as I wrote on.

I know Joe Wilson very well. He has been through deep trouble since the day he brought the double buggy to Lahey's Creek. I met him in Sydney the other day. Tall and straight yet – rather straighter than he had been – dressed in a comfortable, serviceable sac suit of 'saddle-tweed', and wearing a new sugar-loaf, cabbage-tree hat, he looked over the hurrying street people calmly as though they were sheep of which he was not in charge, and which were not likely to get 'boxed' with his. Not the worst way in which to regard the world.

He talked deliberately and quietly in all that roar and rush. He is a young man yet, comparatively speaking, but it would take little Mary a long while now to pick the grey hairs out of his head, and the process would leave him pretty bald.

In two or three short sketches in another book I hope to complete the story of his life.
Source: *Joe Wilson and His Mates*.

Telling Mrs Baker First published: *Blackwood's Magazine*, October 1901. Source: *Joe Wilson and His Mates*.

A Child in the Dark, and a Foreign Father   First published: *Bulletin*, 13 December 1902, under the title, 'A Child in the Dark: A Bush Sketch'. The story was begun in England as a novel, but was broken off and eventually completed after Lawson's return to Australia. *Ardath* was a novel published in 1889 by Marie Corelli, a popular English writer of escapist fiction. Source: *Triangles of Life*.

GLOSSARY

billabong: a waterhole in the bed of a river or creek which flows only after heavy rain.

black-tracker: an Aboriginal working for the police as a tracker.

blucher boots: short boots (half the height of Wellington boots), named after the Prussian field marshal who fought Napoleon at Waterloo.

bluey: bundle carried by a swagman; that is, a swag (possibly so-called because of the blue blanket commonly carried).

bow-yangs: string tied round each trouser leg below the knee, to adjust the length.

brammer: colloquial form of 'Brahma' (from the name of the river Brahmaputra), a breed of domestic fowl from India.

cabbage-tree hat: a wide-brimmed hat woven from narrow strips of the leaves of the cabbage palm tree, which grows along the eastern coast of Australia (the 'sugar-loaf' version had a very high crown).

cotton-bush: an indigenous, drought-resistant, perennial shrub, which grows in a compact shape up to one metre high and wide; its name derives from the white cotton-like growths on its spring branchlets, caused by the action of small grubs.

Crimean shirt: shirt of red or spotted or striped flannel (presumably so-called because worn in the Crimean War).

duffer: in mining slang, a mine that proves worthless.

goanna: large Australian monitor lizard (sometimes confused with *iguana*, which refers to the South American arboreal lizard).

graft: work (in a footnote for English readers of *Joe Wilson and His*

Mates, Lawson wrote: 'The term is now applied, in Australia, to all sorts of work, from bullock-driving to writing poetry').

hatter: a person who prefers to be solitary and appears to be eccentric, if not actually crazy.

humpy: a very primitive hut.

jackeroo: a young man gaining experience on a sheep or cattle property.

jim jams ('the jams'): slang for *delirium tremens*, a state of delusion and terror caused by excessive drinking.

johnny cakes: small flat cakes, made from flour and water, cooked on both sides in the ashes of a camp fire.

larrikin: a hooligan; a rowdy, ill-mannered youth.

lignum: an indigenous perennial shrub, with rigid tangled branches.

lush: (as a verb) to drink alcohol excessively.

Maoriland: New Zealand.

masher: smart, dandified.

moleskin: hard-wearing cotton twill, of which working trousers were made.

mulga: wattles (acacias) found in drier areas.

native apple-trees: indigenous trees, supposed to resemble English apple trees; usually applied to *angophoras*.

Never-Never: country far from the centres of civilisation.

on the track: tramping the country as a swagman.

on the wallaby: the same meaning as 'on the track' (the phrase perhaps suggested by the notion of following the wallaby's track).

Out-Back: a phrase, well established by the time Lawson started writing, to designate the sparsely settled poor country inland from the fertile coastal plain of Eastern Australia (' "Out Back" is always west of the Bushman, no matter how far out he be' – Lawson, footnote to *Joe Wilson and His Mates*).

payable dirt: mining slang for ore-bearing rock or gravel.

post-and-rail tea: cheap tea, which was very coarse, so that stalks and leaves floated on top when it was made in a billy.

ring-barked: descriptive of a tree from which a circle of bark has been cut away, causing it to die.

Royal Alfred: a large, rolled swag, 'with tent and all complete, and weighing part of a ton.' (Lawson, 'The Romance of the Swag')

run: a term used to describe a piece of land worked by a squatter; a synonym for *station*.

sandy blight: the common phrase to describe inflammation of the eye, which produced the sensation of sand in the eye-lid.

selection: a small land holding, created by the various colonial Selection Acts of the 1860s which attempted to promote closer settlement.

shanty: a place where alcoholic drink was sold, usually without licence.

she-oak: not the English oak, but the indigenous casuarina, which has long needle-like leaves.

shooting the moon: leaving at night to avoid paying.

sly grog: liquor sold illegally.

spieler: a glib talker or confidence-man.

squatter: a large landholder.

station: a large landholding used for grazing sheep or cattle.

sundowner: a tramp – that is, a professional swagman – who organises his arrival at a homestead to coincide with the going down of the sun, so that he cannot be asked to do any work for a handout.

swag: bundle carried on his back by a traveller on foot, 'usually composed of a tent "fly" or strip of calico (a cover for the swag and a shelter in bad weather – in New Zealand it is oilcloth or water-proof twill), a couple of blankets, blue by custom and preference, as that colour shows the dirt less than any other (hence the name "bluey" for swag), and the core is composed of spare clothing and small personal effects'. (Lawson, 'The Romance of the Swag')

swagman: a man, with his belongings in a 'swag', tramping the country, ostensibly but not necessarily looking for work.

tucker-bag: any bag used for carrying food.

up the country: inland, away from the coast and the centres of population.

whare: Maori word for 'hut'.

A WINDOW IN MRS X's PLACE
Selected Short Stories
Peter Cowan

Peter Cowan has been compared to writers as diverse as Hemingway and Lawson as he 'explores the responses of individuals to crises in love and work against a variety of Australian, especially Western Australian, land, sea and city scapes.'

This selection by Bruce Bennett allows his work to be 'experienced as a continuity, ranging from stories published in a variety of magazines and collections since the early 1940s. During that period, Cowan has established a well deserved reputation as master craftsman in one of the most difficult art forms'

'One of the finest wo or three short story writers now working in Australia.'

T. A. G. Hungerford,
Weekend News, 1965

'To the negative side of life he is as spring to the bare winter tree.'

Thelma Forshaw,
Sydney Morning Herald, 1973

'Cowan has continued to experiment with the short story form, to test its flexibility, its possibilities.'

Bruce Williams,
The Literature of Western Australia, 1980

STORIES OF THE WATERFRONT
John Morrison

'John was born in England, but no native-born reflects the spirit of Australia more than he does. This country, of which he is so much a part, has absorbed and recreated him as one of its most significant voices.'

Alan Marshall

These imaginative and sensitive stories begin at a time when wharfies turned up at the docks to be picked like cattle, and often went home without work or pay. The events range from personal dilemmas like sharing lottery winnings to coping with pig-headed bosses and the tragedy of sudden death.

John Morrison worked for ten years on the Melbourne waterfront in the 1930s and '40s. His *Stories of the Waterfront*, collected here for the first time, give a realistic yet unusually sympathetic account of the much-maligned wharfie.

Set in the years after the turbulent times depicted in the television film, *Waterfront*, the book provides a narrative of improvement of conditions and the constant struggle to maintain them by a group of warm and down-to-earth people.